Gilhame knew her

as soon as she leaped to her feet. He would have known her anywhere, anytime, not by her red hair and swan throat, not by her green eyes, but by the proud spirit that seemed to shine out of her. Throughout every lifetime he had lived she had been the light of his eyes. But who was she now?

She swept down the aisle of the crowded courtroom and threw her arms around the man Gilhame had just condemned to exile or death.

"Father," she cried . . .

THE DRAGON RISES

ADRIENNE MARTINE-BARNES

ACE SCIENCE FICTION BOOKS
NEW YORK

THE DRAGON RISES

An Ace Science Fiction Book/published by arrangement with
the author

PRINTING HISTORY
Ace edition/March 1983

ISBN: 0-441-16655-5

Ace Science Fiction Books are published by Charter Communications, Inc.
200 Madison Avenue, New York, New York 10016
PRINTED IN THE UNITED STATES OF AMERICA

For many reasons, not the least of which is our common interest in Celtic legend, this book is for Ron.

THE DRAGON RISES

At the back of the North Wind, there is a dark dwelling with many names. The Castle Royal, it has been called, and the Gloomy Castle; the High Castle and the Place of the Perfect Ones. But, for the inhabitants, it is always the Castle of Glass, a prison where the starlight never reaches.

Seven sleepless souls move in the darkness of Glass Castle, silent and filled with memory. The Castle of Glass abounds with memory; and although there is neither air nor water nor light, sound is their constant companion. The seven—the Bull, the Eagle, the Roebuck, the Dragon, the Griffin, the Fox and the Hound—hear the stars sing, and listen to the creaking of the cosmos.

From time to time, one of that company departs, to seek his final release from endless night. The Dragon's disappearance always occasions some small conversation among the others. They speak, usually, by the fountain in the courtyard, where the noise of running water releases torrents of memory, but where no liquid moves.

"Is he gone again?" asks the Eagle.

"Yes. It seems so," answers the Roebuck.

"Do you think this time will be different?"

"Every time is different."

"The poor old Dragon. I wonder what they will call him this time? There have been so many names. Sam, Harata, Arthur, Minoyato, Vlad . . . I can't remember them all.

And I do wonder why he keeps going out. What do you think it is that he does not learn?"

"I know not. That is not my path."

"It does not seem very fair, somehow."

"Fair? No, not *fair*—or even just. But right. Yes, right, somehow. And, perhaps, this time he will make the sacrifice."

"You and your sacrifices, Roebuck. That was your path. Are you so certain it is his?"

"All paths are ways to the offering."

As usual, the Roebuck has the last word.

Gilhame woke. At first he was only aware of the darkness around him and the great chair underneath him. He shook his head to dispel the disorientation he was experiencing, then grinned at himself. No movement of the body could ease the confusion of his mind.

The chair. He pressed his great hands onto the arms, feeling the rows of controls set there. The chair, at least, was right—high, isolated, raised from the surrounding bustle.

There was movement in the darkness. He looked around slowly and saw what seemed to be a great cavern. Above him the darkness was pricked with many points of light, and below him people whispered as they bent over machines.

When he saw the banner hanging on the wall, most of his disorientation faded. The black dragon, crouched on its bloody field, seemed to snarl at him. So, he was returned again from the glassy keep where he waited between wars.

Gilhame sighed. Not free yet? Why? He had done the job—stopped the invaders; saved the world. What world had that been? The details refused to settle into any tidy pattern. There was also a faint query from the personality of his host body, confused by his partial memories of past battles.

'*I am Gilhame ur Fagon. I know nothing of these others, these legends. Who are you, demon?*'

The Dragon ignored the questions as he tried to remem-

3

ber his previous names. What time was this? What war? He knew it did not matter, that he would fight, would win, would defeat the enemy (whoever it was) at the final battle, which was never final, and, with a sense of betrayal, would return to Glass Castle.

Then he abandoned the effort and focused his attention on the situation at hand. As usual, access to the host body's personal memories was difficult and incomplete, though there was no problem securing the entirety of ur Fagon's technical knowledge.

The Dragon activated the computer screen at his right. "Prepared." The word appeared at the top of the screen.

He picked up a tiny contrivance of plastic and metal, tucked the earpiece in and spoke into the tiny microphone. "Biosector."

"Running."

"Ur Fagon, Gilhame." He was surprised at the harshness of his voice. The screen showed a face. That, at least, was familiar. Those gold-green eyes had been his forever; he had seen them in pools of still water, in silvered surfaces, in cubes. The black hair, peak receding from the broad forehead; the hooked nose; the thin, ungenerous mouth were all old friends. The picture vanished and he read the history of the body he now occupied.

The record itself was bloodless, recording only the noteworthy actions of the man, his age, his decorations, rank and marital state. But the reading of ur Fagon's history released memories from his host body, so that when he completed his reading he knew a great deal about "himself."

"Admiral."

Gilhame looked down at the man lifting his arm in salute. A stocky man with the face of an angel. A flutter of memory, then the knowledge that this was Commander Vendare Frikard, his second-in-command.

"Yes?"

"We have some new data on the Coalchee fleet, sir. They are a great deal stronger than Admiral Krispin's information indicated."

"Are they? How much stronger?"

Coalchee? *'Bandy-legged dwarves.'* That was the prejudice of the host body. The Dragon reflected again on the complexity of the mind. Ur Fagon mistrusted his adversary because that race was small in stature, yet respected them as honorable fighters. As the loyal subject of a hereditary monarch, he was contemptuous of them for electing a ruler, their Protector. Yet he found their music and their poetry touched chords in him quite unreached by the carefully structured forms of his own folk.

"About thirty percent."

"I see. All right."

"Any orders, sir?"

"Not at the moment."

"Shall I send a yeoman with some *var*?"

Var. There had been a mention of that in the bio. "Hallucinative mutant with a heavy *var* dependency." The memories which the word aroused were confused. Power, strength and knowledge, and something about a little boy and a dream. "Yes, thank you." Frikard gave him an odd look.

The gallery was full of whispers. Gilhame watched Frikard go to a young woman. "*Curva!* The old man must be worried. He said 'thank you.' Quick, Ottera, get him some *var*." He heard Frikard's words and saw the intimate glance which passed between them.

Gilhame grinned at this. It pulled the muscles tight around the thin mouth, as if it was unused to such facial movements. He listened to the other whispers for a few seconds, then turned his attention back to the screen.

"Fleet status," he said.

"Running. Admiral Gilhame ur Fagon in command of the Twelfth Fleet of the Kardus Temporal Empire, aboard the flagship *Black Dragon*.

"Current strength:
    26 battle cruisers
    19 heavy destroyers
    12 light destroyers
   413 Hawk class fighters
    93 Hawk class scouts

"Position: Subspace 12D492 between Vardar-12 (Kardus) and Vardar-15 (Coalchee).

"Coalchee Ninth Armada currently at 13A612. Group Commander E-varit Gnargol, hero of the Battle of Samnite, heads this fleet.

"Assessment of Coalchee Strength:

    49 battle cruisers
    24 heavy destroyers
    14 light destroyers
  841 Acuma class fighters
    19 Acuma class scouts

"Battle strategy (Admiral Krispin Directive 857/93/D) as follows. . . ."

The Coalchee Protectorate and the Kardus Temporal Empire had been skirmishing along their mutual "border" for three generations now, with neither side obtaining much advantage except to keep their navies out of boredom and, therefore, mischief. All the Ten Nations did that, except the Havassit, who didn't even bother to maintain anything beyond a tiny merchant fleet. The influence of some monarch or leader was extended over one or more planetary systems for a time, then lost again. Ur Fagon knew worlds where the schools taught two tongues against the eventual return of some former government.

The Dragon stared down at the screen now illuminated with the battle plan his superior had issued, and a frown crossed his face. *'There is something wrong, demon.'* The remnant of the host personality stirred, and there was a further integration. *'Why are we having a battle here? There is nothing to gain. A trap?'* Agreement.

Gilhame looked at the screen for a long time, then demanded data on Group Commander E-varit and the battles he had fought.

He completed his study and leaned back, staring blankly at the star-pocked window over his head. There was a faint cough below him.

"Yes?" He looked down.

"Your *var,* sir."

'A pretty female,' he thought. 'Frikard has taste.'

"Thank you . . . Ganna." He gave her a grin which made a death's-head of his face. She handed him a tiny, clear glass cup and scurried away wide-eyed.

'I seem to be playing havoc with my staff's morale,' he thought. 'What kind of a bastard was he before I was in this host body? And where is he going? He's fading already. Where are all the flames whose places I have usurped over the millennia? Do they return when I leave?'

Gilhame gave up his fruitless speculation and looked at the tiny cup, almost lost in his large hand. There was a miniscule amount of gray liquid in the bottom. He sniffed it tentatively. No odor. He touched a cautious tongue to the stuff.

A rush of sensations, swirling, churning, receding—the sense of being yanked from the body he had only just entered, yet of still being in it. A feeling of being sucked away, then the transformation to beast—great leathery wings and a flaming breath in the cold void between the stars where there was no air to support it.

The black Dragon looked back at the body of Gilhame ur Fagon as it sped away between the stars. Fire burned before him as he soared towards the Coalchee fleet. His eyes flamed. Finally he perched like a carrion bird on the great viewport of the Coalchee flagship, staring down at his adversaries, listening to their speech. Then the leathery wings beat a homeward course. The black Dragon covered the still form of Gilhame ur Fagon like a rapist, then dwindled and vanished.

After the hallucination departed, Gilhame sat in his great chair, pondering the experience. He wondered what a full dose of the stuff would have done to him, and again received the confused memories of previous *var* journeys. How accurate was the data he had gotten? '*Very*,' came the distant whisper of his other self.

The use of the drug had given the Dragon more access to the personal memories of his host and he found he did not like the original Gilhame ur Fagon much. His actions had been those of a cold man, ruthless, unorthodox and merciless. The unconventionality he could admire. Nothing else.

Still, if what he had learned was real, not illusory, then

the battle plan must be scrapped immediately. In its current position, the Twelfth Fleet was an easy target, and that he could not permit. Again the sense of agreement from ur Fagon.

He muttered into his mouthpiece for several minutes, studying the information which came up on the screen before him. Finally he said, "By my command."

The computer displayed a battle schema vastly different from the earlier plan. "Implemented," it printed below the picture.

"Frikard!"

"Yes, sir." The man was standing several feet away. He turned and came to the foot of the command chair.

"I have just negated this piece of offal masquerading as a battle plan. I cannot imagine what took me so long."

"But, sir . . . Admiral Krispin has given very strict orders. He won't like this."

"Of course he won't. And neither will Governor Mordell. However, I would like it even less if we all got killed, and you know I always put the needs of my fleet and myself first. Have you ever known me to do otherwise? We fight . . . in this asteroid belt at 12D492.6. Make sure there is no confusion about my orders. Those new mines should make quite a surprise party for Commander E-varit. What's the rewake time on cold-sleep? I've forgotten."

"About forty seconds, sir."

"That should be sufficient. Just make sure our fighters follow my orders exactly."

"Yes, sir. And what shall I tell the Admiral when he comes aboard? We just received word that he will be here almost immediately."

"You won't tell the bastard anything. Just strip the traitor naked and stuff him in the brig."

"Sir? Admiral Krispin?"

"You heard me. This charming little trap, arranged by dear Admiral Krispin, is not going to catch the one for whom it was intended. It will be vastly diverting—after we capture Group Commander E-varit."

"Capture!" The word came out as a squeak.

"Have I ever let you down, Frikard?"

"No, sir."

"Good. Let us continue that way, shall we? Where the devil is Buschard? I want to see him as soon as he arrives."

"Yes, sir."

Frikard stared at him for a long second, then looked at the cup of *var*. His beautiful face registered confusion before he turned and walked into the darkness.

Gilhame leaned back, a little amused. At least the ability to assess information rapidly had not deserted him. There had been a time, he remembered, when he began as a child and grew gradually into these situations. No more. Now he was dropped into them like a stone into roiling water.

But he could still smell a trap. Admiral Krispin! The knowledge of the man's treachery came from the *var*. His superior in the Navy—it pleased him that they still called it that—and his rival in some power struggle as yet undefined. The fast-fading personality of the original ur Fagon registered no surprise at the situation. Gilhame watched his screen and saw the fleet begin to respond to his commands.

A portal opened on one side of the room, its shaft of light shattering the darkness and catching his attention. Gilhame glanced at the man who entered and knew him even as he walked casually across the bridge. No matter what the guise or what name he bore, the Dragon always recognized this man. How many times had they played the tale? He had lost count. Buschard was always there, the trusted companion, friend-in-arms and rival in love. As he always did at first meeting, Gilhame wondered if this person was, like himself, an undying soul or only a mortal flame he always attracted to himself. He could even dimly remember some of the other names, back to that time when they fought together upon rolling green hills against an enemy he had forgotten.

The man who strode towards his dias was tall, broad and fair. His hair was the color of wheatstraw and his eyes the blue of a still lake. Always the lake. The Dragon never thought of the man without thinking of that body of water. Gilhame knew him and loved him, would always love him, even in the last bitter betrayal. He wondered if they had begun to play out that part of the story yet.

"Well, Gil?" Buschard stood below him in a blood-red uniform piped in black. His stance was easy, almost careless. Even at the end, he never seemed to show tension or pain or anything but a kind of quiet serenity.

'I am a destroyer and he is a healer. I conjure loyalty; he creates love. Well, I never did have the common touch,' ur Fagon thought. Suddenly the chair seemed too high, too distant. The Dragon yearned for contact with another living body.

He stepped down from the dias and put his arm over Buschard's shoulder. Gilhame was a head taller than his companion, but leaner. Buschard smiled and silently returned his embrace.

"This is one hell of a mess Krispin has boxed us into," ur Fagon said casually. He savored the manly scent of his friend and the warmth of his muscles beneath the cloth of his garment. There were no embraces in Glass Castle.

"I know. I understand he's coming aboard. What are you going to tell him?"

"Tell him? I am not going to tell the *curva* anything. Look, Pers, I want E-varit's flagship—intact. Will you do it?"

"Take prisoners? Are you out of your mind or just smoky from too much *var*? We haven't taken prisoners outside a war game in nine years."

"Exactly. It has the element of novelty."

"Novelty! Why is it that I mistrust you most . . . when you are most approachable? Gil, no one takes prisoners."

"I have just changed the rules. I need E-varit. Is that clear?"

"Clear as soup. As you will. You want him. I'll get him. Just tell me how, will you?"

Admiral ur Fagon activated a screen nearby. "Here, in this asteroid belt, are our small craft pretending to be debris, one hopes. All along here I have placed the new Sokull mines—the ones that go for prime rhythms. This is the Coalchee formation. Now, when the leading ships have come to this point, they will meet the mines. Confusion will follow. They will spread out, our fighters will activate and engage them. I will have arrived at *this* point, in the rear of their formation, with as much heavy stuff as we can muster. Nothing in Commander E-varit's history leads me to believe he has ever fought a battle from two directions at the same time. So, we will give him three. You will be here. I want you to come up under their bellies and fry them, but get that flagship. And I want E-varit alive, if possible. I hate dead-braining. Nasty piece of technology."

"Do you have time to get behind them?"

"We're lucky. This sector is full of holes in the space warp. Besides, you know my methods, Watson."

"What?"

"Nothing. Never fear. I will be where I say. You may depend upon it."

"Another one of your miracles, Gil?"

"Predictable, aren't they?"

"No, not really. Are you . . . yourself? You seem very unsmoky."

"I am not *var*-bound, if that is what you mean. You can have eight cruisers, ten heavies and four lights. You will get some fighters too, once the shooting starts. He will have four cruisers and six heavies riding escort on the flag. But he will be too busy to notice until you are there. I hope."

"Smoky or not, I think you're crazy."

"Would you rather boil in Krispin's pot?"

"Not particularly."

"Then trust me. Have I ever led you wrong?"

"There was that bar on Estra six years back. . . ."

"And there was that party at the Fridian embassy when you got some mutant weed and started breaking up the place, and I had to haul your carcass out before the shore patrol arrived."

"Fancy you remembering that. You were pretty smoky that night yourself. By your command. Here I go to attack the soft underbelly of the Coalchee Protectorate. This is so mad, it might work."

"Thank you, friend . . . for everything. And good hunting."

Buschard gave him a hard stare, an eyebrow raised above the deep blue eyes, saluted and was gone. Gilhame watched him leave and stood staring at the portal after it closed. Listening to the tinny voice in his earpiece, he walked restlessly around the command center, peering over the shoulders of his technicians and speaking to some of them. He was aware that the original ur Fagon had never talked with his staff, and it amused him to see how his inexplicable camaraderie unnerved them. Fortunately, they were too well trained to remain distracted for long.

"Frikard!"

"Sir!" The man was beside him almost immediately.

"When Commander Buschard is away, I want the rest of the fleet in a sinister-wing formation. Put us *across* to 12D494."

"Sir?"

"That's right. I want to get 'em from behind." He grinned his terrible grin. "Move it!"

Gilhame returned to the dias. Since his first disorientation, he had "found" many of the memories of his host body. Information was still coming in fits and starts, confused by fragments from other lives and times, but now, at least, he had full command of the military knowledge of the real ur Fagon. He realized that however unpleasant the man had been, he was an extremely brilliant and capable commander. At thirty-three he was young for his command, but Nelson had been young too. The thought puzzled him, for he could not recall who Nelson had been.

He used his computer again, ignoring, for the most part, the reports coming into his earpiece. Instead, he read the official biographies of Admiral Krispin, and his own principal staff—Buschard, Frikard, et al. Gilhame read rapidly, familiarizing himself with the habits and careers of the men who served under him. He sensed rather than saw Frikard's approach some time later.

"Sir."

"What is it, Ven?" In the four years that the able and admirable Frikard had served with the original ur Fagon, never once had the Admiral addressed him by his given name. Gilhame saw the slight look of surprise as he used it now unconsciously, and wished that "he" had not been quite such a platinum bastard.

"We are in position as commanded, sir. Their drive units are messing up their sensors; they don't even know we are behind them. And, sir, Admiral Krispin is . . . here. He is very angry."

"Good. Angry men make stupid mistakes. Hmm. I wonder if he would like to see the show? Put him in restraints and have a security team bring him up here. Hand *and* leg restraints, Frikard. After we are engaged—which should be very soon."

"About six minutes, sir."

"I suppose I'd better begin to pay attention now." Gilhame yawned. "Do you know, space battles can be a dead bore? Are they into the minefield yet?"

"Yes, sir. Those new Sokull mines are playing hell with their fighters and light destroyers. Will you give the order to release our fighters from cold-sleep soon?"

"Soon, but not until the Coalchee are well into the asteroid belt. I don't want to lose any more of our men to our own weapons than I must. A double-edged weapon, these prime-rhythm bombs. I wonder what kind of mind invented them? I'll release the fighters as soon as we are engaged."

"Yes, sir."

Gilhame now listened to the earpiece and displayed the battle on his screen. Then they were upon the ships of the Coalchee fleet, torpedoing their drive units from behind and leaving them stalled in space.

The three-part battle unfolded as he watched. At one end of the line of battle his fighters darted in to engage the Coalchee that had survived the Sokull mines. About one third of their fighters and several of the smaller destroyers had been disabled; the Sokull mines continued their mindless slaughter of friend or foe, for there was no way known to allow a machine to distinguish the prime rhythm of one species from another. Individuals, yes; groups, no.

At his end of the battle line there was a kind of inexorable progress as his cruisers and destroyers attacked the Coalchee from the only position in which they were truly vulnerable. Then Buschard's ships appeared, a sudden circle of colored lights almost at the midpoint of the Coalchee formation. They attacked the flagship's escort, then surrounded it and used their tractor beams.

Gilhame laughed. It was a sudden, horrid, grating noise in the quiet room. He enjoyed the realization that he had thwarted Admiral Krispin's plan to have his fleet spread out like decoys on a lake. Instead, it was cutting a superior force into manageable chunks and chewing it up.

Frikard, standing nearby, looked up at the sound. The old man sure wasn't smoky, but he also seemed unlike himself. Frikard puzzled over this. He had fought a number of battles with ur Fagon, but he had never heard him laugh. He looked again at the cup of *var* and could see that it was almost untouched. The flacks would call it another "ur Fagon miracle." The Admiralty would deplore ur Fagon's unconventionality, as they always did. His men would shake their heads and say he was possessed of a demon. They always did. But at that moment, Frikard saw him as a man *dis*possessed. The idea vanished as the portal opened and the security team escorted Admiral Krispin onto the bridge.

Krispin hobbled in in the leg shackles. He was a big man, nearing his fiftieth year, a little soft in the middle and white at the temples of his red hair, but still powerful. His uniform had been torn at one shoulder during his capture, and the color of his face was an unlovely red.

"What is the meaning of this?" he roared at ur Fagon.

Gilhame stopped laughing and turned his head slowly to look down at Krispin. He smiled thinly. "I have brought you here to watch the destruction of your ally, Admiral." He gestured towards his own screen and then pointed at one in Krispin's view. "See? Even now my brave Buschard takes Group Commander E-varit's ship in tow. Tell me, why did you sell out? Did you lose your nerve? Did they offer you rewards? Or did you think to placate them by my death? Pard got your tongue? Oh well, it will make interesting conjecture for my leisure hours."

"Ally? Sell out? What the devil are you talking about, you *curvant var*-freak?"

An explosion shook the *Black Dragon*. It shuddered like a living thing but did not falter. The banner on the wall rustled, and the dragon on it seemed to stir, then settle. The cup of *var* next to Gilhame's arm rattled slightly. Then the room was still for a moment.

Frikard listened to his earpiece. "Only minor damage, sir."

"Good. It felt like the port docking bay."

"Just so, sir."

"Now, where was I? Oh, yes. My dear Admiral, it is obvious to even the meanest intelligence that you were either in league with E-varit or else your battle plan was a piece of the worst miscalculation since the Battle of Nerene. I will know for certain after I see Commander E-varit. Or deadbrain him. Whatever. It matters not. Somehow, I don't think he will defend you."

All the color had drained from Krispin's face. "I'll see you broken."

"*Vragado,* mere *vragado.* You won't see anything but the exile world—if you're lucky; or a penal cell, if you are not. The Diet is rather abrupt with traitors, not to mention His Imperial Majesty. Of course, I will submit the whole matter to the Imperial Adjudicator's office. Hmm. The fun appears to be over. Yes, the remnants are running. I wonder what kind of a reception they will get at home? I don't think it will be pleasant. Do you have any casualty figures yet, Frikard?"

"Forty-one fighters, five cruisers, six heavy destroyers and two light destroyers gone, sir. Another sixty fighters sustained heavy damage. They are being picked up. Two more light cruisers were badly hit, and one heavy. We came off rather well, under the circumstances."

"Yes. Rather well. How many dead?"

"Dead, sir?" That was a statistic ur Fagon commonly demanded, and Frikard always hated giving it. The Admiral often took the loss of men as a personal afront, and Frikard feared a little the rage that followed casualty figures. "More than two thousand, so far. The Healers are pretty busy."

"Make certain they get posthumous recompense and are in my dispatches. That number comes out of the Krispin levy before the Imperium takes its pound of flesh. What shall we call this one, Frikard? You did most of the work. You name it."

Frikard's angular face turned a curious pink. Several of the technicians nearby were unabashedly eavesdropping on the conversation. "Thank you, sir, but I couldn't."

"Name it!"

"Yes, sir. The Battle of the Vardar Straits, then, if you will."

Vardar Straits? Good, very good. The minstrels can do something with that, can't they? We must never forget the poets, Ven. They keep us alive long after we are dust. Have that piece of dogshit taken back to the brig. Buschard will bring E-varit—unless he is dead—aboard. Have him piped on board with full honors. For the moment, he is our guest, not our prisoner."

"I see, sir."

"Bring him to my quarters. I want you there; Commander Buschard; Colmeni; that psycho-historian—what's her name—Darkcut? And get a Witness."

"Yes, sir." At a wave from Frikard, the security team left with Krispin.

Gilhame saw the question in his second's eyes. "Don't worry. I have not lost my mind. Have some *durek* sent up—fruit, cheese. I want it to be a very cozy little luncheon. What do the Coalchee like to drink? I seem to remember they have a fondness for Rurian wine, but I doubt we have any on board. I have some Grentarian brandy in my quarters, but that would hardly be appropriate under the circumstances, would it?"

"No, sir." Admiral Krispin was a native of Grentar.

"Tell me, do we have any of that Nabat elixir?"

"Medic Vraser might have some, sir. I'll ask."

"Fine. If he does, invite him too. I won't take a man's wine without sharing it with him. Besides, he is a truth-seer, isn't he?"

"Yes, he is."

"Let's make it dressy and formal. Full-kit for all our people. You seem bewildered, Frikard."

"No, sir."

"You are a very poor liar." Gilhame grinned, and

Frikard found that the sight became less disquieting with familiarity. "There are many ways to deal with an enemy, Ven. One of the best is confusion. If the Emperor ever gives me a patent, that might be my motto: *Confusion to the enemy*. And what better way to befuddle Group Commander E-varit than to be kind to him when he is expecting just the opposite?"

"Very good, sir." Frikard found himself smiling back at ur Fagon and nearly jumped out of his skin when he noticed it. He spoke into his headset and began arranging the Admiral's little "party."

_____ *Chapter II*

In the end, it was rather a large party. Frikard, sensitive to mood in an almost feminine manner, received the defeated Coalchee Group Commander as he would have greeted an admiral of his own navy. The inclusion of two additional guests, A-gurit, Captain of E-varit's flagship, and an unnamed Havassit priest nonplussed him only a moment. He lead them to quarters where they could wash up and gave them an opportunity to regain some composure before taking them to ur Fagon, though it was debatable that any Havassit was ever discomforted. Certainly Frikard had never heard of any such incident.

When the portal opened, Frikard saw the Admiral. He was standing next to the psycho-historian, Darkcut, his midnight head bent down to catch the tiny woman's words. Principal Medic Vraser, in the deep blue uniform of the Healers, was smoking a large pipe and staring at ur Fagon's narrow back. Buschard had found time to bathe and change into his dress whites, his hair still damp so that its golden color was deeper. In one corner of the room, Culmeni, Frikard's executive officer, was tuning his harp. As he shepherded his charges in, Buschard gave him a glance and a shrug. Neither of them could recall such a gathering under ur Fagon's command. But then, ur Fagon never behaved as one expected. It was what made serving under him such a challenge.

Gilhame ur Fagon turned in mid-sentence to greet them. He observed the three men with Frikard, quirked an eyebrow and stepped forward. "Ah, our guests. Do come in, gentle—persons," he ended in deference to the unknown sex of the Havassit priest. When dealing with a race which has four distinct sexes, the neuter is always politic.

The Admiral looked at the newcomers. The Coalchee were fairly typical of their race: white-haired, pale-skinned and white-lashed around their nearly triangular eyes, short and stocky. Their home world was dim and watery, and they were light-sensitive, so the illumination in the room was low. Ur Fagon knew they counted family before self, clan before family and the state above all; that they built their cities near the sea whenever possible; and practiced the curious custom of salting the bodies of their dead for burial. He felt a slight sadness at the thought of their battle casualties, blasted to bits by the Sokull mines, dead with no chance for the careful rituals they believed would carry them to the Coalchee afterworld. Heaven and hell were mere philosophical concepts to the Dragon, but he had a deep respect for the concepts, harboring a deep suspicion that there was something beyond Glass Castle, if he could only find the way.

E-varit and A-gurit stood stiffly, formally rigid, their short statures emphasized by the taller Kardusians. Only the psycho-historian would greet them at eye-level. But ur Fagon sensed they were righteous fellows, men he could like, and felt a spurt of anger that chance should make them his adversaries.

He indulged in a brief, bitter thought about that ludicrous document, the Ten Nations Compact, and all its foolish predecessors, treaties which made liars of honorable men. All the Compact achieved was limited wars. That it had arisen from the hard necessity of the chaos following the collapse of a dozen or more space-going cultures after the *curthel* invasions did not lessen his cynicism, for the Compact was a marvel of political expediency and special interests. The Coalchee had gotten a very small piece of the pie, and they wanted and needed a larger one. Their preference for cool, watery worlds and an expanding population made it a necessity. This did not explain why they should fight in the Vardar Straits. He hoped to find an answer to that question before the end of the meal.

Gilhame passed from his study of the Coalchee to the priest. The Havassit had the appearance of a stripling male, long hair caught back by clips, beardless, flat—almost invisible—nose, soft brown eyes and generous mouth. The marks on his robe proclaimed him a priest of the second degree, putting his age at seventy-plus. The Havassit were a complete contradiction to him, the smallest of the Ten Nations and the most powerful. They were so powerful that they maintained no navy and remained unscathed. Every fifty years or so, some ambitious admiral would go renegade and try to take a Havassit planet. They would simply vanish—ships, men, everything. There was never even debris. The Havassit were psychics of a high order, traveled everywhere as priests and were widely held to be wizards. Ur Fagon had a not very vague suspicion that they could tell him the answer to the riddle which was himself, but would never do so.

"Group Commander E-varit. I am Admiral ur Fagon."

"I am not unfamiliar with your countenance. This is Captain A-gurit."

"Captain." They bowed formally.

"And this is Lepus con Gessar of the Sceni sect on Harva."

"Your Reverence." More bows. "You have already met Commanders Frikard and Buschard. This is Lieutenant Darkcut. Kessie—Group Commander E-varit, Captain A-gurit, Reverend con Gessar; Principal Medic Farren Vraser and Captain Tchan Culmeni. Why don't we all sit down?"

Frikard glanced around the room. In the corner he saw the hooded form of an official Witness of the Imperial Adjudicator's Office, with the rod and recorder of its position. The shapeless robe of the Witness made it impossible to guess sex, age or anything else. Then he looked at the table.

The long board was covered with a red cloth on which golden dragons danced and capered. Frikard knew that the thing had been embroidered by the Woman of Dalari after the Battle of Kremore, but he had never seen it in use before. What other little surprises did ur Fagon have in store? Bowls of floating flowers and platters of fruits, vegetables and cheeses were placed along the table. Even in the dim light, the multicolored crystal glasses and plates seemed to shine.

Vraser arose stiffly and limped over to the table, his hip joint shattered beyond the Healers' art. Culmeni set aside his harp, and the rest of the party moved hesitantly towards the table.

Admiral ur Fagon took his place at the top of the board and waved Commander E-varit to his right and Captain A-gurit to his left. Lieutenant Darkcut sat beside E-varit, with Buschard on her other side, and the priest took his place at the far end of the table. As it was a meal, Vraser, the Medic, took precedence over the other officers and sat next to A-gurit, leaving Frikard and Culmeni to fill in that side of the table. The empty chair beside Buschard seemed to gape at them.

When they were all seated, ur Fagon asked in a quiet voice, "Reverend, will you bless the board?"

The priest looked at him for a moment with his liquid brown eyes, then began. "Here is quietude. Here is stillness. May the food on this table sustain our bodies and the essence of sanctity sustain our spirits through all eternity." The calm center of the priest's blessing touched everyone with the Havassit gift.

"Thank you, Your Reverence. Some wine, Captain. We have *durek,* Nabat elixir and Kathian wine." Gilhame, after an exchange of glances with Kessie Darkcut, turned his full attention to E-varit's flag captain. She smiled and offered some wine to the Group Commander. She, alone of the people in the room, was as diminutive as the Coalchee, and E-varit found himself looking directly into her eyes. After what seemed to him to have been hours of craning his neck up to converse with giants, he found her attention and friendly gaze curiously restful.

At the bottom of the board, Culmeni asked the priest some questions about Sceni music. Beside him, Frikard and Vraser spoke of casualties. Lieutenant Darkcut drew Buschard into a discussion of wine with Commander E-varit, and within a few minutes no observer would have guessed that any of the people at the table had been engaged in a life-and-death struggle a few hours earlier.

Buschard, having to speak across Kessie Darkcut to reach E-varit, began to discuss a legendary vintage with him. His words reached Vraser. "I drank Ferrea '49."

"I doubt that very much," Vraser interrupted from across the table.

"You may be right," Buschard conceded quickly, for Vraser's knowledge of wines was notorious in the fleet. "I was told it was the '49, and it was quite good, but who knows?"

"*You* don't, obviously. The Ferreans have bottled more '49 than an entire planet can make in a decade. How much did you pay?"

"You old kelt-purse! Let me see. About fifty—maybe more."

"Humph. You got knicked. Sometimes I wonder if there ever was a '49, or whether the Ferreans just made it up to rob fools and snobs."

"Hah! They got you too, didn't they?" Buschard seemed elated by this discovery.

Vraser reached for a platter of cheese, the dim light reflecting softly off his balding head. "Perhaps," he said in a condescending tone, "but I never got taken for any fifty chits."

The portal slid open with a tiny hiss. Everyone except the Havassit priest turned to see who was coming in. The priest had his back to the door but seemed uninterested in who might be coming up behind him. It was one of the five or six unauthorized pards which lived aboard ship. The graceful feline swept in like a grande dame, leapt lightly onto the table and walked its length, fluffy tail erect. It walked up to Gilhame, sat down on his plate, wrapped its tail around itself and yawned into his face. He looked at it, reached out and stroked it under the chin, and was rewarded with an ecstatic buzz.

"Hello, my pretty," he said. The pard flowed off the table into his lap, turned several times, settled down and went to sleep. Gilhame continued to stroke it as he turned his attention to Group Commander E-varit.

"Commander, I have no pretensions to the role of connoisseur of food and wine. I leave that to Vraser and Buschard. I am accounted something of a small expert on music and the dance. Tell me, have you ever heard Grentarian pipes?"

E-varit gave him a slight glare. "Once or twice." Then he looked uncomfortable. "Their sound is not quite to my liking."

"It could not be otherwise, under the circumstances. How maladroit of me. Tell me, what do you think of Lavarin's conducting?"

Ur Fagon smiled. Grentar, Krispin's home world, was famous for many things besides its brandy and fine cloth. One of these was the Grentarian pipes, renown through most of space for their uneasy music. But both men knew that ur Fagon had not referred to the music but to the history of the instruments themselves. The story of the Vrandonian peace conference was well known—how the Grentarians had killed the principal envoy during the meal, to the eerie music of the pipes.

"We live in very odd times, don't we, Admiral?" E-varit answered, ignoring Gilhame's question.

"Odd times?"

"Our cultures—yours, mine, the Nabateans, the Kalurians, most of us except the Havassit—have evolved an entire literature based on deceit and treachery. Have you ever thought about it? We say a man speaks like a Lurian—and we mean he lies. We refer to Risar promises—my daughter used the phrase when her betrothed wed another—and yet the Risar have broken but one oath. But that is all we remember about them, not that Corluss Hruska, the greatest playwright of the last decade, was a native of Risar. My son and I spoke of it one night some years ago. He was about fifteen and doing his psychohistory specials. He wondered that there was no scholarly journal called 'The Annals of Deceit.' "

" 'The Annals of Deceit.' Interesting. He sounds like a

lad with a good head on his shoulders. Does he still pursue his interest?"

"He was one of my fighter pilots," said E-varit, his triangular eyes narrowing. "I am afraid that the mines you used ended any interests he had in . . . anything."

Gilhame stared at his adversary, the tiny golden flecks dancing in his green eyes. "Your sorrow is my sorrow," he said formally. "Let us desire that, upon his return, there will be peace."

The people of the Ten Nations had as many diverse religious beliefs as the nearly four thousand worlds which comprised them. The Kardusians and the Nabateans held to reincarnation after a period of atonement for wrongdoing, while the Coalchee believed that if one was ritually salted, one escaped rebirth. The absence of salting guaranteed that E-varit's son would come back as a member of some other race. To a Coalchee, that was the ultimate punishment.

E-varit nodded and sipped his glass. "No doubt they piped him into the Overworld with the music of Grentar," he said bitterly. "All the allusions we have constructed to prevent us from direct reference. I wonder why?"

"Self-disgust, Commander," said Lieutenant Darkcut. "We are a brutal and uncivilized people, and we know it. The tale of our years is a glorious history of war. Do you wonder we try to pretend that war is forced upon us, not our own deadly choice?"

E-varit turned his head and looked at her a little sternly. "Strong words for one of your profession, Lieutenant."

"Have you ever thought why so few women enter my discipline?"

"No."

"Women have few illusions. And they have none whatever about the glory of war."

"Perhaps. Have you ever been to Shipana?"

"In the Nabatean sector? No, I haven't."

"You, Admiral?" E-varit turned to include his host in the conversation again.

"I think I have heard of it, but I've never been there."

"I visited there—oh, it must have been fifteen years ago.

Strange people. They reverence the Great Mother there, but in a manner so perverse I cannot describe it. The men are very *vragado*—noisy, swaggering louts. The women are the softest, most pliant creatures in the cosmos. They never look you in the face, but simper behind tiny little hands. But they have a play there. Very curious. The play has been performed continuously from time immemorial, if one believes their traditions. They call it *The Loyal Retainers,* and it has more death, deceit and treachery in it than most planets see in a generation. These Shipanii have eight different words for death, sixteen for murder, nine for suicide and I don't know how many for treachery. Some words are poetical, some polite and a few are quite precise, almost bald. Now, this play is a literary work, very rich in ritual and allusion, and yet it only uses the least polite words in their language when they speak of the insult which began the matter and the subsequent murders, suicides and betrayals. Words which any of us in this room would choke to speak. It is as if they have decided not to hide behind words."

"That's fascinating. Why is the play performed continuously?"

"That is the part I do not quite understand," said E-varit. "Their tradition is that they will continue to perform the play until the Lion and the Horse return. Then they will not need to anymore, because the Lion will bring them inner enlightenment, and the end of all things will follow."

"What is the color of the Horse?" asked the woman.

"White."

"I guessed as much. The Lion and the White Steed are a persistent messianic legend on many worlds. I thought about doing my mono on that subject, but it was too large a matter. If I survive to old age, I may tackle it. The play also sounds like the Antrian Creation. I wonder how many worlds have some endless ritual to prevent the end of all things? There's another large subject. Is anything wrong, Admiral?" She looked across at ur Fagon.

He damned her for being so sensitive but said, "No, nothing." The Lion, the Light-Bringer, the Savior. Why did the mention of this legendary creature disquiet him? The Dragon had seen him in uneasy dreams since the beginning of time, though he had never met him. But the Lion's ruddy beard and eyes like great black stones, eyes like the depths of space with no white in them, had disturbed his sleep many times.

The pard in his lap sensed his unease and lifted its head. It stared up at him with its large blue eyes and purred to comfort him. Gilhame stroked its head and wondered if the Lion would return in this lifetime and if they would finally meet. "Everyone is waiting for the Messiah or someone like him, aren't they?"

Kessie Darkcut smiled at him. "Of course they are. We can't save ourselves, so we want someone else to do it."

"Culmeni!" Gilhame said abruptly.

"Sir?"

"Some music, please."

"Certainly, sir." Culmeni rose from the table. He wondered what the old man was up to, being polite and petting that pard. 'In fact,' he thought as he went to get his harp, 'what the devil was that pard about?' Usually they bottled their tails and hissed at ur Fagon's approach. He noticed that Frikard and Buschard seemed puzzled too. The old man was positively affable. Then Culmeni sat down with his harp and began to play.

By prearrangement, the rest of ur Fagon's people rose from the table and sat on the cushions around Culmeni. A-gurit joined them after a moment, leaving the priest in solitary state at the far end of the table. He seemed to have fallen into a silent meditation. The little witness brought the rod and recorder to the table, sat down in the empty place next to the priest and waited.

Gilhame looked at E-varit and stroked the pard. "Since you seem in favor of plain-speaking, shall we two simple men of war essay some?"

"I am at your service."

"I only wish you were. I realize what an intolerable position I have placed you in. You won't be welcome at home."

" 'No one loves the vanquished.' "

"I suppose not. We are still exchanging literary pleasantries, Commander."

"Yes, Admiral, we are." The little Coalchee reached for his glass.

"Could you bring yourself to call me Gilhame? 'Admiral' and 'Commander' are so formal for men who have broken fast together—even enemies. There are no Risar promises here, no Grentarian pipes."

"And Esarian harps?" E-varit referred to the famous siren instruments of that world.

"Culmeni? A more honest man I would be hard-pressed to name. Or do you mean me? I am hardly as seductive as Esarian harps."

"What do you want?"

"A little quiet conversation."

"In exchange for what?" E-varit was wary.

"I have nothing to offer you except the opportunity to remove yourself with dispatch—after we have talked."

"After you get the information you require."

"Precisely. Now we are getting down to plain-speaking."

"I know a guest's right. I did not ask to break bread with you."

Gilhame laughed, quietly this time. "I use everyone, do I not? That is the secret of control, E-varit. Never waste an opportunity to learn. I could have had Buschard remove you and had you dead-brained. That would have given me the information I wanted, but then we two would never have known each other. That, my friend, is the role of food in history. It is why the guest's right is rarely betrayed. Eating is our only vestige of civilized behavior. Even the interaction between the sexes is a kind of combat."

E-varit grinned, displaying even teeth as white as his hair. "True. My wife and I have been fighting to a draw for years. You have never married?"

"No, never. I made my sister-son, Hamecor, before I left Faldar and entered the Academy. Women are delightful creatures, but their logic quite astounds me. They are, you know, the most logical thinkers in the cosmos, illusionless, as Kessie pointed out, but their leaps and bounds, their ruthless reshuffling of the data to suit their own ends, exhausts me. It is like pursuing a running hart over rough terrain on foot. The odds are not to my liking, in any case."

"There are very few spacemen from Faldar, Admiral."

"At least try 'ur Fagon.' The word will not choke you, I promise. The Faldarian dream is not for everyone, E-varit."

"My wife says, if she ran the cosmos, there would be no war."

"Perhaps. But what would males do to occupy themselves then? No, if war did not exist, we would have to invent it."

"There are many things—art, music, poetry."

"Come now. You must agree that no man has written a book worth reading in over a decade, or painted a picture worthy of the canvas. I don't know if we could ever learn that."

"Turn our ships into shovels? I find that a curious but attractive notion. Men have created beauty in the past, but I suspect you are correct. The course we are on is rushing head-over-heels to destruction. Listen. Your harpist is playing such a strange song. I wonder how old it is?"

Gilhame listened intently for a moment, drifting back through the flotsam of his many memories, sifting the overlay of millennia from the song until he could hear in his mind the first time he had listened to it. "It was written, according to legend, by al-Richar, the demon warrior, during his captivity in the Endless Tower on the Mother World."

"That old? I would never have suspected you of an interest in ancient music . . . ur Fagon."

"There is much ancient music on Faldar. My sister Corinda . . . made it part of the dream. Poor Faldar. A world living in a past which will never return."

"I have heard that." E-varit drained his glass. "I find that I am weary. What do you wish to know?"

"Anything you are *willing* to tell me."

"You are very unlike your public image, ur Fagon. In fact, I would say your current behavior is completely out-of-character."

"Then you did have a psycho-tape on me. You had an advantage I lacked."

"Three, actually."

"The devil you say!"

"It was one of the assurances which convinced the Protector."

"Krispin is going to live to be a very sad old man." Gilhame sighed. "The why of it still puzzles me."

"I would guess he was afraid of your growing success, ur Fagon."

"Ambition? Strange, but that is a drive I think myself devoid of. Does that surprise you?"

"No. But I have studied your tapes. A man doesn't have to be ambitious to be dangerous. Sometimes efficiency is a greater threat than glory. No one would ever deny that you are a fine killing machine, ur Fagon."

"What a bitter epitaph you have written me, E-varit. No more than I deserve, certainly, but bitter nonetheless. What rewards would the Protectorate reap for being Krispin's assassins?" He twirled the stem of his wine glass in his left hand. "Besides my death, I mean?"

"The Island Worlds. In fact, a flotilla is probably already there. The Protector was anticipating success."

"Then, unless there was double-dealing on Governor Mordell's part—for such a concession must have arisen with him, not Krispin—you have three planets which suit your race nicely. Still, I suspect your colonists found a rather nasty welcome. Mordell would know that the Protector couldn't holler cop."

"Cop?"

"An archiac word for peacekeeper."

"Oh. You are probably right. You can't trust a traitor, can you?"

"No, you can't," ur Fagon said. "And Mordell would be a great hero for warding off a Coalchee invasion. Clever man, Mordell. It's a wonder he hasn't cut himself before, he's so sharp. Tell me, since your welcome at home is likely to be cool, if not fatal, would you consider staying on with me while I shove the bastards' treachery down Krispin's and Mordell's throats? I will not restrain you, of course, if you want the short way out now. I gave my word. But I thought you might enjoy the fireworks."

"You mean my son might still be alive if Krispin had not tried to have you ambushed? I agree that the final responsibility is his. You and I, after all, are only tools. But after that, what?"

"Whatever you will. You are a brave and loyal warrior. You may live out your allotted span however you wish. I would be honored to accept you into my service. Or, I could arrange for you to settle on one of the Imperial domains and make a new life for yourself there. You may take the short route to the Overworld, of course."

"I have always had a fondness for fireworks, Black Dragon."

"Good." He filled both their glasses. "Let us drink to Old Hag Death cheated of our company for a while, then. It is good to toast a surety."

"To Death!" They raised their glasses.

Chapter III

The audience hall at the principal city of Vardura V was ancient and immense. It was several millennia older than the Kardus Temporal Empire, by the archeologists' best guesses, and appeared to have been scaled for a race of giants. That the giants had been manlike was evidenced by splendid murals on the two long walls, but beyond that no clue to their existence or fate had ever been found. No skeletons, no artifacts of that vanished race had ever been reported.

The walls rose eighty meters from the floor. The roof was made almost entirely of glass in a curious, pleasing pattern of abstract shapes and colors. Unlike the walls, which showed the giants at work and play, the ceiling lacked any underlying theme and seemed at variance with the ordered black and white hexagonal slabs of stone, mortared in red, which made up the floor.

Governor Inawe Mordell sat on the dias at one end of the hall, waiting. His elegant hands traced the intricate carving in the arm of the chair as he tried to quell his rising anxiety. Something was certainly up. It was Krispin's silence which disquieted him the most. The only communication he had received from him was that the battle was over and that the fleet would be at Vardura that day.

Of course, Krispin had planned to bring the fleet home, the remnants of it, after the destruction of Admiral ur

Fagon. They had agreed on that. But Mordell could not shake his sense that something was wrong.

He was a handsome man, tall and well-proportioned, with black hair and dark eyes. Those eyes were restless now, flickering from the murals to the ceiling to the floor and back again. The presence of the Imperial Temporal Adjudicator did nothing to ease his mind. One didn't, of course, ask a man of that office what the devil he was doing, landing in one's provincial capital and demanding one's presence, however tempting or desirable that might be. It was the Adjudicator's job to be present at all disputes concerning the great families, planetary infringements and just about anything else which he chose to meddle in.

So, Mordell waited, surrounded by his guards, hovered over by his secretary and watched by his wife. Halba Armanda Mordell sensed her husband's unease, but she stood beside him calmly. A beautiful woman, not quite forty, Armanda was tall, full-figured and fair-skinned. She wore a full gown of dark green embroidered along the eight seams of the robe with rust-colored flowers on long, light-green stems. Her straight red hair fell almost to her waist beneath its curious diadem. Her eyes focused on her husband's restless hands.

The enormous doors at the end of the hall swung open, and a squadron of men-at-arms wearing the uniform of the Imperial Marines marched in under the charge of a downy-cheeked lieutenant. They marched down the hall, lifted their arms in salute to the governor and wheeled off to the right. The door remained open. After a minute, the Marines were followed by a disorderly gaggle of clerks carrying chairs, desks and recording equipment. They did not salute or even acknowledge Mordell's existence, but scurried about setting up their gear. Two men staggered in, carrying the Adjudicator's iron-studded wooden chair. They placed it in front of the clerks' equipment and adjusted its position at some direction from the Principal Scribe.

Horns blared. Mordell jumped at the sound. From without the gaping door six robed priests entered, followed by the Adjudicator's legal staff, twenty men and women in the distinctive black robes of their office. After them came Lorus fan Talba, Imperial Temporal Adjudicator, in his clinging robe of silver.

Fan Talba walked casually behind his staff, cooling his skin with a pleated paper fan, for the climate of the city was humid even in winter. His movements were indolent, and he seemed to have no concern in the entire cosmos. He was a neutral-appearing man, hair and eyes of no distinctive color, face unmemorable, body neither tall nor short, slim nor fat. Surely a man one would forget as soon as he was gone from sight, and hardly a figure to be acknowledged the finest legal mind of his time. He went to his chair without a glance at Mordell on the dias, certainly with no sign of recognition.

The Office of the Adjudicator—Imperial in Kardus, Protectoral in Coalchee—was written into the Ten Nations Compact. It was, in fact, probably the best portion of that dubious document. It crossed the boundaries of the members, arbitrating between monarch and president, between master and servant. Its Witnesses might be anyone from peasant to king, for a Witness is an anonymous, sometime job that many were trained for and few actually performed in a lifetime. But as navies absorbed reckless spirits too rowdy for a conservative society, so the Adjudicator's Office made certain that the inequities natural to such societies did not become oppressive. The unwritten motto of the Ten Nations was "Make litigation, not war." And when that failed, they let the navies kill each other and kept the planetary populations intact.

Mordell knew that it was the purpose of the Adjudicator and his staff to create a feeling of uncertainty in anyone having contact with them, but he still felt nervous. The simple fact that the Adjudicator had not approached him told him he was not here to witness some mere squabble over an estate boundary. As Governor of Vardura, he was supposed to be present at all sessions of the court, but he rarely actually attended unless summoned.

'What could it be? Of course, my beastly brother has begun another of his legal battles,' he thought. He hadn't heard a peep out of Devar in months, which was remarkable in itself. Perhaps he was suing the Imperium to abandon Vardura as interlopers upon the property of the long-vanished giants. It would be just like him. Such nuisance suits were Devar's food and drink, and the Adjudicator's office treated them with the same gravity it treated everything. There, the Adjudicator was studying the walls. It must be a matter concerning Devar.

The relief he experienced at this conclusion was short-lived. It was swept away almost immediately by the arrival of four squadrons of Imperial Troopers in the red uniforms of naval combat. They assembled themselves on the left side of the hall.

Then Mordell saw Commander Pers Buschard, elegant in his white dress uniform, beneath the blood-red cape with the black dragon embroidered on it. Buschard marched up the hall, but so easily did he move that he appeared to saunter. The multicolored ceiling made a moving mosaic across the white uniform and fair hair.

Buschard arrived at the foot of the dias and stopped. He looked up at Mordell and slowly removed the white gauntlets from his hands. He slapped them down on the bottom step of the platform.

"For two thousand of my comrades, fallen in battle!" His strong voice echoed up and down the hall. He turned and marched away.

Mordell watched the dragon flutter on Buschard's cloak as he marched away. He glanced up at Armanda, but she seemed to have withdrawn from him. The hall was almost silent.

Two squadrons of Coalchee combat troops in blue-and-green uniforms goose-stepped into the hall, counting stridently as they marched. They wheeled into position next to Buschard's men. Then two officers of the Coalchee Armada entered and strode up to him, each bearing a small golden arrow.

As they came to the foot of the platform, he recognized Group Commander E-varit. The man looked up at him, the pupils of his triangular eyes narrowed to slits. "For my son's life!" E-varit said, putting his arrow down on top of Buschard's gloves.

"For the lives of eight thousand of my comrades," added the other officer, placing his arrow parallel to the first. They marched down the hall to their men.

Mordell could feel the sweat running down under his arms. E-varit, here? What had gone wrong? The plan had been foolproof. Krispin! The bastard must have ratted.

A security team urged Krispin forward now, ignoring his leg restraints. The Admiral looked exhausted, his uniform stained with sweat and dirt, but otherwise he looked as he always had. He glared at Mordell when the security men let him stop moving.

Mordell heard Armanda sigh. He looked up at her, but her face told him nothing. Only her hands showed her agitation as she looked across the hall at her older brother, Krispin. Then she looked at Mordell, and he saw something in her eyes he could not define. Disgust? Loathing? Hatred? Not his Armanda. She was incapable of hating anyone.

He was trying to puzzle it out when the sound of footsteps coming towards him arrested his attention. For a moment, Mordell saw only a blur of red.

Gilhame ur Fagon stopped at the foot of the dias. In addition to his formal red uniform adorned with the black dragon on his chest, he wore a black-winged red helm of archaic design and red gauntlets. The visor of the helm was shaped like a bird's beak and shadowed the upper half of his face. All that was visible was the thin line of his mouth and the jut of his jawbone.

He looked up at Mordell and smiled. Very slowly, ur Fagon removed the gauntlets, but Mordell was mesmerized by the square, white teeth. Putting one foot insolently on the bottom step, ur Fagon cast the gloves down directly at Mordell's feet, ignoring the white gloves already there and the arrows on the step near his foot.

"For the lives of my men wasted in battle, I claim recompense!" His voice echoed around the great hall. Ur Fagon walked down the hall to stand near Buschard and some officers who had followed him in.

The small figure of an Adjudicator's Witness trotted halfway up the hall, panting beneath its black hood. It looked around, then darted across to one of the clerks and handed over the recorder as if it were burning hot. The clerk smiled at the nervous figure, reached out and patted it on the shoulder, then said something which appeared to calm the Witness.

The Imperial Adjudicator stood fanning himself for several seconds after ur Fagon had gone to his place. Then he sighed, shifted his shoulders to reset the fall of his robe and handed his fan to a clerk. He placed the black cap of his office on his head and cleared his throat.

"You may descend the dias, Governor Mordell. This tribunal is called to order," he said. His voice had a reedy quality. No one sat while the court of the Imperial Adjudicator was in session.

Mordell rose and offered his arm to his wife. Halba Armanda laid her hand so lightly on his arm that he could not feel it. She looked straight ahead, the diadem of flowers in her hair hardly stirring as she walked beside him.

"Don't abandon me," he whispered.

"You should have thought of that earlier!" she hissed. "Now is too late."

As they took their places facing the Adjudicator, Mordell tried to think of some way of shadowing the truth, of making himself the hapless victim of his brother-in-law's schemes. A cautious glance at Krispin's face destroyed that hope. So he waited with as much equanimity as he could muster for the principal clerk to read the specific charges to the court.

The doors of the audience hall crashed shut.

It was the purpose of the challenges and charges offered before the opening of the tribunal to diffuse the anger of the complainants and bring a spirit of neutrality to the proceedings. It frequently sufficed, but not on this occasion.

Gilhame listened to the angry denials and even more furious affirmations of the evidence. He alone offered no comment out of order, even when Krispin resorted to direct lies concerning the events of the Battle of the Vardar Straits.

"These proceedings are incredible, Magistrate. I am

shocked that you should allow yourself to be a party to them! I am no traitor. It should be obvious that this ambitious subordinate of mine has cooked up this entire scheme with that renegade Coalchee. In fact, I do not understand why I am here at all. It is ur Fagon who should be in the dock for disobeying my orders." Krispin sent little bits of spittle into the air as he shouted.

"You . . . swine's rectum!" E-varit roared.

"Gentlemen!" the Adjudicator said firmly as his clerk banged a staff on the floor.

"May it please the court," Commander Frikard said.

"Yes?"

"I have here copies of Admiral Krispin's battle plans and the details of our strength, as well as a similar document pertaining to the Coalchee Armada. Both were issued by his office and are initialed in the Admiral's own hand."

"Forgeries!"

"It does please the court, Commander Frikard. Give them to the clerk. How did you obtain these documents?"

"From the ship's files, Magistrate."

"Can you testify that Admiral Krispin placed them there?"

"I cannot, sir."

"Of course you can't! They are forgeries." Krispin's face was red with fury.

Commander E-varit mastered his anger, for the Coalchee regard truth as one of the primary virtues, and to call a man a liar was a blood insult. "If it please the court, I offer the following documents from my own files. I have here the Kardusian fleet's position as dictated by Admiral Krispin, and three psycho-tapes on the personality of Admiral ur Fagon. Please note the date upon which these battle lines were transmitted to me. I believe I received these battle plans in advance of those received by Admiral ur Fagon."

"So, you had some spy steal the plans!" Krispin yanked at the restraints on his wrists.

"If we were not in a court of law, Admiral, I would cry blood-insult and kill you where you stand. The Coalchee are neither thieves nor liars."

"You gutless, under-sized weasel. How would you reach me? Have your *var*-crazed friend hold you up?"

"Enough!" The Adjudicator snapped. "One more word and I will have you gagged, Krispin. Give the documents to the clerk, Commander. Can you tell the court how you came into possession of these psycho-tapes? From the seal on it, one appears to be the official Navy tape. That should be gathering dust in the Document Center on Gantar VI even now."

"It was put into my hands by the Protector himself. He told me that Admiral Krispin had 'arranged' for us to have them."

"That is hearsay," said Mordell.

"Yes, it is," answered the Adjudicator. "And the Protector is not a person upon whom this court can call for affirmation." He bent his head to one side to speak to a clerk. The clerk held the Truth Rod of the Witness's Office in his hand. "However," he said, straightening up, "Commander E-varit speaks the truth of his experience. Tell me, Commander, have you always enjoyed the Protector's confidence?"

The Coalchee did not hear the sarcasm in fan Talba's question. "To some degree, sir. We share a common grandam, although we are of different generations," he said seriously. A sort of sigh went round the hall. Coalchee blood-ties were a serious business even at their most dilute, but first cousins were counted as siblings.

"Goodness. That close, are you?" Fan Talba give E-varit a tiny smile. He spoke to a clerk again. "The documents appear to be very much in order. Indeed, a more damning set of papers I am hard put to recall. And Governor Mordell's involvement in this nasty little affair?"

"Again, I must speak hearsay, Magistrate. The Protector informed me that in exchange for the removal of Admiral ur Fagon, Governor Mordell was prepared to allow the Island Worlds to come into the hands of the Protectorate. As the Magistrate surely knows, those planets have long been desired by my people, their environment suiting us much more than many worlds in this sector. I am only a simple fighting man, and I have no pretensions to a knowledge of politics, but those planets have an emotional place in the Coalchee heart."

"I have never heard such nonsense," snapped Mordell. "The Protector seems to have deluded himself on a grand scale. I am very sorry that you were caught in his machinations, Commander E-varit, and that it is you who will pay the consequences of my libel suit." Mordell felt he had introduced just the right note of bewilderment and sorrow into his voice. He had decided to let Krispin take the whole blame. The man was lost anyhow.

Krispin had apparently come to the same conclusion. "May I speak, Magistrate?"

"Yes, of course. As long as you confine yourself to the matter at hand and refrain from showering abuse on anyone."

"Yes, Magistrate. I wish to make a full and complete recital of the events which led to this tribunal. And although it pains me to say this—for my sister will suffer the consequences—the complainants were correct in placing their challenges at the feet of the Governor. I can produce tapes of all the negotiations between the Protector and the Governor. These meetings took place on the pleasure world of Artenii five weeks ago. Governor Mordell's posture of ignorance and innocence is pure masquerade. I will not be sacrificed for him . . . or anyone. I also wish to make clear that my sister, Halba Armanda Mordell, had no knowledge of these matters . . . unless Mordell talks in his sleep."

"Be that as it may, wives and children suffer for the errors of husbands and fathers. Where is this documentation?"

"In the music room at my townhouse here in the city."

"Please tell the clerk the exact location of your home and the tapes."

"Yes, Magistrate." Krispin whispered in the ear of one of the Adjudicator's staff. After a moment, two clerks crossed the hall and left by a small side door. Admiral Krispin looked less tired now. He had come to his decision, and his tension had dissipated. He thought a little sadly of his three daughters, safely away on Grentar. Another clerk came up to him with a recorder, and he spoke into it calmly.

The Adjudicator looked over his audience. It was not the kind of hearing he enjoyed or which commonly made up his workload. Of course, if he handled it well, it would mean much more rapid advancement than he had anticipated. He looked at ur Fagon, the helm now removed, who seemed to have fallen into a standing doze. He remembered the curt demand for his appearance on Vardura, which had reached him some thirty-six hours earlier. Ur Fagon had cried treason, rightly it appeared, but now seemed to have lost interest in the matter.

If Lorus fan Talba had any ambition—and men were chosen for the position of Adjudicator for their lack of that curious emotion—it was to be appointed a Law Lord and to spend the balance of his colorless existence researching the history of the legal system which he now represented. That goal seemed closer now, but he was not sure he liked the means by which it would be achieved. He enjoyed the variety of a circuit magistrate's life, but space travel upset his bowels and he longed for a permanent home.

"Admiral ur Fagon," fan Talba began in his neutral voice, "you have been curiously silent in all this. Since you began this matter, it seems appropriate that you should interact in it."

Gilhame shifted the helm from his right arm to his left. No man covered his head in the Adjudicator's court, any more than they sat. He had been staring at fan Talba, speculating as to whether he had been chosen for his job because he was so colorless, or whether the blandness was an outgrowth of the role. He drew himself slowly to attention.

"I meant no offense to the court, Magistrate. It seemed to me that my former foe, Commander E-varit, and my former allies were sorting the matter out between them nicely. How may I serve the court?" He made a graceful bow.

"A curious attitude for the victor of Haran's Deep, I must say."

"I appear to have outgrown my youthful need for direct

vengeance. Besides, flaying the hide off Krispin would not bring back a single one of my men and women, sir, or Commander E-varit's. I have learned that not all matters are best served with a weapon." He smiled at the Adjudicator. "Perhaps I am becoming mellow in my middle years." He wished that the real Gilhame had not left him with such a record of ruthless violence. At Haran's Deep he had had three hundred men skinned alive for disobeying orders. Of course, one only needed to do that sort of thing once to get complete obedience and a reputation for brutality.

"Very true, Admiral. Tell me, what suddenly caused you to forego Admiral Krispin's battle orders? You appear to have found no fault with them until shortly before the fight."

Gilhame understood the implication of the Adjudicator's question. Had he been a party to the conspiracy in some way? And, of course, he was not about to mention his *var*-created knowledge. "The Admiral's plan was eminently suitable if our strength had been greater than our enemy's. As soon as I learned that this was not the case, that the data we had about their numbers was in error, I scrapped the plan. Let us say I saw a trap and chose to avoid it."

"I see. Commander E-varit, have you anything to add?"

"I *believe* that Admiral Krispin was fully aware of my Armada strength, Magistrate."

"Krispin!" The Adjudicator nearly barked.

"I knew the number of the Coalchee force." He sounded weary.

"For what reason were you willing to sacrifice the lives and arms of the Emperor?"

"Fear? Ambition? Envy? I don't know any longer. I have long had a sense that ur Fagon would be my downfall. I appear to have been correct. He was rising too fast. I couldn't stand the thought of serving under the brute. And, if I were His Majesty, I would be concerned at the success of men like ur Fagon."

"The seeds of our own destruction are within us, Admiral."

The side door of the hall opened, and the clerks returned

with Krispin's microtapes. For the next ten minutes the Adjudicator listened intently to them. He was about to speak, when there was a heavy thud against the great doors of the audience hall. It was repeated. He said, "What is that infernal racket?"

Four Imperial Marines trotted down the length of the hall and opened the inward-swinging-doors. A second later, three young women, carried forward by the momentum of the large piece of drainage pipe they bore, tumbled in and fell to the floor.

Chapter IV

Gilhame knew her even before she had leapt to her feet. He thought that he would have known her anywhere, anytime, not by her red hair and swan throat, not by her green eyes and strong nose, but by the proud spirit which seemed to shine out of her, always. Throughout every lifetime he had lived, "she" had been the light of his eyes. But who was she now? Certainly, the original Gilhame did not know her.

Once on her feet, she was magnificent. She was tall and white-skinned, and she carried herself with great pride. Then he looked at the two women with her and for a moment wondered if he was having a hallucination, for the three were so like in form and countenance that they might have been triplets. *Was* it "she"? For a moment, he was unsure. Then he watched her sweep down the hall, ignoring the filth on the hem of her gown and the dirt on her face, to fling her arms around Admiral Krispin. The older man was gray now and looked as if he had been kicked in the groin.

Still breathless and very white with anger, she swept the assemblage with a contemptuous glare of her wide green eyes. "What is the meaning of this outrage!?" she shouted when her gaze came to rest on the Adjudicator. Fan Talba was listening to something being said by one of the clerks who had gone to Admiral Krispin's house.

"You will moderate your voice instantly, Halba Krispin! You cannot come bursting in here, interrupting the business of the court. Get those blasted doors closed!" The Adjudicator was suddenly tired of the whole matter. He hated this great barrack of an audience hall, he hated all the people in the room and he hated his job. Although he was aware that the emotions he was experiencing were really just indigestion, he took a moment to savor them in full before motioning to a clerk to give him a stomach dose.

Gilhame watched the three women. The two who had not spoken touched the arms of their sister and drew her away from their father. The three stood together, and now he could see that one had hair of a darker red and one was shorter than the others. They did not speak to the magnificent creature who had shouted at fan Talba, but the expression on her face changed slowly. It was a tremendously mobile face, with a soft mouth and wide eyes. The chiseled nose might be deemed a little strong for real beauty, and the square jaw certainly so, but to Gilhame she was and always would be the only woman in the cosmos. He was so taken with admiring her that it took him a moment to realize that the three women were almost surely communicating mind-to-mind.

Quite suddenly, she gave her father a look of such violent dislike that it was almost palpable. Halba Mordell walked over to the girls and drew them to her one by one, kissing them lightly on the brow and smoothing their hair. Their likeness to their aunt was quite striking.

"Identify yourselves for the court," said the Principal Clerk.

"Halba Armanda Krispin," said the one with darker hair.

"Halba Derissa Krispin," the shorter one answered.

"Halba Alvellaina Curly-Krispin." Gilhame noticed that she had a good voice when she wasn't shouting, and then realized that her additional name meant she was the eldest daughter and an heiress through her mother.

"The court did not require your presence. Why have you burst in here like a bunch of . . ." Fan Talba's reedy voice failed as he searched for an elusive metaphor.

Derissa Krispin bowed. "We beg the court's indulgence. We had just arisen from the table when your clerk demanded entrance. He informed us that our father was before the Imperial Tribunal. Naturally, we came here straightaway but found the door closed against us. I regret that our natural filial anxiety overcame us, Magistrate, and we acted without thought." As she ended her speech, two of the Marines put the drainage pipe the women had carried into the hall down against the wall with a hollow thump that echoed around the room.

Gilhame silently applauded Derissa's diplomacy. It was almost a shame that she was not the one. But, no, Alvellaina, red-headed termagant that she was, was the only woman he desired. There had been a time, long before, so long that he could not remember a name for the place, when he had wed all three sisters. Not this time. He suspected that one would be almost more than he could handle.

He glanced over his shoulder and found Buschard also staring at the women with undisguised admiration. He felt a pang of anger and then realized that Buschard's attention seemed to be fixed on Derissa. Would that prevent the final betrayal? Could he alter the pattern even that much? He hoped so. Perhaps, just this once, his domestic life might be tranquil, though looking at Alvellaina's now stony face, he doubted it.

The proceedings of the court continued, but Gilhame was almost unaware of them. He answered such questions as were put to him with half a mind, the rest being occupied with the problem of how he could get close enough to Alvellaina to secure her attention. He was impatient for the Tribunal to be done.

"Admiral ur Fagon, before the court makes its final disposition, have you any requests or recommendations to make, other than those in your original suit?"

"What?" As principal plaintiff, he had the right

of personal recompense as well as the privilege of setting the basic terms of the general one. "Oh, yes. I do not feel it excessive, sir, that personnel be drawn from the levies of the estates of Governor Mordell and Admiral Krispin to replace not only the more than two thousand of my people who died at Vardar Straits, but those of the Coalchee dead as well. I leave the division of the matter to the Magistrate's discretion. And, since it seems to me a dreadful waste that such lovely females should languish upon the exile world, through no fault of their own, I would accept one of the Admiral's daughters—the noisy one, there, Alvellaina, I think—as personal recompense for the attempt to terminate my existence." There. He had done it. Not gracefully, but there was no charming way to demand the enslavement of another creature. If she followed her father into exile, it would be the devil to get her out again.

Alvellaina made a faint croak. "Please, no!"

"May I inquire why, Admiral?" fan Talba sounded curious.

"Any woman who would try to batter down the door of this mausoleum is just to my taste, Magistrate. Besides, I believe she might just be worth the five cruisers I lost." A ripple of laughter tinkled around the hall.

"A five-cruiser woman! You insolent, underbred bastard." Alvellaina pulled herself from her sisters' embrace. "How dare you!"

"Is it too little? I can add the rest of my lost ships, if you like. Let me see, there were . . ."

"I am not some country lass to be bartered for cows or ships or anything. Please, please, stop this."

"Control yourself, Halba. Your wishes are of no interest to the court. The Admiral is quite within his rights. A little tactless in his speech, perhaps . . ." Fan Talba was having some difficulty in restraining his smile.

"Tactless? Arrogant and unmannered is more the truth!" she shouted, her breast rising and falling in anger and a faint flush of red coloring her cheeks. She looked splendid.

"Commander Buschard, do you wish to speak?" The

Adjudicator ignored Alvellaina's outburst.

"Yes, Magistrate. It seems to me that these sisters are very close, women of a single mind almost. It would be cruel to separate them. There has been enough unkindness in the matter already. Therefore, I would request that I be permitted to take the one called Derissa. I am unbound and would be glad of some companion. The other . . ."

"Yes, Captain . . . Culmeni?"

"I also . . . would rather see these sisters . . . remain together."

"Is that an offer to undertake the responsibility of Halba Armanda Krispin?"

"Yes, sir."

"I see. Well, you do have the right of secondary plaintiffs to make these requests, unusual as they are. Commander E-varit, you lost a son, did you not?"

"I did."

"Then you have recompense before the others. What will you?"

"These daughters of the Admiral's are very handsome women by the standards of your race, but they are . . . rather mammoth to my taste, sir." Laughter followed his statement. The shortest of the Krispin girls was more than a head taller than the Coalchee.

"I see. Governor Mordell has sons, if a son is your desire."

"Nothing can take the place of Furtlar, but to have a young man near me would be a comfort."

"Halba Mordell?"

"Yes, Magistrate." Her voice shook.

"Ennumerate your offspring."

"I have two sons and two daughters. My oldest son, Behar, is at the Academy on Darin, and my second son is six years old. His name is Kurwen. My girls are twelve and eleven, Mirra and Falga. The younger children are here on Vardura."

"It is very hard for you to bear the brunt of your husband's folly. I must admit that the laws concerning matters of recompense seemed very unjust to me when I entered my profession. Why should the innocent suffer for the actions of the guilty? I have asked myself that question many times. I will ask it many times more.

"Throughout our history we have tried many methods to discourage crime—particularly crime against the state. Death used to be the punishment for such crimes and many others. Before the Ten Nations Compact brought us a uniform legal code, it was possible to be executed for stealing a bit of string, and yet to retire in great comfort to one's estates, if one had money. This is one inequity we have removed.

"But we are a culture with strong bonds of family. We now hold that the suffering of the guilty party's family is a deterrent to crime. Few persons are so dead to family feeling that they would wish to endanger their innocent wives or husbands or children. This, at least, is the theory." He gave Mordell and Krispin a quick, sharp glance as he continued to speak. That too was part of his job, to remind the populace of the nature of the law.

As fan Talba's voice fluted on, Gilhame thought of all the times and all the places where people had been a mere commodity, little different from kine or wheat. It was a harsh system, one which discounted the individual, but individuality was often an extravagant fashion for a culture. How far back did the practice go, he wondered? To the home world, to the times when if one was responsible for the death or crippling of a son, one took his place. Not for murder, of course, but accident. As systems went, it worked as well as any, and the victim was at least not ignored. It would bring him Alvellaina, unwilling prize of war, but she had been that many times before. He forced his eyes away from her proud profile and back to the Adjudicator.

"It is not the desire of the court to create further victims. The Empire will take whatever is not used to itself, which will leave you very much alone, Halba Mordell, unless you choose to go into exile with your . . ."

"Certainly not." Armanda Mordell snapped the words out, then flushed with embarrassment. "I find the Commander's request for my son . . . a reasonable one, for I am sure he will treat him well." She was terribly pale now.

"Then the child Kurwen Mordell shall be given into the care of Commander E-varit Gnargol." Governor Mordell made a sound like a man being strangled, but fan Talba went on inexorably. "As Admiral Krispin is a widower, and we have settled the matter of his issue, there remains yourself, Halba Mordell, and your two daughters." He gazed at her, then glanced around the room at the audience.

She looked across to her husband, her face unreadable. "I shall go wherever my girls do. My place is with my children. Is it permitted that I return to my mother's people?"

"I hardly think you would be welcome there," fan Talba said dryly. That was the worst part of the system, the part over which the court had no control, the behavior of the families of wrongdoers.

"Sir?"

"Yes, Commander E-varit."

"Halba Mordell spoke quite correctly that a mother's place is with her children. I would welcome her and her daughters too, if they would choose to come."

"Halba?"

"Yes." The word was a whisper. Then she spoke more clearly. "I would prefer to be with my son, even among strangers."

Motioning his clerks to him, fan Talba conferred for a long time, occasionally waving forward one of his legal staff. Then the Principal Clerk read the decisions of the court. They were very much as set out by the plaintiffs, with the exception that the two estates were levied at two men for every one killed on both sides and the residuum of the estates was confiscated by the Empire.

After the judgments had been announced, Adjudicator fan Talba said, "This tribunal is now closed."

He removed his cap of office and again became a very ordinary little man. The Marines took Krispin and Mordell into custody and removed them. The Adjudicator noticed that his indigestion was unimproved and knew that the homeward journey would not make it better. He sighed, rose from his chair and broke wind audibly. 'That,' he thought, 'sums it up nicely: The whole matter stinks.'

_____ *Chapter V*

Gilhame twirled the stem of his wineglass and smiled, remembering the odd sorting out of parties in the audience
hall after the Adjudicator's departure. Culmeni, looking
like a man shaken awake to find that his dreams had come
true, had approached Halba Armanda Krispin and stood
looking at her as if she had sprouted an extra head or two.
The girl herself had seemed in a similar state of shock.

Culmeni, coming from a culture which believed firmly in
magic, wondered if he had been enchanted. He could not,
for the life of him, discern what had prompted him, a confirmed bachelor, to ask for the responsibility of this female.
Finally he had asked, "Are you musical?"

"Somewhat, Commander." She had smiled very sweetly, and Culmeni had entertained several dark thoughts
about witchcraft.

"Then I suppose we will manage."

Armanda had laughed in his solemn, worried face.

Buschard, with Derissa, had been quite another matter.
Quiet as Pers was, he could charm the birds from the
trees—or even the devil. And he remembered E-varit,
bowing gracefully before the other Armanda, Halba
Mordell. She was somewhat shorter than her nieces, but
still a good seven inches taller than the Coalchee. She had
left the hall like a magnificent ship escorted by two sturdy
tugboats, E-varit and A-gurit.

51

Halba Alvellaina Curly-Krispin was neither charmed nor resigned. Gilhame had stood for several minutes, watching her still outraged countenance, then he had given several quiet orders to the invaluable Frikard. After that he had walked outside the hall into the pale sunlight, sat on a bench, and puzzled over the situation for a long time. He could not recall Buschard—all the faithful Buschards who had been his companions before—ever taking a wife, or even exhibiting an interest in any female except she whom the Dragon favored. Was there to be some other rival? And never, since that time so long before, had there been three. This alteration in the pattern disturbed him. Finally, he had laughed at himself and taken the shuttle back to his ship.

Now Gilhame looked up from the spinning golden liquid in his glass to his silent companion. She still wore the soiled white gown, but her hair was tidy and her face and hands had been washed. The gown, he thought, was a calculated insult, for he had ordered Frikard to have all the women's effects brought on board. She had not eaten, drunk or spoken since her arrival thirty minutes past.

"I had no idea, looking at you, that you were quite so spoiled," he said, remembering how she rose to the bait of being traded for five ships.

The portal slid open to reveal the empty hall, and the white pard entered. She walked daintily into the room, leapt onto the table and came to Gilhame, demanding attention. "I wish I knew how you did that trick, my pretty," he said as he stroked the animal. "I must tell you, halba, that closed portals are as nothing to this pard. It puzzles me, for the controls are well above her reach, and yet no one is ever there except her. Besides, I doubt any of my staff would dare to open the door to my quarters to let in . . . anything. She seems to have adopted me, which I rather like. Perhaps 'commandeered' me is more accurate. She obviously views reality from the slave-master position— and I think I am the slave. But at least she is not completely spoiled." He smiled at his silent companion.

"I am not spoiled!" Alvellaina said through clenched teeth.

"Aren't you? Well, then, perhaps just in the habit of getting your own way. It is a very bad habit to fall into, for it offers one the illusion of control. Nasty stuff, control; quite as addictive as any drug and much more dangerous. It always deserts you at the critical moment. Still, it is good to know that you haven't forgotten how to speak. You can stop searching the utensils for a weapon. A fruit knife makes a very poor killing device. You might apply to Medic Vraser for some poison. The Healers use some in their work, don't they?"

She looked directly at him, her big green eyes narrowed a little from tension. "There isn't a poison slow enough to punish you."

"Isn't there? What a shame. No doubt you have given the matter some thought. Then we must just hope I contract some slow, wasting disease beyond the Healers' art, mustn't we?"

"Yes."

"But why are you angry with me? I did not cause your current situation, except by my intervention. Surely you are not still piqued by my five cruisers? Your father and your uncle brought you to this pass, m'alba, and the faster you accustom yourself to that reality, the quicker you can get about the business of your life. Believe me, you would not have liked Munsor very much. The exile world is filled with bitter people and . . . well, never mind."

"*You* should be there, not my father."

"I applaud your loyalty, however misplaced. I did not conspire against the Kardus Temporal Empire, my dear, and he did. That is the entire tale."

"*You* called the Adjudicator." She banged her hand flat on the table, making the giltware jump. The pard, still sitting before Gilhame, gave her a scornful look and slid into his lap.

"There, now, you've upset the *ghat*."

"*Ghat*?"

"An archaic word for these graceful creatures," he said as he chucked its chin and it buzzed passionately.

"The devil take the pard!"

"Don't be hurt, my pretty. She didn't mean it. I see your

attitude now. I should have covered the whole mess up. Now, tell me this, why should I exhibit clemency to a man who has declared himself my foe? Why the devil should I wait for Krispin to try to stick another knife in my back? That really is asking a great deal too much."

"You did it out of envy."

"Envy?"

"Our family is very well-connected."

Gilhame laughed his noisy laugh. "Silly girl. I would not care if you were the Emperor's sister. No, I take that back. The Emperor's sister is a great deal of trouble, always up to some mischief or intrigue. But no man tries to kill me and goes away unpunished . . . not the way he tried it."

"What is that supposed to mean?"

"My men, m'alba, my men. The battle was intended to be a slaughter—a slaughter of the men in my care, in my charge. That is an inexcusable crime. If your father had tried to cut my throat in a blind alley or had me alone poisoned, fine. That is fair by my lights—one on one. But my fleet? No. That is unforgivable."

"Your men? What do they matter? They are replaceable."

"I see you are indeed your father's child. And the Adjudicator said he had no sons. How little he knew. My men, forty thousand of them, are no small matter. They are not machines to be tossed away when broken. They are flesh and bone, as you or I. They have wives and children, even as your father. How can you think that anyone not nobly born is less than you are?"

"That is precisely the kind of egalitarian claptrap I would expect from an underbred peasant like you."

"Poor, poor Alvellaina. Welcome to the greater cosmos that exists outside the high walls of your father's estates. I think you will find that stiff-necked pride is very brittle stuff in the real world. No accident of birth makes one man better than another."

"But, my father said . . ."

"A great deal of nonsense, clearly. Look at Buschard. You know, the officer who took Derissa. On his home world, he is a duke. His bloodlines are much better than yours, my dear. His great-grandmother was an empress. And yet, he chooses to serve with me, the underbred mongrel you despise. I did not coerce him into my service. He asked to be here. I could not find a more able or loyal second. And Frikard: Ven is entitled to estates as magnificent as your father's, although he is a younger son. He does not count himself demeaned to serve me. Those two men are my right and left hands."

"You have some hold over them."

"That is true. I think they love me."

"They only serve with you because of your success. Lose a battle, and they'll desert you in a flash."

"Perhaps. But I doubt it. They were both with me at the Siege of Calfara."

"You are in league with demons."

"A commonly held superstition. Any man who is successful is held to be blessed by the gods or to have sold his soul to the devil. As if natural ability had no meaning. Darkcut was right. We are not a civilized people."

"Who?"

"One of our psycho-historians, Lieutenant Kessie Darkcut."

"She must be an idiot."

"Do you know, Halba Krispin, that you are extremely tedious? You have all the social graces of a street urchin, and none of the charm. I find I prefer your sullen silence to your uncouth speech."

"How dare you speak to me like that!"

"I would get up and give you the spanking you so richly deserve, but I don't want to disturb the pard."

"You wouldn't dare. I am your responsibility, and if I get damaged, you'll pay for it."

"Child, I could beat you from here to the Havassit League and back again, and it would not be in violation of my contract with the courts. I see that you still do not comprehend the full extent of your position. You are mine, my personal female, my possession, to do with just as I please, for the rest of my life. Now, if something happens to me, you go to my sister-son, Hamecor, on Faldar. I don't think you would like that. Faldar is not a comfortable world even if you are born there. You are about the same age as my son, I imagine. Eighteen? No, you are a bit older. Whatever possessed your father to marry so late? Never mind. Sometimes my curiosity is almost as great as a pard's. During court today, I found myself wondering about the giants who built the audience hall. Where was I? Ah, yes, your position. Legally, you are my chattel, a portion of my estate, a piece of inheritable property. I may treat you however I choose. Do you understand?" He knew he was overstating the letter of the law considerably, but he could think of no other way to get her complete attention.

Her face was white. "That's barbaric."

"I just said we are not a civilized race."

"But . . ."

"Did you sleep through your Imperial law specials? Or don't they teach law to the daughters of the aristocracy?"

"Derissa took the class for all of us."

He chuckled and scratched the pard. "Your sister has the makings of a splendid diplomat. She and Buschard should deal very well together. What have you been doing all your life?"

"Nothing. Why should I?"

"No reason, I suppose, except that ignorance creates more destruction than knowledge. I suppose you were waiting for your father to arrange a suitable marriage for you?"

"No," she said frowning down at her plate, as if seeing the fruit on it for the first time. "I never thought of marriage. My sisters are my world—and my father." Her voice was very pensive. "How did you bribe the Adjudicator?"

"I didn't."

"You must have."

"I see your mind still refuses to accept the truth. I *am* sorry."

"What if I say I knew of my father's plan to destroy you?"

"Do you know, when you lie you get two red spots on your cheeks? Your skin is so white, they look like little suns."

"But, if I claimed I had knowledge, the court would have to send me to my father."

"I doubt they would believe you, anymore than I do. Oh, it would cause a little trouble. You would have to be examined under *truth*. That is extremely unpleasant. You would find yourself entirely stripped of any defenses, facing your internal trueness. It is not a course of action which recommends itself, believe me. The little illusions we build around ourselves are necessary for our sanity. You never forget what you learn from *truth*."

"How do you know?" She was interested and curious now.

"It was necessary for it to be used on me after the Calanpor Mutiny."

"Why?"

"My superior officer, Commander Whitby, made certain claims about my part in the mutiny which the military court could not ignore and which could not be settled by the simple use of the Witness Rod. Basically, Whitby tried to throw the blame on me. I demanded the use of the drug. I could have done the thing as well with a truth-speaker like Vraser, but I had a youth's violent need for extreme measures. You might say it woke the Dragon in me. No, I would not recommend *truth*."

"Oh? Did it hurt?"

"Only myself. It was after that that I began to use *var* with greater frequency. The hallucinations it produced were a more acceptable reality than the one inside my skull."

"I am not like you."

"No, you are not. I think you have a great many more illusions about yourself and life than I did. You have much more to lose."

"What do you mean?"

"Are you willing to discover that your father was less than the great and good man you believe him to be?"

"I wouldn't find that!" The two rosy spots came back to her cheeks.

"Are you quite certain? Here, tell me something. How

came your father to be a widower? The Healers can cure almost any illness. They can even encourage wounds to heal, unless the energy of the sinew is disrupted. Then they must use mechanical methods which are less than satisfactory. That is why old Vraser stumps around on that steel hip of his."

"His wife died."

"How? Was she slain in a riot? Was she hit by a vehicle, trampled by a horse? What happened to her?"

"I was very young when she died. I don't know what happened."

"M'alba, you do know. Part of your mind which is fenced off knows. You do not wish to confront it—and I will not press you. But, if you take *truth,* you will know, and you will not be able to forget."

Alvellaina looked at him for a long moment. "The servants whispered that she wasted away, trying to give my father a son."

"I am sorry. And you have tried to be that son, have you not?"

"Do you know, Admiral, I never, never think of her? She deserted us. At least, that is how I *feel.*" She picked up the wineglass and drained it. "You are the devil," she said as she put it down, "dragging that out of me."

He refilled her glass. "Self-knowledge is never immediately pleasant. Now, do you think you could clear up a little puzzle for me? What the devil were you doing on Vardura? I saw your father's face when you entered. He could not have been more surprised—or horrified—if the Emperor himself had battered the door down. He obviously thought you were somewhere else. What brought you to Vardura?"

"Fragments." She began to peel a piece of fruit.

"Fragments?"

"That is what I call them—the dreams I have. I *knew* my father was in danger. And I knew it was your fault. At every corridor of my mind, I saw your death's-head smile and your bloody hands. We arrived at my father's house on Vardura the day before yesterday. I tried to get in touch with my aunt, Halba Mordell, but I couldn't. The Governor's Palace was not accepting any communications. It was

very strange. I was going to go see my aunt that day . . .
this day . . . when the clerk came and told us Father was in
before the Adjudicator's Tribunal."

"I see. Have you always had these 'fragments'?"

"As long as I can remember."

"Have you ever been tested for fore-seeing?"

"No. My father would not permit it."

"And your mother? Did she have this talent?"

"I think so."

He had a quick flash of the limited telepathy which
sometimes came to him without the use of *var*. It lasted
only for a moment, but it left him chilled. "She was tall,
fair-skinned, yellow-haired, and she had a little mole over
this eyebrow, did she not? Very blue eyes—almost
purple—with a tiny iris. She loved blue gowns edged in
gold. Yes?"

"Yes. Did you know her?"

"No."

"Then how . . .?"

"You might say . . . we share a talent for fore-seeing,
m'alba. Your mother has walked the corridors of my mind
for almost twenty years. Do you know, you might be right?
Perhaps my hands are too bloody for redemption. For, she
saw me too, I think, in her mind. What did you call it—a
death's-head grin? Well, I never was fair to look upon. I
suppose knowing that I was one's own child's fate might
frighten one to death. How long have you seen me?"

"Always."

"A face to frighten children. When will I be released?
What am I doing . . . well, no matter. Perhaps I will solve
the puzzle . . . in time."

"Puzzle?"

"Of my existence. A very boring metaphysical problem.
It is nothing."

"I did not expect a philosopher, Admiral."

"No. You never do."

"Riddles are very amusing, but only if two are playing.
What does that mean—'I never do'?"

"Forgive me. I was talking to myself aloud. I have the curious illusion that we two have met before."

"You are lying." Her eyes were narrow with intensity.

"As you wish."

"It isn't an illusion. You believe—no, not believe, you . . . *know*."

They looked at each other for a second, and then he looked away, wishing that he had not raised the issue. He wondered what the extent of her talent for reading minds was. Probably, from what he had seen in court, it required physical contact and some familiarity. But he couldn't be sure. And he wished, just this once, that he might be known. That other "she," if she too was an immortal, might know and recognize him. It was so lonely always to recognize her and never be known.

"You are not what you seem, are you?"

"Is anyone?" he answered lightly.

"How old are you?"

"Thirty-three. A very symbolic age."

She paused and drank some wine and ate a piece of fruit. "No, you are very much older than that. Tell me, *Admiral*, is it very cold *there*?"

"There?" The silence that followed his response seemed to stretch on forever. 'Well,' he thought, 'I have gotten my wish. She knows, something.' How much he was not certain, but it did not matter. She "saw" something—his resting place between times, the Glass Castle. Now he must decide how to answer. "I would say it was rather chilly," he said finally.

"Then you *are* a demon."

He laughed softly at her statement. "I suppose you could call me that. I would not, but you might. What do you know of . . . Ker Vidor?"

"That it is the resting place of heroes. And heroes are men with blood-stained hands. So, you are free again. Yes, I do know you, and I wish that I did not. You are Chaos masquerading as Law. Yes, I remember. Yes, I know you. How will you use me this time?"

There was such bitterness in her question that he almost wept. So, this was the price of knowledge. She knew who she was, had acknowledged her own immortality in a single chilly sentence, without struggle or hesitation. 'It was so like a woman,' he thought, 'to give in when you would fight, and fight when you would surrender.'

"I don't know. I cannot foresee the events of my life from here. But the pattern is altered. Shattered, almost, for never before have . . . have I been recognized."

"All my life you have been there—the fate I most sincerely wished to avoid. And I ran right towards it. So, I seem to be betrayed by my own foreknowledge."

"That, at least, you cannot lay at my feet in blame." He gave her a half smile.

"Certainly I can. You need never have existed. Or you could have gone away long ago. But something prevents that. What?"

"I don't know, m'alba." He sipped his wine.

"I don't either. And, do you know, I have the greatest reluctance to once again be the subject of any romantic lays. Even though until a few minutes ago I did not 'know' who I am . . . was . . . whatever, I find I am very tired of the role already."

"That, I think, makes two of us. Perhaps this time we will make an end to heroes and wars—and romantic songs. Perhaps this time I'll find out what *not* to do."

"Will you? I wonder. I, too, am blind in the matter. Will you promise me something?"

"What?"

"Don't ever touch me."

Gilhame looked at her proud face. So, she had not completely accepted her role. He frowned a little. "As you will. Too much blood on me, I suppose, to be attractive."

"Much too much."

He bowed slightly, forgetting the pard on his lap. The little animal promptly put a clawed paw into his stomach and pushed. He chuckled and straightened up. "It seems I will live under the sign of the *ghat*'s paw for a time."

"Do you know, I hope this time you really die. I am going to bed. All this has given me a headache."

"Good night, m'alba."

"Good night, demon." She swept out of the room, and the portal whispered shut as it closed.

"A pretty pickle, isn't it?" Gilhame said to the pard.

"Well, beginnings are never easy, are they? Still, this one was better, under the circumstances, than many. Do you remember that time—when was it—well, sometime, somewhere, she slashed me with a knife and I bore the scar for the rest of that life? Right here, on my cheek. I can still almost feel it. Or the time she got drunk on honey wine and came to me almost willingly? No, of course you don't remember." The pard woke up and gave him a sudden, wide-eyed stare. "Or do you?"

It yawned, curling a pink tongue in his face, and resettled itself into some obscurely more comfortable position. It looked at Gilhame again, then closed its eyes and took its secrets away into feline sleep.

Gilhame stepped out of his shuttlecraft into the shadowy docking bay of the Coalchee flagship. A rather bored-looking subaltern scrambled to his feet and made a curious hash of a salute. Gilhame was amused rather than offended, for the young man could hardly be blamed for confusion. One day he was serving the Coalchee Protector, and the next the Kardusian Emperor, no one asking him whom he wished to serve, or even if he desired to do so.

"Good evening, sir," he said in slow, formal Kardusian.

"Good evening. Am I very tardy?" Gilhame smiled quietly at the young man, noting that the Coalchee insignia had been removed from his uniform and not yet replaced by Kardusian ones.

The Coalchee blushed under his pale skin. "I was not informed that you were coming, sir, and I believe the dance has already begun."

"Perfectly understandable. Now, where is this dance?"

"In the mess hall, sir. Level 3, Corridor G."

"Very good. As you were," Gilhame said with another grin. He was aware of the young man's eyes following him as he left the bay and wondered just what the subaltern's tale of his meeting would be like.

Ur Fagon's fleet, with its newly added Coalchee contingent, was still in the Vardura system, awaiting orders from the Admiralty. Three "days" had passed since the trial, and Gilhame was now restless from forced inactivity. Alvellaina was keeping to her quarters, emerging only at the dinner hour to continue their exchange of insults. He had spent his days working through the stack of reports that was the natural aftermath of a military encounter, until the sight of one of those thick, yellow-bound things began to make him queasy. Unlike many of his peers, he did not shove off the task of perusing reports on a subordinate, as was certainly permitted, but forced himself to study each one. As a result, he knew the capabilities of his ships and their commanders as well as anyone could.

He suspected that E-varit also was chafing under the lack of activity. The Coalchee commander had begged permission to hold a dance. Gilhame had said yes, for while a dance was not a major activity, it was something to do, and Gilhame loved dancing. Still, he had been of two minds about putting in a personal appearance. The sight of the hefty document from Captain Unaga of the destroyer *Sureswift* had decided him. He had dropped it with hasty dismay, removed his working grays, bathed, put on his dress blacks and commanded a shuttle. Unaga was a worthy and able captain, but he was also the dullest reporter of ur Fagon's acquaintance.

Gilhame took the lift to Level 3 and began looking for Corridor G. He heard the faint strains of drum, flute and *kibla*, a sort of guitar, well before he found his way. In the pale light of the Coalchee ship, the music had an eleven-hill quality to it, and Gilhame chuckled to himself at his conceit. However small in stature the Coalchee might be, they were not fairies dancing in the night to lure unwary mortals to their doom.

Finally he found the correct passage and followed the sound of the music. He entered the open portal and stopped for a moment, watching the dancers. They were doing a round dance of nine persons, five-and-four of each sex, though some of the seven circles in the room had five men and some five women. Nine was the most sacred number of the Coalchee faith, and the dance had both a social and a religious significance.

The mess hall was a great dim barrack. Unlike the

Kardusians, the Coalchee always ate communally, even the Commander taking meals with his men. Gilhame, who hated the clatter of large numbers of people eating, shuddered a bit and was grateful for his own race's choice of dining in small groups. He could imagine how the hall sounded at mealtimes.

The musicians saw him, and the music began to falter. Again, he had the sense of frightening fairies at their dancing. He peered into the dimly lit room, trying to spot E-varit, and wished that the Coalchee were not so light-sensitive. He saw a movement in the shadows across the room, and the music ceased. The dancers, both his own people and the Coalchee, stopped and stared at him silently.

"Please, continue the dance," he said clearly. Now he could see E-varit standing next to Armanda Mordell on the far side of the room. He moved between the circling dancers as the music began again, and crossed the room. Gilhame made his bow before E-varit and the woman and felt a cold hand slip into his. He looked down and saw a child, a sturdily built girl with red hair and great dark eyes. She smiled up at him.

"Are you important?" the girl asked. Halba Mordell began to rise, but ur Fagon motioned her to stop.

"I'm not sure," he replied.

"Well, who are you?"

"I am Gilhame ur Fagon."

"Oh." The girl studied his face without any self-consciousness. "You don't look very scary. Why did they stop dancing when you came in?"

"Quite a little question box, aren't you, m'alba? They stopped because I am the highest-ranking officer in the room. It was a matter of precedence, very grown-up and very boring. Now, you must tell me, are you Falga or Mirra?"

Her eyes seemed to widen further. "I am Mirra, but how did you know?"

"It is my job to know many things. I heard your mother mention your name . . . once." He didn't feel it tactful to repeat the circumstances under which he had heard her name. "Do you like Commander E-varit's ship?"

"Oh, yes. It is ever so much more fun than that dumb old school. I have been in the drive room, and the engineer says I am not a pest but ask very intelligent questions. And I have been in the sick bay, but no one was there but the Healer. I thought I would get to see sick people."

"I see. Tell me, is that your sister peeping out from behind your mother?"

"Yes, that's Falga. She's older than me, but she's dreadfully shy. Mother says I am not shy at all. 'Ur Fagon?' Does that mean you are from Faldar?"

"Yes. Why?"

"We were studying Faldar in our metaphysics class. Tell me all about the Dream."

"I cannot, Mirra. I have never entered it. That is why I joined the Navy. You might say I am *from* Faldar, but not *of* it."

"But why didn't you?"

"Mirra," said her mother, "that is quite enough. The Admiral did not come here to be quizzed by a schoolgirl."

"I *want* to know." The child stamped her foot.

"It is alright, Halba Mordell. The search for precise knowledge is vital and should be encouraged."

"The last thing my daughter needs is encouragement."

Gilhame laughed. "I am sure you find her a rare handful. Now, Mirra, tell me, can you see all the colors in the cosmos?"

"That's funny. I thought I could until I came here. I couldn't figure out why it was so dark everywhere until the Healer explained that the Coalchee see different . . . spectra than we do. Does that have anything to do with Faldar? I never heard that it was dark there."

"In a way. As you cannot see the same colors as the Coalchee, so I could not perceive the Dream of Faldar. I am . . . sort of a cripple, in terms of my people." He sensed a distant stir of the original Gilhame, deep in his mind, at the pain that admission cost.

Mirra looked up at him thoughtfully, then glanced at her sister. "Are you trying to give me a sneaky lesson?"

"Of course not. You are clearly on holiday from school."

"Humph," she said with a facial expression which put him much in mind of her cousin Alvellaina. "I can tell when someone's . . . preaching at me." She removed her hand, gave her sister a hard stare and marched away stiff-backed, her long red hair bouncing over her tidy bottom.

Ur Fagon wondered what the import of her look was. The other child, Falga, seemed to shrink back behind her mother. Halba Mordell was stifling a laugh, and E-varit had lifted a hand to cover his mouth. "Ah, the dignity of youth. That is quite a child you have there, halba. She is going to cut up your peace like anything by the time she is fifteen."

Falga peered out again, apparently recovering from her shyness a little, and he saw that she was as slender as her sister was stocky. 'The Krispin genes must be very strong to place their mark against the darkness of their father.'

"Sir, can I drink the punch?" asked a voice near his kneecaps. He looked down to see who was speaking. It was a small boy, slender and dark, dressed in the uniform of a Coalchee student. He was looking at E-varit, not Gilhame, but ur Fagon felt he had seen the child before.

Then he remembered the dream. There had been a child, a boy like this one, but not this very child. It was the dark hair and light eyebrows that deceived him in the half-light. He was glad, for there was something terrible about that dream and that other little boy.

E-varit smiled fondly. "I don't think so, Kurwen. I believe that the chef has some fruit juice for you."

"That's not fair. Mirra drank some of the punch."

"Goodness. Did she? The wicked little thing," said her mother. "I don't need to wait until she's fifteen, Admiral."

"I see that."

"Gil?"

"Buschard. Nice to see you."

"I should have known a dance was the only thing that would drag you off your old reports. I've asked the musicians to play 'The Elves' Parade.' "

"I can always depend on you, Pers, to remind me what dances I enjoy. Now, a partner." He scanned the room, then turned his eyes back to the family beside him. "Halba Falga, would you do me the kindness to stand up with me in the 'Parade'? You might almost be an elf yourself, you know." He bowed gravely as the child shrank back again.

"Do I have to?" she whispered to her mother.

An expression of concern crossed Armanda's beautiful face. She looked from the girl to ur Fagon and back again. "It is very rude to refuse such a gracious request, my dear."

Falga pressed her lips together, pulled her shoulders back and stepped out from beside her mother. "Thank you very much," she said in a tiny voice.

"You are very brave, m'alba. Come, we shall show everyone here how it should be done." He reached down and took her hand gently. "Think how jealous your sister will be to see you dancing with an Admiral."

He was rewarded by a grave smile, very like Alvellaina's. He led her out to form the long line of the dance. The musicians played the opening refrain, a soft, wistful melody in a minor key, offered by the flute alone. When the dance began, the flute was accompanied by a tiny drum to keep the beat for the dancers. The drum had a minute crystal bell attached to it, so that there was a brilliant tinkle of sound with each beat.

Gilhame bowed to his partner and she curtsied, spreading her lavender skirts gracefully but without coquetry. They joined hands and walked three short steps, ur Fagon carefully measuring his long stride to his short companion. Then they joined both hands and walked slowly in a circle. Three more steps, and Gilhame pivoted, leading Falga around him. Step, step, step. He took her in his arms and swung her around waltz-style.

Falga concentrated on her movements, but soon relaxed somewhat. As the dance progressed, Gilhame gracefully led her into the more complicated figures, going down on one knee to lead her around him. There, eye-to-eye with him, she gave him a sweet smile, and he returned the gesture. The next time he swung her around, he asked, "Easy, isn't it?"

"Yes, sir."

"You must call me Gil. All my dancing partners do."

"I couldn't!" Step, step, step.

"Be brave and try it." Turn, turn.

"Yes . . . Gil."

"You see. It didn't hurt at all."

"Does . . . my father—the Commander—call you that?"

"No. But then, he has not danced with me yet." Step, step, step.

He was rewarded by a tiny giggle. "Do you often dance with men?"

"Only when there are no partners as lovely as you in the room."

"Do you really think I am pretty?"

"Don't you have a mirror?"

"Yes. But . . . I only see white skin and red hair."

"Halba Falga, you are a lovely girl. You will grow into a beautiful woman, a very beautiful woman. Believe me. I am something of an expert in these matters. In fact, if my heart were not already promised, I would be tempted to wait for you to grow up."

"Is she very beautiful?"

"Yes, very. You look very like her."

"I do? Who is it?"

"Can you keep a secret?"

"I think so."

"Ah, wise as well as beautiful. Never promise something until you find out what it is. Just between you and me . . . it is your cousin, Alvellaina."

"Really? I thought . . ."

"What?"

"That it was just political. I heard . . . I was listening when I should have been asleep."

"Let me give you a piece of advice, m'alba. Politics is a game for . . . underbred persons. Once you begin to play that game, you become corrupt. Every decision you make is based on how it will further your interests. Your heart rots in your chest, and you become a creature of expediency."

"Like my real father?"

"Another word of advice. Never take a general statement personally."

"Oh." She fell silent as they ended the dance. He took her hand and began to lead her back to her mother. "I'll keep your secret . . . Gil. Does *she* know?"

"Yes. But she doesn't like it much."

"Why not?"

"Your cousin is not of a romantic mind, perhaps."

"Mother says she's Grandfather Krispin all over again."

"Is that good?"

"I don't think so. Are you a good dancer?"

"I am accounted to be."

"Then that must be why I didn't stumble over my feet once."

"Nonsense. You should have a greater appreciation of your own abilities."

He watched her blush. "Thank you very much for the dance . . . and all the advice."

"It was my pleasure, m'alba. You'll be fine, once you get your ship's legs. And don't let your sister bully you. It's not good for her—or you."

"I'll try, I promise." She gave him a deep curtsy, one worthy of royalty, and slipped behind her mother again.

Armanda Mordell looked at him and smiled. "Falga, don't you want some juice?" Her daughter exchanged a look with Gilhame which clearly said she understood that her mother wished to talk behind her back.

"I am a little thirsty."

"No punch, now." Armanda waited until her daughter was gone. "That was very good of you, Admiral. I never suspected you of being good with children."

"I'm not."

"I am a better judge of that than you. Do you have children of your own?"

"I have a son, Hamecor, by my sister back on Faldar, but I have never seen him. My principal exposure to the young happened years ago when I helped escort the inhabitants of the LeMonteen Royal Creche into exile. It was, as I remember, a horrendous experience. We were on an old slug of a cargo vessel, the Navy having nothing more suitable for transporting seven thousand children and young adults. Our drive units went haywire in sub-space. One of the refrigeration units malfunctioned, and we had a rash of food poisoning. It hit most of the Healers as well as the children. I, being so much super-cargo, got pressed into nursing duty. My worst nightmares were nothing compared with trying to deal with six hundred very sick little Monteenarins. I am happy to report that most of them lived, but I doubt they can look *keefa* bread in the face to this day. I know I can't."

"*Keefa* bread? But it smells terrible when it goes. Didn't anyone notice?"

"As near as I can tell, the creche nurses are bred for stupidity."

She laughed. "You might be right. It was very kind of you to be nice to Falga. You seem to have coaxed her into having a good time. This has all been very hard on her. She was devoted to her father, and she is terribly shy."

"Shy? I found her to be a very thoughtful young woman. Don't worry. She'll blossom at her own pace. She only needs a little self-confidence. I take it there is some problem?"

"I . . . I assumed you knew. When you spoke of your inability to see the Dream . . . how stupid of me. She's . . . a hidden Flame. She can't read minds, nor can she be read. And in my family, that makes her handicapped."

"Strange. I never would have taken you for a fool, halba. So, she's thought deaf? I wonder, is she really? Or has she just chosen to remove herself from the field? I must remind you that Blessed Amalina was unable to hear even her own thoughts for a great portion of her life. Not that I predict sainthood for your daughter."

"I don't think the Krispins could produce a saint."

"No. They are much too intelligent for that. How do you find it, living among strangers?"

"It is not as difficult as I might have imagined. The Commander is everything that is kind, and he and Kurwen are getting to be friends."

"You don't regret your decision?"

"I am not given to vain regrets, Admiral. I count myself fortunate to have had a choice."

"Good. It sounds like they are about to end this set. Will you stand up with me in the next?"

"I should be honored." She stood up slowly. "Mean as it might be judged, I was a bit jealous of Falga. She seemed to be really enjoying herself. And you are very graceful."

"I know. No one thinks of a spider-shanks like me as anything but awkward. It should teach one not to judge by appearances."

He led her out, noting the dark blue gown embroidered around the hem with white flowers. The music began, and they danced a brisk contra-dance, much too quick for polite conversation. They were both a little breathless at the end, so he led her towards the refreshments.

He had just handed Halba Mordell a glass of punch when an anxious-looking yeomen came up to him. The young man carried a still-sealed message pack. He saluted and offered the object to ur Fagon.

Gilhame looked at it and saw the seal. "I see the mills of the Admiralty have finally ground out something. I was beginning to feel neglected. If you will pardon me, halba."

"Certainly," she answered.

The yeoman stood nervously nearby as Gilhame broke the seal and read the enclosure. "Go get yourself something to eat or drink, yeoman. This doesn't require an answer."

"Yes, sir."

Ur Fagon give Halba Mordell a quick bow and walked across the room to where Commander E-varit was speaking to Frikard and the yeowoman Ganna Ottera. He noted that she was even more attractive in her formal uniform than in her working one.

"Gentlemen; Ganna." He bowed slightly. "Our orders have finally come through. We go, I regret to say, to the Island Worlds. The Admiralty wishes us to dislodge any

Coalchee colony, politely, and send them home. I am sorry, E-varit, truly I am. It's a damnable position to put you in."

"But hardly unexpected, ur Fagon. If the Island Worlds were less strategic to Kardus . . . but they aren't."

"I can arrange to leave you behind. No one expects you to act against your own people. Or you can precede us to Attira for refitting." He looked at the Coalchee's face, trying to discern the man's thoughts.

"No. I made an oath to you two days ago and, by proxy, to the Emperor. An oath is an oath, not just empty words. Besides, I am already a traitor to my people. I might as well finish the matter." His voice was sad and a little bitter.

" 'Honor makes hard choices.' " Frikard said quietly.

"True. But, 'Oath-breakers die unsalted,' and I might loose my way to the Overworld without a proper burial. I have never seen the Island Worlds. When do we leave?"

"Frikard?" Gilhame asked his second.

"Eight hours to form, another six to get us to the jump point. Shall I signal general orders now, sir?"

"No. It will keep a little longer. After the dance is over."

"As you command, sir."

Amara, Culiba and Helvira, the so-called Island Worlds, were actually the moons of a gigantic planet orbiting an eclipsing variable star. The total land mass of the three moons did not equal more than a small continent on most worlds, for they were mostly covered with water. Life, such as it had evolved there, was still tied to the seas.

To the Kardus Temporal Empire, they represented only a strategic outpost close to the Coalchee sphere. To the Coalchee, however, they were worlds of great beauty and desirability—worlds such as the Mother brought forth when she was creating the cosmos described in their legends. Ur Fagon was not surprised that the Protector had jumped at the opportunity to get them under his control, for he was an elected ruler and had to make political decisions or risk losing his position.

To ur Fagon, looking at the enormous gaseous planet

with her escort of seven moons, four lifeless rocks and three sea-covered orbs, there was no emotional response. He sat in his chair on the bridge and looked at the screen. But he knew that E-varit and all the Coalchee in their ships experienced a sense of homecoming he himself associated only with green hills and yellow sunlight.

He wondered a little at the wisdom of bringing the Coalchee so near to temptation. Still, to have left E-varit and his ships behind or ordered them to Attira would have so dishonored them that all future cooperation would have been impossible. He cursed the Admiralty for bone-headedness and waited for some response to his fleet's presence. Several radio messages had gotten no response.

A planet had a curious advantage over a space fleet. Its very vulnerability was a kind of defense. The weapons of a fleet were intended for use in space. In addition to a widely-held reluctance to use such devices against any planetary population, there was the problem that between no action and total devastation there was no middle ground. One carried troopers and marines for planetary encounters, but Gilhame knew that, well-trained as his people were, they would be out of their element on the watery worlds below. And, although there was no indication of any vessels, the system they were in was large enough to hide three fleets.

His commlink beeped. He touched his headset. "Yes?"

"Who is this?" said a tinny voice.

"Give me a visual!" he replied.

"Who is this?" the voice repeated.

"This is Admiral Gilhame ur Fagon, commanding the Twelfth Fleet of the Imperial Kardus Empire. Show yourself."

Silence followed. "Why are you using a Coalchee hailing frequency?" the voice finally asked.

"By the Emperor's beardless face, I'll see your bowels in a cauldron if you don't show yourself!"

He heard a gulp, and a picture began to form on his little screen. A very handsome young man looked out at him. He was dark-haired and was wearing the insignia of the

Kardus Diplomatic Corps. He also looked about ready to cast up his accounts, so greenish did his pale skin appear.

"Well? Just what is the meaning of this? We have been hailing you for nearly an hour."

"Are you from Governor Mordell, sir?"

"No. I am not."

"Then, why are you here?"

"Young man, I am here at the bidding of the Imperial Navy. Now, who are you?"

"I am Coolan Niyarkos, of His Majesty's Diplomatic Corps. What is your business?"

"Well, *Harvar* Niyarkos, my business . . . is the Emperor's business. Why didn't you answer?"

"It's *Kentinus* Niyarkos, Admiral," he said, naming himself as a hereditary count.

"I don't care if you are the Nabatean Empress. Answer my question."

"I answer only to Governor Mordell."

"Do you now? Strange. I had not known that the diplomatic corps answered to provincial governors. The memorandum must have escaped my attention. You will have to go a long way to answer him, young man. He's on Munsor by now, contemplating his sins, one hopes."

"In exile? Are you certain?"

"Since I was instrumental in sending him there, yes, I am."

Niyarkos turned a little greener, though Gilhame would not have thought it possible. "Why?" he gasped.

"For treason."

"Treason!"

"Yes. We were given to understand that he had permitted a Coalchee invasion of the Island Worlds."

"As you can see, sir, there aren't any Coalchee here. There must have been some mistake. We're all Kardusian."

Ur Fagon pondered this for a moment. The young man was obviously worried to death. What was going on? Krispin's documentation had been sufficient to convince the court and, unless the Coalchee had developed a method to befuddle the Truth Rod, E-varit had spoken honestly. Had the Protector had second thoughts before the battle about sending his colonists? Still, there had been a curious listlessness about Mordell's self-defense which had nagged at him.

"You have not been invaded?"

"No, sir." Gilhame sensed that he was being evasive.

"I see. Well, it seems to have been a false alarm. I am sorry to have disturbed you for no reason. Why don't you join me for dinner and some wine? I'll send a shuttle down to get you, say, in an hour."

Niyarkos had recovered some of his color, a fish-belly white. He gulped again. "I should be honored, sir."

"The honor is mine."

Ur Fagon sat thoughtfully in his chair after the screen went dark again, staring up at the larger screen where the Island Worlds circled their primary. "Curiouser and curiouser," he said aloud.

"Frikard!"

"Admiral?"

"Do you know, you have an absolute gift for being here when I want you? Get some scouts across to the area where the Coalchee would have entered the system. I want the area searched . . . very carefully. And send a shuttle down to Helvira to pick up a Kentinus Niyarkos about an hour from now. Tell me, Ven, do you feel . . . as if there's something looking over your shoulder?"

"No. But I am sadly lacking in imagination."

"You think it's just my nerves? Perhaps." He opened the intra-ship comm and punched the number of Alvellaina's room.

"Yes?" The screen remained dark.

"M'alba? Do you think you could . . . do me a small favor?"

"Do I have any choice?" The screen lit up, and she stared out at him defiantly.

"Yes, of course you do."

"What is it?"

"I am planning a small entertainment this evening. Do

you think you could bestir yourself to act as my official hostess? I have no doubt that you have done so for your father. Put on a pretty dress." Every night, she wore the same soiled white dress in which he had first seen her, although he knew that her entire wardrobe had been brought aboard. It was a red flag he had chosen to ignore until now. "And ask your sisters if they will also join us. Let me see. You and I are two, your sisters are four, Buschard and Culmeni are six, our guest makes seven. I cannot leave Frikard out. So, eight. That poses a little problem. Shall I make the numbers unbalanced or break precedence?"

"Eight is not unbalanced."

"No, it is not. But five men and three women is. You see, Frikard's particular is enlisted, not officer, class. Still, it seems unfair to deny Ven the pleasure of his special friend when all the rest of us have ours. And our guest is of such estate that he probably will not come alone. You'd better plan for twelve."

"Who is this guest?"

"*Kentinus* Coolan Niyarkos." He watched her eyes widen. "Is something wrong?"

"No."

"Do you know him?"

"By name only."

"And?"

"He's a *neemus*-cousin," she said slowly. She used a term which indicated a relationship by marriage, not blood.

"Really? He's the diplomatic representative here. How is he *neemus* to you?"

"His mother is Mordell's sister."

"My, it is a small cosmos, isn't it. Just as well I didn't plan to invite your aunt and Commander E-varit. Will you do it?"

"Yes. Since you asked so graciously. Dinner for twelve. When?"

"In about an hour."

"An hour? *Curva!* You are worse than a husband," she said and closed the link.

"Such language, m'alba," he said to the darkened screen.

As such occasions go, ur Fagon's impromptu dinner party was neither a success nor a failure. By that magic of which only women are capable, food appeared on the table, flanked by flowers and wine. When ur Fagon entered the room, leading his ranking officers and escorting Niyarkos, his wife and a sour-faced individual introduced as his secretary, Illnos Caraheen, he found Alvellaina, her sisters and Yeowoman Ottera awaiting them. All the women were wearing gowns, including Ottera. He raised his brows in question and began the introductions.

When they were done and he seen Niyarkos and his wife safely into the sphere of Derissa Krispin and Buschard, he slipped over to Alvellaina. "Ganna is out of uniform. Why?"

"Gowns have no rank. It seemed less insulting than presenting him with a yeowoman."

"And I thought Derissa had all the diplomatic talent in the family. My compliments, m'alba, on the room, the food and yourself. You look quite lovely."

She blushed faintly. Alvellaina was wearing a dark-blue gown embroidered with silver, high-necked and long-sleeved. It was very conservative compared with the Kentinessa's asymmetrical shift of filmy gold stuff, but he liked it. It made Alvellaina seem older than her years and more dignified. Her sisters were wearing equally unrevealing garb—Derissa in white to match Buschard's dress uniform, and Armanda in pale lavender. Gilhame was no expert on the vagaries of female clothing, but he knew that Kentinessa Niyarkos was in a recent fashion of the Imperial capital and that the little yeowoman's was a year or two out of date, but in very good taste. It was a dark burgundy, draped robe which set off her dark hair and eyes to advantage.

"Did you dump the white dress down the disposal?" he asked.

"Certainly not. I save that for special occasions. Like

dinner with you," she answered sharply.

"You are a jewel among women, m'alba. I thank you most sincerely for your efforts. Everything looks wonderful."

She smiled at him. "Your wine cupboard leaves a great deal to be desired, but the ship's kitchens were very helpful."

"Good. Ottera looks a little uncomfortable. I'll go and set her at ease. Do you think you could . . . uh, engage your *neemus*-cousin in a little polite conversation? I think Buschard is telling them a tedious story. Or perhaps Niyarkos always looks like a constipated camel. And if he asks you, as I am certain he will, how you came to be here, you may tell him anything you wish."

"Why?"

"The truth is sometimes more disquieting than any falsehood." He walked across to Yeowoman Ottera.

"Ganna?"

She jumped a little at the sound of his voice. "Yes, sir?"

"You look lovely tonight. Smile, do your duty and do me proud and I'll give you a field brevet. I can't have my chief officers . . . uh . . . consorting with the enlisted personnel. It's the very devil with precedence, you know."

She gave a glance, then a smile. "I would prefer to rise by my own merits, sir."

"I see. Call me Gil for this evening and I will let you do so."

"Would you be so kind as to define my 'duty,' Gil?"

"Laugh, be charming, be witty and don't drink to excess."

"Should I be witty to anyone in particular?"

"Try that rat-faced secretary of Niyarkos over there. Let me see. Illnos Caraheen. That's his name."

Ganna gave him a curious look. Then she looked at Caraheen. "He should be worth at least two grades in rank," she said, and drifted across to Caraheen.

Later, they sat down around the table. A mess servant filled the soup bowls, removed them when they were empty and departed. Ur Fagon watched the platters being passed along the table, smiled at Alvellaina at the opposite end of the table from him, and filled Niyarkos's glass again.

As the guest of honor, he had Niyarkos at his right and the Kentinessa Niyarkos on his left. Derissa sat beside Niyarkos, talking charmingly, with Buschard, Ganna Ottera and the secretary Caraheen ending that side. The secretary seemed to have unbent somewhat under Ganna's attentions and was actually smiling. Frikard sat beside the Kentinessa, with Armanda Krispin and Culmeni beyond him.

Quite suddenly, Gilhame was depressed. He forced himself to answer some pleasantry from the overbred camel of a diplomat on his right. Then he realized that he had not heard anything the man had said and wondered if his answers had made any sense.

Ur Fagon looked at the women at the table. The Kentinessa he dismissed as an empty-headed beauty. The three sisters were each making proper small talk with their dinner companions, and Ganna was proving herself worthy of any rank in the service she desired. She had that curious mixture of intelligence and sexuality which is either very attractive or very frightening to men.

But he was using these people. The depression passed away as anger took its place. It was inward-directed rage, but he saw Alvellaina look at him sharply. While appearing to hang on every word of Caraheen's, she quirked an eyebrow at Gilhame. He gave her a small shrug in response. He knew she had picked up the anger. Time, always time. He had to buy time, he who had all the time in the cosmos on one level, had spent endless hours of untold lifetimes delaying people, confusing them, always waiting for that moment of perfect balance when all the energies came together. Then he would win. He always found the crux; he always won. Why did he feel so empty now?

He sighed, recognizing post-conflict doldrums, and stopped himself just before he began to drum his fingers on the table in boredom. If the ladies could endure this tedium, so could he.

"And then we had this curious infestation of small, flying, blood-sucking mammals. Nobody knows where they came from. They just appeared suddenly, hung around attacking anyone who came out after dark and vanished about three weeks later. I tell you, I'll be glad to get off these damn backwaters. Between the boredom and the strange animals, it's been hell.''

"I can see that, Kentinus. Small, flying, blood-sucking mammals, you say. It sounds as if some cargo ship left a zoo crate behind. Those things obviously aren't native to the Island Worlds. Backwater! Hah! Very good. I missed the joke when you said it.''

'Great bleeding cosmos,' he thought as he saw Niyarkos's supercilious smile, 'I've convinced the bastard he's a wit. Well, perhaps I've convinced him I'm an idiot at the same time. I've got to know what, if anything, happened to that Coalchee flotilla. Blood-sucking mammals? Bats? On Helvira?''

"A zoo crate?" yelped Niyarkos. "You know, I never thought of that. There was a small freighter through just before the things appeared. But why did they disappear?''

"I suspect they starved to death," Gilhame answered calmly. 'If they had to survive on your thin blue blood, I'm sure they did, or died from the contact,' he thought.

Alvellaina passed the dessert platter around the table. She smiled at Caraheen in a way that made Gilhame want to break the man's neck. The thought elicited another hard stare from her. 'I can't have it both ways,' he decided. 'Either I use her or I don't, but I can't be angry when she does what I ask.' He noticed Frikard silence a beeper and turned his attention to the Niyarkos woman. Frikard arose from the table, bowed gracefully to the women on either side of him and left the room. So, the scouts were finally back.

"Tell me, Admiral, have you seen the latest fashions from the capital? It's been months since I've heard a word.''

"Why, yes, Kentinessa, I have." Anything to shut her up. In addition to being stupid, she had a voice like a blackbird. Just how much outrageousness could he get away with? "The last time I noticed, about six weeks ago, it was all paint and jewels.''

"Paint and jewels, Admiral?''

"The very *highest* fashion leaders, I believe, are shaving off all the body hair, painting their forms in interesting patterns and then covering the whole with electro-nets of gemstones. I was quite shocked the first time I saw a female on a dance floor dressed so, but I'm a bit old-fashioned. I like a woman to have hair on her head. But it sort of grows on you. One must have an absolutely perfect body, of course, but with electro-nets, anything is possible. The head is, I seem to remember, also adorned with a fantastic headdress. The cloth manufacturers are furious."

"How delicious. Lani," she purred across the table to her husband, "did you hear what the Admiral said? They're not wearing anything but paint and jewels in the capital." She gave Derissa's simple gown a contemptuous glance. "It's a shame that . . . everyone can't wear such finery."

Gilhame followed her glance, had a pleasurable moment imagining Derissa decked out in the manner he had described and then said very solemnly, "It would be very inappropriate on a fleetship, Kentinessa. What would the Admiralty think? Of course, that raises the question of whether the Admiralty ever thinks at all."

She leaned towards him, and he got a whiff of her scents. There was perfume, normal body odor and, under all, the faint musky smell of a woman in a rutty frame of mind. She thinks she's seducing me, he thought. "Admiral, of course one couldn't have ships' women dressed like ladies. I must admit I am a little shocked at their presence. Are they all yours?" Her voice was conspiratorial.

"Mine? If you mean, are they all attached to the fleet, yes, but so is everyone in this room except you, your husband and Harvar Caraheen. What do you mean by ships' women?" He knew precisely what she meant and he wanted to strangle her for it.

The Kentinessa made a moue of her mouth. "You know. Prostitutes." She said the word as if it dirtied her.

"My dear Kentinessa, how very provincial of you. It is strictly against Admiralty policy to have personnel of that nature on board ship. Oh, occasionally an individual officer or enlisted person is prostituted through the fleet, but as punishment only. Men and women. I cannot imagine how you could leap to the conclusion that persons of such obvious quality as the Krispin *halbara* and *tema* Ottera might be anything but what they are—part of the ship's complement. I am shocked. You must think the fleet is a mobile debauch.''

By the time he stopped speaking, the Kentinessa was red with mortification. ''But, I've heard . . .''

''I consider the matter closed, Kentinessa.''

''Is there something the matter with the Kentinessa's dessert?'' Alvellaina asked from the end of the table.

''No, nothing, m'alba,'' he replied before the woman could open her mouth. She was too stupid, he realized, to give up the subject. Nor was her attitude uncommon. Many assumed that all females of whatever rank on fleetships were actually there solely for the sexual convenience of the male complement. He was angry again, at himself this time, for putting Alvellaina and her sisters in an intolerable situation. Still, she had better learn how to handle it, and the sooner the better. ''She mistook you for a . . . grand horizontal, and I was just setting her straight.''

The look that Alvellaina gave him would have frozen a steaming swamp. Then she gave a laugh which sounded almost natural. ''How droll. Wherever did you get such a curious notion, Kentinessa? With my carroty hair and flat chest, I really am complimented. Redheads are quite out of fashion these days, you know.''

''Yes,'' Gilhame cut in. ''I was just telling the Kentinessa how all the fashionable ladies are shaving their hair off and painting themselves various colors. You would know better than I, Alvellaina, what is *the* most fashionable color?'' He gave her high points for handling the insult offered her so gracefully, and higher points that she did not laugh at his description of the fashionable female. Her sister Armanda had her lower lip caught firmly between her teeth, and Derissa appeared to be memorizing the pattern on her plate. Ganna Ottera gravely raised her napkin to her lips.

''Why, blue, of course,'' Alvellaina said solemnly.

"Right, right! It shows off the white stones to such advantage," he added.

"True," Alvellaina continued. "A female without white stones is quite out of fashion." He saw a curious expression in her eyes and realized that she had picked up his mental picture of Derissa wearing almost nothing. Then her face changed subtly. "If we have finished, shall we leave the table? I am certain all this talk of fashion is quite boring to the gentlemen." She gave Gilhame a slight nod.

He stood up, signaling an end to the meal, and tried to discern what Alvellaina's nod had meant. Ignoring the Kentinessa, Gilhame walked to the end of the table to pull Alvellaina's chair out for her.

The portal opened behind him and Frikard returned. Gilhame could see that the man had something of importance to report, and drew him aside.

"Sir, they have a Gamester dreadnaught," Frikard hissed.

"What?"

"That's right."

"But, they're proscribed, and with very good reason." Gilhame could feel the hairs on the back of his neck respond to the terror he was feeling. "How?"

"We don't know yet. Apparently, what happened was that the dreadnaught was placed at the entrance where the Coalchee would exit into the system. They came out, and it gobbled them up. We've found some debris, not very much, but enough to indicate that between twelve and fourteen ships were in the flotilla."

"Twenty thousand people! And that bastard sitting over there acting like . . . Alright. What in the cosmos was Mordell thinking of? The use of a dreadnaught is an act of war. And the very last thing Kardus needs right now is a *real* war. The man must have been out of his mind. How long will it take a fast packet to get to the nearest Admiralty office and back? I don't want this to be broadcast."

"I should think not, sir. Let me see. The nearest is Calma II. That's two jumps and three hours of maneuvering at each. Presuming anyone can be found capable of making a decision, the packet might return with orders within a day."

'A day,' Gilhame thought, remembering that a day was now thirty hours of fifty minutes each. "Good. I think Buschard better go. Now, what the devil am I going to do about our 'guests'?"

"We still have no idea who is in control of the dreadnaught."

"I have a pretty good idea. This is one battle I would gladly walk away from, Ven. I think I'd better end this little gathering right away. Go get a packet ready. Oh, and Ven, I do like your Ganna very much."

He got one of Frikard's rare smiles. "So do I, sir."

Chapter VII

Gilhame sat silently in his now-deserted quarters. The table had been cleared, and he sat at it in his great carved chair, staring down into an empty wineglass. The portal opened, and the pard walked in, sniffed the air and spat.

"You are so refined, my friend," Gilhame said to the animal. "She did leave quite a stink in here, didn't she? And since you have learned to open my door, why haven't you learned to close it?"

"Who left a stink?" It was Alvellaina, still wearing her simple gown.

"The Kentinessa. Or perhaps it was her mate. Anyhow, I can still smell it, and you can see that it offends the pard."

"You were sending the strangest stuff tonight. Are you still angry with me?"

"Angry with you? Do you care?"

"No."

"Little liar. I was not angry with you. In fact, I was very pleased with you and your sisters. You handled the Kentinessa like a seasoned veteran. I am sorry that you had to be exposed to her malice."

"It doesn't matter. My nurse always told me only married women can afford to dress like whores, and it seems she was right. I wonder if she will shave her head and paint her body?"

"Without a doubt. It should look very well . . . where

she's going." He didn't want to speak of the exile world
directly.

"That's the third time tonight I've gotten a clear impression from you. Is Munsor really that dreary?"

"Yes."

"Can you tell me what is going on? I saw you speaking to
Frikard. That's when Derissa dumped her wine all over
Niyarkos."

"A man with you three girls behind him could go far, if
he were inclined in that way. You were invaluable. I thank
you again."

"And you are not going to tell me what's going on?"

"Why are you interested?"

"Because you are afraid. I want to know what the great
Gilhame ur Fagon is terrified of."

"Very few things in the cosmos. A Gamester dreadnought is high on the list."

"What's that?"

"A very large, very old, very deadly machine. The Emperor has proscribed their use in Kardus space, but there is
one in this system, apparently functioning. It was used to
destroy the Coalchee when they entered the system. It is
quite capable of taking out half the fleet. And that young
popinjay knows it's here."

"Where did it come from?"

"Who knows? There have been a dozen or so found,
here and there. A few have been operational. The rest
were derelict. The Gamesters left a number of interesting
artifacts. I've never seen one. I don't wish to see this one. I
don't think I have any choice."

"Why do they call them Gamesters?" Alvellaina seemed
very curious, but he was almost too preoccupied to notice.

"I keep forgetting how little you have traveled. All over
this arm of the galaxy there are huge cubes, like dice. They
can't be entered or x-rayed. They are even marked with
dots on the sides, like dice. So, we call the makers
'Gamesters.' "

"Why can't we get into them?"

"I don't know, not being a technical specialist. I only
know that teams of engineers and archeologists have spent

generations trying to get in, with no luck."

"Why have I heard nothing about them?"

"No nation likes to admit there is anything they cannot understand, do they? I think, personally, the Havassit know how to broach the damned things, and I think they don't because what is inside those cubes is just too dangerous to have around. The Havassit have been trying to protect us from our worse natures since the *curthel* invasion. It must be terrible to have the whole responsibility for all our petty little nations."

"What are you going to do?"

"Wait until Buschard gets back from Calma with some orders, unless Niyarkos loses his nerve and starts shooting before that."

"I see. Is it very bad?"

"It could be. We're rather like fish in a barrel."

"Then why don't you attack it immediately?"

"Because I cannot risk the fleet without orders. There are too many lives at stake to do it on my own responsibility. It is conceivable, just barely, that the Admiralty might tell me to leave it alone."

"Something else is bothering you."

"Alvellaina, what do you know about the Ten Nations Compact? Or did Derissa take that class for you also?"

"My, you are in a foul mood. Let me think. No, I remember. You mean the part that says, 'No member nation shall use weapons of war which are beyond its capacity to fabricate'."

"Precisely."

"And if the Protector finds out . . ."

"There will be a war."

She got a glass and a fresh bottle of wine from the cupboard, sat down at his right and refilled his glass. When she had poured herself some wine, she said quietly, "But . . . I thought . . . you liked war."

Gilhame sent the bottle of wine flying across the room to slam against the wall. It did not break but fell to the floor and gurgled its contents out onto the rug. The veins stood out on his neck, and he made a wordless bellow. Alvellaina pushed her chair back from the table and scrambled away.

She ran towards the portal, then stopped short.

"I'm sorry," she said.

Gilhame mastered his rage a little. "Fighting is what I *do, not* what I like."

"Then, why do you do it?"

"You might say I have been cursed."

He could see by her face that she had forgotten or suppressed her knowledge of that part of him which was undying. He did not blame her. If he could have forgotten, he would have also. She looked as if she had been struck. Then she opened the portal and ran out of the room.

The thing was immense. Gilhame, looking at the dreadnought on the overhead screen, wondered what powered it and how it had been constructed. He had spent some of the time while waiting for Buschard's return studying the available documentation on this and other Gamester artifacts. Buschard had not returned. Instead, a single message had been broadcast from Calma II. "Destroy at once." It was signed with the name of the sector Vice Admiral.

That was easy for him to say, far away and safe. Gilhame was still trying to decide how he was to accomplish the task. The documentation had been informative but not very helpful. All the indications were that the thing was self-powered and that it "ate" anything small enough to go into its maw. The set of things which would fit into that opening included any ship in Gilhame's fleet.

For the moment, he kept his fleet out of range. He hoped his technical staff would be able to give him some method of attacking the thing without sacrificing most of his ships. He wondered too if Niyarkos was in control of the thing or if it had somehow been programmed. The whole situation reeked of the kind of careless politics which Gilhame had come to despise over the centuries.

Mordell had assumed that he could use the dreadnought with safety. He must have thought that no one would discover it. Ur Fagon was puzzled how a man capable of masterminding a deal with the ruler of a sovereign nation could be at the same time stupid enough to believe that he could hide the use of a thing like the dreadnought. Still, if he had died at Vardar Straits, no one would ever have been the wiser about the Coalchee in the Island Worlds system. He wondered for a moment if the real Gilhame would have seen the trap.

He decided to do something he knew was dangerous and even foolhardy. Gilhame relaxed and let his memory drift back into the many previous existences of the Dragon. Who were the Gamesters? Had he ever been one? The horrible, wrenching disorientation which accompanied this activity made the sweat pour down his underarms and face.

Floating. He was a speck in the cosmos, a tiny flame surrounded by the screams of dying men. That, of course, was the danger, the courting of madness. The Dragon survived by integrating his personality into that of his host body, by suppressing as much as possible the individual memories of his lives. To remember the millions of men he had led into battle and death, to recall his own body deaths, was more than pain. All the flames seemed to have one question: Why did *I* die?

He drifted back, hearing the deaths of thousands of years of war and seeing the pale face of his jailer, the Lady of Glass Castle, as she carried him from the field time and again. Her eyes were two tiny blue stars, cold and severe, and her hair was as black as a starless night, long and straight and caught back at the brows with silver brooches in the shape of nine-spoked wheels; her lips were the color of blood, drawn back in a smile of welcome. Always, with each new death, her silent look conveyed to him some sense of failure, of rebuke.

Worlds flowed past—green rolling hills, brown empty deserts, pitching seas; suns of many colors shone on him. Then blackness. Again and again he commanded ships, great arrays of spaceborne vessels filled with men and women. They rose and fell like fields of grain.

Finally, he glimpsed the Gamesters, great, busy men worshiping their machines. These, perhaps, were the greatest engineers of all time. They had perfected a method of chaining the mind to the machine and had created a sort of harmony between the two. The machines, thus, had acquired a kind of sentience. And then the harmony was broken. The man-machines revolted, destroying the Gamester civilization and leaving the remnants in planet-bound barbarism for centuries.

Gilhame saw the little wars that he had fought on worlds with no names. He saw the rise of other cultures, the constant scrabbling to reach the stars. Always the stars, and always the war.

"Sir? Are you alright?" The question brought him back. The return to this time and place seemed to last forever, but only a moment passed in reality.

"Thank you, Ottera," he said when he focused on the little yeowoman. He realized that he was shaking all over, hot and chilled at the same time. "I will be in a moment. How about getting me a cup of . . . something hot. I don't care what."

"Certainly, sir."

Gilhame watched her move off into the semidarkness of the bridge. He wiped his forehead with his sleeve and twisted his neck from side to side. Finally the shaking began to subside. He thought of the face of the woman of his vision and hoped that he would never see her again.

Then he looked at the dreadnought on the big viewscreen again and forgot his clammy physical discomfort and his jailer and the voices of the dying. He knew nothing more about the actual technology the Gamesters had used than he did before, but at least he had a clearer idea of what his fleet was confronting. How could he turn that into an advantage?

That thing out there had a mind of sorts, but it must be a very old mind. Senile, perhaps? Had it taken orders from Niyarkos? Should he risk asking the Kentinus if he controlled the dreadnought and, if he did, have him turn it on the fleet? Or was there another way? In fact, if Niyarkos had control of the thing, why hadn't he attacked already?

Ganna returned with a steaming cup. "Thank you again. Ugly, isn't it?" he asked referring to the dreadnought.

"I don't know. It's just a big ship shaped like a worm to me, sir."

"A very nasty worm. What the devil are our technical people up to? Running in circles, I'll bet. Not that I blame them. Take my advice, Ganna, and don't become an Admiral."

She covered her mouth to stifle a giggle. "No, sir. I won't."

"Where the devil is Ven?"

"I think the Commander is harassing our technical staff."

"At least he has something to occupy him. Tell me, Ganna, do you like him?"

"Why . . . of course, sir."

"Of course? It has been known that . . . advancement sometimes pursues affection. I had a lover like that once. She climbed on my coattails and hung on until I was forced to disengage her rather—violently."

Ganna pulled herself up proudly. "Then I must assume your question is from cynicism, not from rudeness."

Gilhame looked at her. Slightly flushed with anger, her eyes fixed him with a stare unbecoming her station but not her person. Her voice had betrayed no anger, only a chilly disdain. He admired her for standing up to him and wished with a faint pang that he could inspire something like it in Alvellaina. "I am, indeed, a confirmed cynic. I beg your forgiveness for doubting your integrity. I should have more respect for Frikard's judgment than that, shouldn't I? After all, he chose to serve under me."

"Yes, sir."

"Here we are, exchanging pleasantries under the shadow of that . . . thing. How curious a device is man. He will talk of love in the shade of the gallows, and of death on the couch of love. Still, after that, what else is there to talk about? And you almost certainly think I am the vainest man in the cosmos."

"Yes, sir," she replied, giving him a tiny grin.

He didn't want her to stop talking to him, Gilhame realized with a start. As, a few nights earlier, he had not wished the dance to end. Why? Because without the close companionship of a female, he felt incomplete. And Alvellaina had made it quite plain that she could not abide either the man he was or the man he had been. Until his outburst the night before, he had thought they were making some progress towards friendship.

"I am, you know, but only about the things which are worthy of my vanity. Not my looks, of course, or my manners, but my skill in the field. There I take a second place to no one."

"Yes, sir."

"Clever girl. You allow me to convict myself of all the sins in the cosmos and then quite properly agree with me. Is that Frikard?"

"Yes, sir. Shall I get you some more *feoan*?"

He discovered that the cup she had given him was empty. He had drunk it without noticing. "Is that what it was? I would have sworn it was bird pee. Yes, another cup, please." He stuck his tongue out expressively as Frikard came up to them. "Gah! Well, Frikard, what have the geniuses to say about our little friend out there?"

Commander Frikard, after giving Ganna a curious glance, handed up a thin leaflet of laboratory reports. "It doesn't look too promising, sir."

"It never does." Gilhame flipped through the pages of technical data as fast as he could, going back once or twice to reread a passage. "Is this right? About the molecular structure?"

"That's what our analysts think. We won't know if it's right until we start fighting it."

"We could pull it apart with our tractor beams, except we don't dare get that close. So, scratch that one." He was looking at the last page whereon the technicians had listed some possible means of attack.

"Commander E-varit is . . ."

". . . ready to leap down the dreadnought's throat, no doubt. No, no suicide missions until we have exhausted all other possibilities. At least the thing isn't completely invulnerable."

His viewscreen winked into life. He saw the distinguished face of the head of his technical staff.

"Well?"

"We just picked up some very faint life-readings from

the dreadnought. There was about a thirty-second burst, then it was gone. We thought we'd better inform you."

"Was it from within the dreadnought?"

"Yes, sir."

"Can you pinpoint a location?"

"Of course, sir," the man said in an offended tone of voice.

"Then do it, Halvar Morshull, and put the display on my screen. Frikard, I think you'd better send a detachment of troopers down to Helvira and bring me back that Niyarkos character."

A curious tune began to play in his mind. For a moment he thought it was "The Elves' Parade," the dance he had done with the little Mordell girl. Then he realized that it was not a piece of music at all, but more a progression of sounds like the tiny crystal bell that accompanied that dance. The bell-like sound in his mind was painfully shrill. It became more and more clear until it was a maddening tone almost beyond the range of his hearing. He tried to will it to stop, but it went on and on, the pitch climbing higher and higher, beyond his ability to hear it, but still sensed as bright lines of agony in his mind. Then there was a groaning noise, like a house creaking in an earthquake, followed by a sort of splitting rumble. Then he heard nothing but the normal sounds of the bridge.

Ganna Ottera returned with another mug of the nasty-tasting tea. Gilhame took it from her and stared down at her for a long second, wondering what that series of sounds meant. "Thank you, Ottera. Is there any word from Buschard?"

"Yes, sir. He is just returned."

"Good." He stared up at the dreadnought as he drank the *feoan*. Finally he realized that the sounds he had heard were one of those occurrences of clairvoyance which usually occurred with the use of *var*. He had not recognized it as such, for it had been unaccompanied by any visual images. He always "saw"; he had never "heard" before. He wondered what it meant.

Then Gilhame remembered a curious war, a war fought with sound, not explosives. He could not recall where it took place, but it had been as devastating as any other conflict. He felt suddenly exhausted, as if he had relived every battle of his many lifetimes in a moment. He knew that the fatigue was from his own search for an answer to the Gamester dreadnought, but that did not lessen his weariness. Then he thought, as he always did, of the thousands of people whose lives depended upon his knowledge and judgment, and he let the exhaustion pass from him, tucking it into a distant corner of his mind and dismissing it from his consciousness. He had the answer to the problem, if only he could discern it.

An hour had passed since he had sent Frikard off to get Niyarkos. He was surprised at the passage of time. He picked up the technical report from his lap and read it again.

He finished his rereading and called the lab. Morshull answered, looking as distinguished as always. "Sir, I still don't have any idea."

"I think perhaps I do. That thing is articulated, like a segmented worm."

"A picturesque way of putting it, but accurate enough," Morshull replied.

"Don't get snotty with me, Aram. Is there any indication that the thing is armed at those joints?"

"No. But on the other hand, I don't know of any weapon we have that could blast through the stuff the dreadnought is made of."

"I was not thinking of explosives. Try to restrain your genius impatience, will you? Now, how high-pitched a sound do you think it would take to start breaking up the molecular structure of that beast?"

"Sound?" Morshull's eyes got a glassy look. "Sound," he whispered again. His hands moved down onto his keyboard as he mumbled formulas. "It's a little out of my line. Cursoni! Come here."

Gilhame could hear a few words as Morshull spoke to one of his technicians, but none of it made any sense to him. After a while the head technician turned back to the screen. "We'll work on it," he said, and blanked out his screen.

Buschard came onto the bridge, looking bleary-eyed. He had a stubble of beard on his jaw, and his usually neat uniform was filthy and rumpled. "What the devil happened to you? A pard wouldn't drag you in." Gilhame said.

"My food processor pitched a fit on the way back. The inside of my scout looks like a giant puked in it. I was up to my neck in a mixture of stew and pickles."

"Isn't modern technology wonderful? Go change. Pugh! Much as I love you, wonderful you do not smell."

Buschard looked up at the screen. "Big, isn't it?"

"Yes, very. Go away, and don't come back until you smell less like the aftermath of an eating orgy."

"But . . ."

"But, nothing. I promise, you won't miss a thing. You're very anxious to be in at the kill, I know, and you will be. But I don't think it will be quite what you imagine."

Buschard gave him a curious look, a broad grin and a salute. Then he glanced at the screen again and left. Gilhame marveled again at his ability to inspire such trust and faith in his subordinates. Then he went back to studying Morshull's technical report.

Most of another hour passed before Morshull reported back to him. "I think we've worked out something that would indeed break up the molecular structure of the dreadnought. Are you just planning to stroll over and pop one into the thing's mouth?"

"Hardly. We will need about eighty gadgets . . . I don't suppose you have a name for the thing yet? I'm going to put them on magnetic probes and rain all over the dreadnought's parade."

"Eighty! What do you think I am, a magician?" Morshull screamed. "It will take me days, and I can't even test the damned things for fear I'll shatter the lab. Probably the whole ship would go."

"Then you'll just have to work a little harder. Don't worry about testing them. We'll test them on the dreadnought. If they don't work, well, we're back at square one. Just think how your reputation will increase when you take out a dreadnought without firing a shot or losing a man."

"Do you really believe that thing is just going to noodle

around out there until I'm ready? And why eighty?"

"I don't know if it will go on ignoring us, but maybe. My alternative is to try an assault as soon as possible, and your report has convinced me that would be not only futile but costly. Now, stop having hysterics and go to work."

Morshull cut his comm, and Gilhame rose from his chair and stretched. He was stiff and felt filthy. He could smell the stench of tension-sweat on his body. 'And I was complaining about Pers,' he thought. He also realized that he was ravenously hungry.

Frikard materialized before him. "Sir. They'll be bringing Niyarkos aboard in about ten minutes. Actually, it's the whole household."

"Clever of you, not to leave anything to chance, Ven. Good. Very, very good. I'll be in my quarters for a while. Stick our guests in the brig, and let me know if that machine out there starts anything."

"Yes, sir."

Thirty minutes later, ur Fagon entered the security quarters of the *Black Dragon,* showered, freshly uniformed and with a cheese tart warming his stomach. The guards jumped to attention as he came in, snapping smart salutes. Gilhame looked at the cubicles—upright cylinders of some smoky colored glass stuff. The other Gilhame had spent a time in that environment and remembered the odd dreams which it had created. The security cells sent one into a kind of twilight sleep, leaving one vaguely aware of the habitat and totally uninterested in doing anything about it.

"Get me Niyarkos."

"Yes, sir." One of the guards opened a cubicle and yanked out the inhabitant. Niyarkos stood there, blinking in a bemused way as awareness returned to him. He looked around the room, gaped at Gilhame and twitched all over. His fine tunic was torn in several places, and one side of his jaw was swollen.

"I demand to know what the devil you think you are about, Admiral!" he squeaked.

"You are not in any position to demand anything, Kentinus. In fact, if you come through this with a whole skin, I shall be very surprised."

"You can't go around arresting persons of my station and expect to get away with it."

"Shut up! I know all about your little pet and about what happened to the Coalchee fleet. Now I just want to know whether you control the dreadnought."

"What dreadnought?"

"Oh, dear. Are you going to be uncooperative? I did hope I would not have to resort to the various methods of persuasion which I have available to me. Those that are painless are so frightfully destructive to the mind. And I hate to hear a man scream. It seems so undignified. Still, in the service of my Emperor, I will dare anything." Gilhame grinned, fully aware of how disquieting that expression could be on his face. He turned to one of the guards. "Have you any special recommendations, sergeant? I'm afraid that the extraction of information is a little out of my line." He said this in a bland, almost lazy way.

"Yes, sir. I think *truth* would be the most direct. Of course, the aftereffects are a bit troublesome. Or, we could use *ulmai*. Except that it usually kills the subject within twelve hours, it's quite effective. It destroys the red blood cells, you see," he added in an informative voice. "There are the physical methods too. I can usually make a man tell me anything I need to know inside of twelve hours, but it does leave the subject rather the worse for wear."

"Stop! You can't do this. I claim diplomatic immunity."

"I don't know if we have time for out-and-out torture," Gilhame answered reflectively, ignoring Niyarkos's protest.

"I don't think he'd last long, sir. Twelve hours is what I would require for someone like yourself, not a little maggot like him."

"Do you have a preference?"

"Well, I do hate to destroy a mind. You might say it goes against the grain, sir. Besides, one never really knows if one has asked all the necessary questions. I remember once on Latis Station, we had a saboteur to work on, some religious fanatic. I was only a private then, and my sergeant used *ulmai*. We found out where this fellow had placed all of his bombs, but my sergeant forgot to ask if he was working with anybody. By the time he thought of that, the saboteur was dead. It turned out he *was* working with someone else, and we lost almost a third of the station. My sergeant went up with the bomb. He was lucky, I guess. If he had lived . . . well, sir, ever since then I've been partial to the old-fashioned methods, if you see what I mean."

"I do, indeed. Very wise, too, I am certain. Still, time is our enemy in this. I don't believe I can wait twelve hours. And while I am sure you could break our captive in less time than that, I hesitate to risk it."

"Just as you wish, sir. *Truth* or *ulmai.*"

"Have you ever used *pentos,* sergeant?"

"Well, sir, I have." He rubbed his jaw reflectively. "It's a bit chancy. The subject can tell you what you want to know, but the problem is in sorting out the data. We could just kill him and dead-brain him. It's tidy, and there's no doubt that you'll get all the stuff."

"True. Still, it smacks of sorting through a garbage bin."

"Yes, sir. But I don't have much squeamishness left, not after twenty years at this business."

Niyarkos was huddled against a cubicle, white-faced and shaking. His spit glands seemed to be working overtime, for he was dribbling on his torn garment.

"There now, sir. A fellow what gushes at the mouth like that can usually be persuaded to spill his guts just by pulling out his teeth one at a time. Give me an hour to try it, won't you?"

Niyarkos clapped a trembling hand to his mouth and his skin took on the unhealthy greenish tinge which Gilhame remembered from their first encounter on the communicator. A moment later he cast up the contents of his stomach. He sank to his knees, coughing and choking as he fouled the floor. One of the guards hauled the man up abruptly.

"Caraheen," gasped Niyarkos. "He . . . controls the machine."

"How?"

"There's a device . . . oh, *sanctess*," he prayed and vomited again. "In my library. It's a box, sort of dull gray. He has to contact it every *decan* and assure it he's safe. It won't listen to anyone but him. I know; I've tried. I wanted to control it, but I couldn't. Only Caraheen."

"When did he last make contact?"

"At midday."

"Planetary or Imperial time?"

"Imperial."

Gilhame looked at his timekeeper. "And what happens in seven hours if it doesn't hear from him?"

"I don't know. I . . . think it will start looking for enemies."

Gilhame folded his arms across his chest and drummed his fingers on his biceps. "Think we'd better have a little chat with Halvar Caraheen, sergeant."

Chapter VIII

Ur Fagon's "chat" with Niyarkos's secretary, Caraheen, was brief, unpleasant and informative in a chilling kind of way. Men had been dispatched to recover the dreadnought control box from Niyarkos's library. Morshull had been told he had less than seven hours to complete as many of his little gadgets as possible. The man had called Gilhame a number of unlikely, rude and downright impossible things in seven different languages before storming off to harass his underlings. Gilhame didn't blame him a bit.

He strode down the corridor, aware of his body's again-unpleasant odor. 'Next time, I'll change *after* the interrogation,' he thought grimly. Then he entered Farren Vraser's quarters, off the medical section of the ship. The old Healer was puffing away on his pipe. He grunted and began to rise as ur Fagon entered.

"Sit still. Who do we have in Medical who can manage *dominance?*" He snapped the question.

"*Dominance?* Have you taken leave of your senses? That's strictly proscribed." Vraser frowned and shook his large, bald head.

"I know that. I didn't come here for a quiet course in Healer's Ethics. Unless you have a real urge to get munched up by the dreadnought, I suggest you forget about the legalistics of the situation and tell me what I want to know."

"You always begin in the middle and try to bully me. Tell me why you have need of a *dominant?*"

Gilhame sighed. "The dreadnought . . . can be communicated with by means of a device. We'll have it here in a while. This device appears to be keyed to the thought patterns of one individual, Illnos Caraheen, the diplomat's secretary. He is currently down in the brig, recovering from a mild dose of *truth*. He has to talk to the machine at the next *decan*. If he doesn't, I don't know quite what the thing will do, and right now we are essentially in the position of having nothing more deadly than rocks to throw at the machine. We need time. I need a telepathic *dominant* who can take over Caraheen's mind, restore it to its normal state, or as close as can be."

"Couldn't we just go hyper until we are ready to fight the dreadnought?" Vraser asked.

"We could, if I were certain that it wouldn't begin to attack the planetary population on the Island Worlds. The problem is, Caraheen doesn't know what the thing will do if he doesn't tell it everything is right. He says it's . . . sort of senile and timorous. That's subjective, of course. But I don't want to chance the dreadnought's deciding to jump on anything in sight. Morshull *thinks* it has the capability to go hyper within the limits of a planetary system. Now, be a good fellow, and tell me who could do it."

Vraser tented his large hands and rested his chin against them thoughtfully. Gilhame knew that as Principal Medical Officer, Vraser had access to that portion of the psychotape information which was closed to himself. He also knew that he was asking the man to violate both the sacred confidence which that knowledge carried with it and his medical ethics. *Dominants* were rare even among telepaths, and most of them were psycho-conditioned so that they did not know their talent themselves.

"There are a few," Vraser began slowly. "Yourself, of course. I have often thought it was a good thing that you could not enter into the Dream of Faldar. It would have become such a bloody nightmare under you." The man sighed and leaned back in his chair, picking up his pipe and relighting it. "But you are *too* strong for the task I think you suggest. You cannot conceal yourself. You want a subtle *dominant*. Let me see." He looked off into the air with a bemused expression on his face. "A man would be better than a woman. It is hard for a woman to color herself with a male subject's patterns. But . . . no, there isn't a man in the fleet who is effacing enough for the job you outline. But, which woman?" He tugged at his beard, then pulled his earlobe.

Gilhame stood and waited. There was no rushing a man who carried a whole fleet's psionic knowledge in his head. Finally, Vraser swung his chair around and punched the keys of his computer console. Data, encoded, flowed over the screen. He studied the numbers and signs on the screen for a while, then closed the line.

"Normally—if your request could ever fall into the classification of 'normal,' which it couldn't—I would recommend a member of my staff. Unfortunately, she is recovering from a bout of *elemin* fever. Do you realize that almost every world has an indigenous fever that is almost beyond the Healer's art? Funny, isn't it? We can lessen the severity of the attack, but we can't cure it. This leaves us with two possibilities, of which I think Halba Alvellaina Curly-Krispin is the most possible. The tones of her mind are most near to the masculine. It will require her to use one of the invading mind-drugs, of course, since she is quite untrained."

"Who is the other possibility?"

Vraser made a face. "I've told you too much already."

"Who else?"

"Her sister, Armanda Krispin."

"Really? I would have guessed it was Derissa."

"Halba Derissa's talents lie elsewhere."

Gilhame knew better than to press the matter. "But you favor . . . the older girl."

"I do."

"Thank you. I will try to forget we ever had this conversation. I wasn't aware that you had psycho-tapes on. . . ."

"I did them as soon as they came on board. It was my responsibility."

"Well, you have given me the devil of a problem. Let's

hope that Morshull can figure a way to diddle the box so that I don't have to use . . . to ever need to know what you've just told me."

Gilhame stood uneasily outside Alvellaina's portal. He had never invaded the sanctity of her quarters. Always, she came to him. There was not, of course, a portal on the ship which would not open at his command. He could not decide whether to retreat to his own rooms and request her presence, to beg admittance to hers or to ask to meet her in some neutral place.

The pard butted against his legs, buzzing mightily. He looked down at the fluffy white beast. "Do you think you could do your trick and open m'alba's door for me, little friend? Or should I just forget it and go find Armanda?"

The animal responded after the manner of its kind, opening its mouth and exhaling but making no sound. Then it looked at the portal, puffed its body fur up and gave a curious keen. The entrance whispered open, and the pard bounced across the threshold.

"Alvellaina? May I enter?" he called.

There was a sound from the inner chamber. "What? Oh, it's you."

"I was just passing, and the door was open," he said mendaciously.

"It's your ship," she replied.

"Not this part."

"Stop being thoughtful and polite. I prefer you when you are slightly menacing. Come in."

He entered a suite of rooms identical to his own and those of his high-ranking officers. But where his room was hung with the curious momentos of a hundred worlds, and Buschard's was decorated with the stuffed heads of the beasts he hunted whenever the opportunity presented itself, this room had a transient quality to it. There was no personal litter, nothing except a bowl of flowers on the table to show that anyone resided there.

Then, in a shadowy corner of the room, he saw a tiny household shrine of the kind which was usually dedicated to the Mother of All Living. Alvellaina followed his eyes and crossed quickly to the object, pulling a bright blue cloth down over the structure.

'How profane my eyes must seem to her,' he thought.

"Should I apologize for my display of temper last night?" he asked.

"No. I have thought about it a great deal, and I see that you are, in your own way, an honorable man. I feel I must beg pardon for being so . . . childish."

"M'alba . . ."

She cut him short. "Save your sweet phrases for someone else. What do you want?"

"Must I want something?"

"No, but you do."

"I have a task which you are most suited to, but which I have no doubt will be distasteful to you."

"That will be true, however you use me."

"Yes." He outlined the problem to her slowly, explaining what had happened in the brig, and finally asking for her help in controlling Caraheen.

"I don't want any part of your schemes. This is your mess, not mine," she replied.

"That is inaccurate. The mess, as you call it, is more of your uncle's making than of anyone else's—your uncle's and your father's. Quite a family affair."

She flinched. "Why should I help you?"

"If you don't wish to, I shall ask your sister Armanda. Vraser doesn't think she is the most able tool for the job, but at this point I'll take whatever I can get."

"No! I won't have her entangled by your . . . And I won't do it either."

"The Gamester machine has two potential targets, Alvellaina: This fleet and the planetary population on the Island Worlds. If you refuse me, and Armanda fails me—which I believe Vraser's cavil indicates she might—and that thing attacks either target, then it is on your head. There are fifty thousand souls on the Island Worlds, perhaps more. Your pretty white hands would be as blood-stained as mine, then, wouldn't they? Do I ask too much—that you should control one miserable man for a few minutes so that no one might die needlessly?"

He was standing very close to her. He watched her white skin turn rosy. Her eyes seemed to dilate until there was very little green showing, but only the deep black of her pupils. She swept her hand across his face too fast even for his fast reflexes.

"You unspeakable bastard!" she screamed, striking at him again. He caught her arm and twisted it behind her. He could smell her sweet scent and feel the trembling of her body as she struggled against him. She stiffened suddenly, and he knew that she was feeling his acute awareness of her. "Let me go!!"

He released her, stepping back. "You are even more spoiled than I thought, m'alba. The next time you strike me, I'll turn you over my knee. You deserve a beating."

"I could cut your heart out, your balls off. I . . . I'll see you eaten by vermin!" she screamed and shrank back at the same time, clutching her shoulders with her hands. "You filthy animal."

"I promised to keep my hands off you, not to let you batter me. Now, if you really want to roast my heart over an open fire, I suggest you calm yourself and then go see Medic Vraser. I wouldn't want to deprive you of the sight of my testicles on a spit. Just think, we might have to play this whole dreary scene over again . . . as other people."

Alvellaina went pale at the thought. "Do you always have it your own way?"

"No, I don't."

"Get out. I'll go see Vraser. You . . ."

"If you are short of expletives, I suggest you apply to Chief Technician Morshull. He has a rather colorful supply." Gilhame beat a hasty retreat on that note, well aware that his beloved was looking for something portable to throw at him. He took a deep breath as the portal closed behind him. Somehow, it was comforting to know that Alvellaina was no happier in her immortality than he was in his. He wondered where she rested between times. Not in Glass Castle, certainly. Then, his mission accomplished, he put her from his mind and went towards the bridge.

Caraheen slumped over a console on the bridge, half conscious, with Alvellaina's hands on his shoulders. The odd gray box sat before him. Gilhame watched the tableau, thinking of Morshull's reaction to the thing. "Give me a month, or maybe six, and I might be able to figure it out. But three hours? I am not that much of a genius, you old camel-bugger," he had said. Well, Morshull had always been less respectful than most of his staff.

He felt sad that Alvellaina had been forced to do his bidding, yet glad that she might begin to understand the way in which he treasured the lives of the people who served under him. Then the box changed color, and he forgot his reverie as he watched Caraheen and Alvellaina. There was a stillness on the bridge for perhaps a minute, then the box went back to its dull gray.

Alvellaina took her arms away from Caraheen's body, and the rodent-faced man slid down and out of his chair onto the floor. Alvellaina bent down and touched the secretary's throat. Her lips were quivering when she stood up.

"He's dead. You . . . have ten hours. The machine was uneasy about your continued presence in the system, but I don't . . . I don't think it will do anything for a while." She rubbed her hands together uneasily. "It's confused. But, I bought you . . . a little time. And I think I killed him." She gasped the last sentence, turned, and fled the bridge, white and shaking.

Nine hours later, Gilhame once again sat in his great control chair, watching the screen. The Gamester machine rippled slowly through space, almost eellike in its sinuosity. A swarm of tiny objects which Gilhame knew he was not really "seeing" sped towards the dreadnought, a flight of mechanical gnats which Morshull had christened "screamers," attacking the thing broadside. There were forty-seven of them, not the eighty he had asked for, and he did not know if it would do the job. But all he could do now was wait.

Out of the corner of his eye he could see his console screen rattling off numbers as it tracked the screamers to their destination. The bridge was filled with whispers as most of the technicians watched the screen. The computer flashed a message, and he knew that contact had been made. For several minutes nothing happened.

The gray box beside him on the arm of the chair became translucent. Gilhame picked up the electrode and pressed it to his forehead, listening. He could "hear" the machine asking questions of a sort. "What? How? Why? Pain. Terrible pain. Why? I am impregnable. How?" Then the dreadnought vanished.

About forty seconds later it reappeared at the left flank of ur Fagon's fleet. The great mouth of the thing swooped down on a destroyer. Gilhame watched with a kind of sick fascination. A tinny voice on his headset told him the *Sureswift* was gone. Then a section of the dreadnought began to sheer off, as the ships nearby the *Sureswift* attempted to maneuver out of range. The "head" of the machine turned from side to side, snapped up a scout, then seemed to stop, the little ship still hanging in its maw. Gilhame could see the midsection of the dreadnought begin to separate and float away from the main body.

The box beside him glowed red for a few seconds, then went back to dull gray. There was no sound on the electrode. He removed it, remembering the sort of agonized scream the dreadnought had made, glad that he had made the decision to concentrate Morshull's gadgets around the section where they had picked up life-readings of a sort, but vaguely sorry he had had to kill the old machine. He watched the scout ship slip out of the still open mouth.

Gilhame felt tired; even his bones ached. He made a silent prayer for the dull but able Captain Inaga of the *Sureswift* and the eight hundred people who had been with him, gave a nearby yeoman a few curt orders and left the bridge. 'What a thing I am,' he thought as he strode down the corridor, 'to have saved my fleet and yet caused the invention of a new piece of weaponry potentially more dangerous than the dreadnought itself. Why can't I just stop fighting, stop spending lives to save lives, just die, once and for all? Every time I spend a man, it gets harder.'

Chapter IX

The little boy ran into the square. He was a sturdy lad of five or six, with black hair slanting from a widow's peak, reddish eyebrows and great green eyes with flecks of gold in them. He wore a gray single suit with a red dragon stitched across the chest. The child looked up at the sky and screamed, "No, Father, no!" Then there was a blinding flash of whiteness.

Gilhame woke. He sat up in bed, sending the pard sliding off his chest, and flicked on the light. He was shaking and sweating. The pard said several things in extremely low feline as she rearranged herself at the foot of the bed.

The dream again. When had it begun? Gilhame was not certain. Ten days earlier? Two weeks? He propped himself up on the bed, picked up an empty pipe from the nightstand, stuck it in his mouth and sucked meditatively for a while. Gradually, the trembling in his body ceased.

His son. He kept killing his son. A child who did not exist, yet who kept calling to him. In all time, he had never had a son by the woman he loved, only the sister-son so often sent against him, or a child by some other woman. And her son too. Alvellaina's. Where did the child come from? Was his lust to overcome him? No. He would never rape her, never break his word. How then? But he kept seeing the child's pleading face before the dreadful light came. What was that light? 'My son, oh, my child!'

The faint whisper of the portal caught his attention. He

tensed a little, removed the pipe from his mouth and held it in his right hand in such a way that the stem made a provocative little protrusion. It wasn't much of a weapon, but ur Fagon had killed men with less.

Alvellaina seemed to drift into the room. At first all he saw was her white face in the darkness beyond the bed. Her red hair seemed to have a life of its own, surrounding her face like a nimbus. A dark green cloud flecked with silver floated below her long throat, making her seem a disembodied head. For a moment he wondered if he was still asleep.

"What is it?" she asked quite sharply. She moved closer to the bed, and the green cloud became a nightgown of transparent stuff offering tantalizing glimpses of her long legs and small, high breasts.

"Nothing." He didn't want her here, not *now*.

"Why, you've been crying."

Gilhame lifted his hand to feel the moisture on his face. He did not remember weeping. Damn her and all women to perdition, particularly all women with foresight. How dare she come floating in like some ancient sea sprite, almost naked, and notice his tears. A faint hint of her scent touched him. 'There is nothing like the smell of a warm, healthy woman,' he thought.

"Have I been?"

"Are you ashamed to cry?"

"No. Should I be?" He noticed the pipe clenched in his right hand and released it, putting it back on the nightstand.

"I heard you cry out."

"Through the ship's walls? You must have very good ears indeed. I had a nightmare—nothing more." She had been on the ship for nearly two weeks now, and they had fallen into the habit of a kind of tense rudeness. He had left her to herself a great deal as he wrestled with the problem of revamping his fleet's maneuvering capabilities to accommodate the eighteen ships he had acquired from Krispin's disbanded fleet and the ten from the Coalchee.

She sat gingerly at the foot of the bed and rubbed the sleeping pard between the ears. The little beast rumbled with pleasure but did not wake. "Do you always cry during nightmares?"

"Certainly. It is much more efficient than at any other time."

She giggled. It was the first time he had ever heard her laugh, and the sound delighted him. "You *are* ashamed to cry. It is not unmanly, you know."

"I am not concerned with my masculinity—no, not that."

Alvellaina looked at him, clearly nude beneath the silky coverlet, stared thoughtfully where his waist disappeared beneath the blanket and stopped smiling. "I see that."

"Did anyone ever tell you that you smell like roses?"

"Roses?"

"It's a flower."

"Yes, I know. But they are scentless. We have many on our estate. They have no smell."

"They did once. Once they were the very smell of love."

"Oh." She was uncomfortable now.

"I am not much on ladies' garments, but is that thing you are wearing for sleeping in?"

"Yes."

"What a shame. It really belongs on a dance floor. Except, of course, that every woman in the place would want to scratch your eyes out and every man . . . well, it is an incitement to riot."

"Is it?" She sounded pleased.

"Yes, it is, my innocent. I cannot tell if you are vain or naive. All women are vain in varying degrees, I know. But that is not an appropriate garment to wander around the corridors of the ship."

"From my portal to yours is six steps."

"Is that all? Then retrace them."

"No. Not until you tell me what woke you. It is not the first time I have heard you call out. Is it a very bad dream?"

"Only my conscience pricking me for my numerous misdeeds. These sanguine hands you are always taxing me about."

"You cannot lie to me, Admiral."

"I suppose that is true. For a woman who hates my guts, you certainly avail yourself of the inside of my skull with great familiarity. It was an ugly dream about the death of someone I love very much. It will not come to pass. They do sometimes, you know, these twisted visions of possible futures."

"Yes. I do know. How many of yours happen?"

"About half."

"And this one?"

"Will never be. Now, go back to your room and go to sleep. I shall try not to wake you in future."

"It must be quite dreadful, if you won't tell me." She looked at him for a long second. "I could cook you in your own juice, you know."

"Oh?"

"What I learned on Caraheen . . . I could do it without any drugs now, if I wanted to."

"I cannot believe that you are so hungry for answers that you would risk finding out more than you wish to know about me. I remember our little tussle in your rooms. You didn't like what you picked up at all, did you? Still, someday, it might be amusing to learn which of us is the stronger."

"You are, of course. But I think I am crueler." She pursed her lips together. "I promise I won't walk around in the corridors in my nightgown again—but, your dream . . . it hurt!"

"I am sorry, m'alba, I seem fated to pain you, don't I? But, why . . . how can you be so ignorant in matters of dress? You wore just the right thing at that dinner for Niyarkos."

She gave him a shy half-smile. "I asked your Lieutenant Vaverly, your protocol officer, what would be appropriate. That is, Derissa told me to ask her, and I did."

"Your sister is a clever woman."

"I know. She's not as headstrong as I am, either."

"No, she isn't."

"You might think this looks like a dance dress, but since I have never been to a dance, I really couldn't be certain.

Oh, I've seen tapes of the Imperial Cotillion, two years out of date and seeming like a dream, but I have no personal experience.''

"Why?"

"Admiral, I have lived my entire life on either my father's estates on Grentar or on my mother's. I have been to tea at the Governor-General's on Grentar, and to chapel. That is the sum of my social experience. Until that night two weeks ago, I had never eaten a meal alone with a man. Do you know, one of the officers invited me to attend a musicale on Deck 3, but I didn't go. Derissa went. She said it was wonderful. She said Armanda and Culmeni sang together. But I don't know how I am supposed to behave, so I just keep still. Am I the Admiral's woman or the Admiral's slave? I mean, I have hardly spoken to anyone but my sisters and my aunt and you. Oh, yes. Lieutenant Darkcut has made a point of dropping in every day or so. She seems to be a very strange person. She is always talking about the forces of history. She gave me a book-tape about the Kardus Temporal Empire. I now know a lot about history, but I am still very confused about everything else."

"I see that. And what am I going to do about it? I have been neglecting you—no, I haven't. I have kept my distance at your demand. Why the devil have you never been to a dance. And what have you done to your hair?"

"My hair? Oh, this is how it really looks. I usually wear an electro-net to make it straight."

"I like it this way. In fact, I have a hard time believing it's the same stuff I have been seeing at dinner every night. An electro-net, eh? Amazing. To me, the nets are part of the technology which powers my ships, not a cosmetic doodad. Why no dances, then?"

"My father did not wish us to associate with just anyone."

"Why?"

"He said one met all sorts of upstarts at social functions—especially embassy balls. He had a violent aversion to ambassadorial events."

"Really? And yet, I can remember meeting him at any number of them. I wonder."

"What?" Her eyes were alight with curiosity.

"I am not accounted a social man in the ordinary way; war has been my life. But ever since my cadet days, the single exception has been dances. I like to dance. I enjoy meeting people in those circumstances. In fact, just before we left the Vardura system, I stood up with your little cousin Falga. And embassy balls are quite a favorite of mine; you meet such interesting people there."

"Do you think you haunted my father too?"

"It would certainly explain a great deal about his recent actions, wouldn't it?"

"Yes, it would. Then, it would be your fault that I've been cooped up for years and years. I've never even been presented at court, although Aunt Armanda has offered repeatedly."

He grinned at her. "If the stars wink out in the night, you will no doubt find a way to lay it at my feet. I cannot make retroactive compensation for the pleasures you have been deprived of, but we go to Attira for refitting as soon as I am satisfied with the way the fleet is shaping up. We will be invited to a number of functions—including balls. You are quite welcome to attend them. Ask Buschard to teach you some dances. He is a good dancer and a good instructor. Talk to Lefair about your clothes. He's the ship's tailor. We shall stand up in at least one pattern dance together. As for your status, you are neither my woman nor my slave. Within reason, you have the freedom of the ship. I don't want you tinkering with the drive unit, as your cousin Mirra seems likely to do, or trying to conn the ship. I am sorry I did not define your role. I have been busy—and I suppose I assumed you knew your place. I keep forgetting how young you are. Your sisters have . . . adapted themselves so well, I did not realize that you were having difficulties. Always remember, m'alba, that you can ask me anything."

"I haven't given you much of an opportunity to notice me, have I?"

"Well, we do seem to spend our time together arguing about cosmic reality. That doesn't leave much energy for any personal dealings."

"Am I really very spoiled?"

"Just a bit."

"My nanny used to say I could out-sulk the devil."

"I bow to her greater knowledge of you."

"And Derissa says I am a fool," she said with an air of making a clean breast of the matter.

"What an unkind thing to say, to be sure," he replied with a slight smile.

"I am not good at resigning myself to my fate. Should I have submitted to your will instantly?"

"Little one, I truly have no wish to . . . dominate you. That would demean both of us. You may sulk in your rooms until the end of time, if it suits you. You know who I am and what I am. That has never happened before. I hope that you might, in time, come to value me—or at least tolerate me. It would have been easier if I were just a man like other men. And I am, on one level. If you cut me, I *will* bleed. But if you are angry with that other me, the one that seems to be eternal, then you must take your grievance to a higher authority."

She shook her head. "Don't you see what it is? Admiral Gilhame ur Fagon *was* indeed a man—a ruthless fighting man, but only a man. But you, now, are all the fighting men who ever existed, using people, spending lives to save the world or galaxy or cosmos. You always fight for right— or, at least, it turns out to be right, because you always win. You *seem* to hold back the darkness, but really you *are* the darkness. I cannot reconcile myself to that. You would kill anyone for a just cause, whatever the cause is, even your own offspring. Wouldn't you? To save the world?"

"I always have, yes."

"And then, when it is done, you die a hero and leave the rest of us to pick up the pieces."

"True."

"The Cosmic All seems to be to be a pretty poor planner."

"If men will stop making war, I will cease to exist."

"No. You can't get out of it that way. You *are* war, the very spirit of it. I have thought and thought, and I think it is the fact that you have existed that inspires men to deeds of valor. You make killing romantic."

"Do I? Perhaps. What would you have me do?"

"Make it all so ugly and sickening that no one would ever wish to fight again."

"I see. I did that once at least, as I recall, and obtained such a reputation for savagery that I was a name to frighten children with for centuries afterward—the Undead Prince of Darkness, a man who lived on blood; that is what I became. But I remained a hero. You cannot lay the whole blame on me, however neat and tidy a solution that seems. I am more a result than a cause."

"I don't want to be used to glorify you and what you stand for."

"Fine. And I don't want to use you."

"You already have."

"Yes. Everything is always the same and always different, m'alba."

"*Curva*! Here I am, shrilling on about cosmic reality again. I see I can't convince you, yet. Goodnight, Admiral."

"Goodnight."

He watched her drift into the darkness. He was glad now of the distance she had placed between them. The child of the dream, the fine boy who looked so much like Kurwen Mordell, would never exist, and therefore would never die begging for his father's mercy. He turned off the light and slid down in his bed, to try to sleep dreamlessly. And such dreams he had were of roses and green eyes and red hair.

_____ *Chapter X*

The refitting Station in the Attira was a series of hefty asteroids in the orbit of what had once been a planet. It was an ideal place for the rehabilitation of ships too large to land on a planet's surface, and indeed, that was the principal industry of the place. Although it was in the Kardusian sphere, it was officially neutral, and the workshops would outfit the ships of any of the Ten Nations.

Ur Fagon's swollen fleet settled into their assigned sector at the trailing end of the asteroid belt. Work crews swarmed aboard as Gilhame's people departed for one of the asteroid-cities for some recreation. Two other fleets were being refitted, as well as a large number of merchant vessels.

"We pulled Seven, Gil," Buschard said when they met in the shuttle hanger.

"I know. So?"

"Well, Gyre is here and he's assigned to Seven, too."

"Just what I needed to make my week complete. I thought he was clear across the sector."

"The poop is he got his ass kicked by the Nabateans."

"Then I doubt I'll find him in a charitable mood."

"Gil, where you are concerned, Gyre has nothing but ugly moods. He's never forgiven you for that thing on Feebus IX."

"Did Frikard try to get our assignment changed? I don't

particularly want any trouble."

"Sure. No room. It's Seven or nothing. And we can't stay on board."

"Then, we must just hope that dear Guthry remembers that Attira is neutral territory."

"I would not like to wager on it."

"Neither would I. What is his strength?"

"About thirty thousand—but it's you he'll be after."

"A man who would carry a grudge about losing a war game would do anything, anything at all. How is Alvellaina coming with her dance lessons?"

Buschard understood that the matter of Admiral Guthry Gyre was closed. He grinned. "She's a quick study. Got the pattern dances in nothing flat. It's a shame she's too old to train for navigation. I suspect she'd be a natural. And in the *onteem*, she's brilliant. I must say, she doesn't seem to like them much, though. Kept making me feel as if my hands were dirty whenever I touched her, but very light in the hand, for all of that. Maybe she'll enjoy the *onteem* more with you."

"I doubt I will have the pleasure. What do you think of her?"

"Alvellaina? Very reserved, compared to Derissa. I don't know. I wouldn't call her animated or lively, but she's smart enough. Sharp-tongued, too. I suppose she keeps herself apart too much for my liking. Derissa jumped into the routine and has my people eating out of her hand. Her sister doesn't have any tact, at least not compared to my Derissa."

"You sound besotted. And Armanda?"

"Lovely girl. Imagine an ugly old man like Krispin fathering those girls. They must take after their mother."

"And their aunt. I hope E-varit is satisfied with his part of the bargain."

"Well, you saw them at the dance. Quite a family, already."

"It will help make his exile tolerable."

They stopped talking as they climbed into the shuttle. Gilhame fell into a reverie during the trip, considering why the presence of Admiral Gyre was both unexpected and

disquieting. It was odd, he realized, that he had had no pre-
science at all of the trip to Attira. Usually he got brief
glimpses of an impending event, and certainly he would
have foreseen the presence of such a vigorous rival as
Gyre. Then he shrugged his shoulders and listened to the
chatter of the people in the craft with him, enjoying vicari-
ously their anticipation of the pleasures that awaited them.
For the other major industry of Attira was tourism, and
while it was not a fantastic fleshpot like Artenii, neither
was it an exclusive haunt of the very wealthy. An enlisted
man could have a very good time on his credit.

They arrived at City Seven, disembarked the shuttle and
found air taxis. Buschard and Gilhame shared one to the
apartment complex where they would be housed during
their stay. He entered his suite and looked around.
Alvellaina and her sisters had come earlier in the day, but
there was no evidence of her presence except a dress flung
down on the bed in one of the sleeping rooms.

He prowled around his own room for a while, unpacked
his uniforms, then bathed. Redressed in fresh grays, he
caught a glimpse of himself in the mirror as he walked to
the communicator. The somber color of his uniform
heightened the whiteness of his skin. He sighed. He felt a
tiny tinge of envy for Pers Buschard's flashy handsomeness
or even for Frikard's more ordinary good looks. He knew
that nothing in the way of dress could make him look other
than what he was—a fighting man—and he saw nothing attractive in his lean body and prominent features. He
straightened the black belt around his middle, then slipped
a little knife into his sleeve. Parts of the Attira complex
were rough enough that a knife could come in very handy,
and other weapons were strictly forbidden.

He punched the message button on the communicator
and waited. The machine warbled happily to itself for a few
seconds, then began spitting out cards of various sizes. He
picked them up and sorted through them, enjoying the ar-
ray of heraldic devices which adorned them. The intercom
from the hall clicked on.

"Admiral?"

"Yes, m'alba." He released the doorlock, which he had

put on "no entry" during his bath, and Alvellaina entered, her arms full of packages. "Out spending my hard-earned prize money, I see," he commented.

She blushed and smiled. "Yes," she said as she dropped her burdens on the couch. "I have resolved to reduce you to penury." Then she shook her head. "Not really. I have a line of credit from my mother's estate. I'm so ignorant, it took Derissa to point it out to me."

"I would have given you a blank check, in any case. I've never been able to spend all the money I've gathered over the years. What did you buy?"

"A nice sturdy robe for sleep-walking in." She grinned again and showed delightful dimples.

He looked at the nearly dozen packages. "Did it come in pieces, then?"

"You beast! I didn't really buy a robe."

"I should hope not, when Lefair could make you a good one at no cost to me or you."

"I got a fan and three hats and several pairs of shoes— the ship's cobbler doesn't make very nice dancing slippers—and two purses, no three, and a tea dress I liked. That's all. I've never had so much fun in my life."

"Good. And what will you wear to the ball we are invited to this evening?" As he said this he thought how sad it was that she could not remember anything more pleasurable than buying a few trinkets.

"My nightdress, of course."

"Then I am glad I have a cloak to cover you with in the streets."

"I see you won't be baited. Whose ball is it?"

He waved a card in his hand. "I fear your father would not approve. The Kalurian Embassy invites us tonight." He flipped over another. "And tomorrow there is a costume affair at the Havassit ambassador's; a tea, also tomorrow, at the C'sildan consulate. I have not looked at the rest."

"So many? No wonder Lefair insisted I would need more than one gown. Do you always get so many invitations, or only when you have just won a battle?"

"On Attira it is the principal business of embassies to

host a diversity of entertainments. The notion is that you get your enemies smoky on neutral territory and then pick their brains. Speaking of enemies, one of mine is here. Sub-Admiral Gyre of the Eighth Fleet. He would like my head on a pike almost as much as you would. You should get along famously."

She shook her head. "Having a common enemy doesn't make people friends. Besides, he has an even nastier reputation than you do. My father disliked him."

"But you have found, have you not, that reputations often lie?"

"Yes, but better the devil I know . . ." She shrugged, sat down and removed her shoes with a sort of happy sigh. "Can I open the rest of the invitations?"

"Certainly." He placed them on the table beside her. "How are your sisters?"

"Fine, I hope. I got lost twice finding this room. This place is a regular warren. Are all cities like this?"

"Some. What is the biggest city you have been in before?"

"Larista on Grentar."

"Was I ever there? No, I think not. It's small, isn't it? A garden city, I seem to remember. Seven is pretty typical of sport-port towns—not as exotic as some, not as big as others. There's Grettry, the world-city. I suppose it's the largest continuous habitation in the cosmos. Even its oceans are covered. And Bentil is probably the tallest city—sixty miles square and four high—an engineering marvel. And Velyn, the Emperor's winter home. That's rather pretty. Perhaps we'll go there sometime. Find anything you like?"

'Anything,' he thought, 'for me to stop sounding like a travelogue.'

She looked up from the invitations. "What's a *kevar*?"

"Festrian Embassy?"

"Yes."

"Unless you have a taste for group sex, I suggest we pass on that one," he said dryly.

"An orgy?"

"At the very least."

"The least?"

"It is a Festrian custom to die in ecstasy."

Her eyes got wide. "Why?"

"I have no idea. Consult the ship's library if you are curious."

"Does anyone come to their *kevar*?"

"Yes."

"Why?"

Gilhame shrugged. "For the same reason people gamble, I suppose. Excitement."

"Have you ever gone to one?"

"Yes. I was a downy-faced ensign on my first leave. I was much too terrified to be ecstatic—or even aroused. One should not mix one's pleasures."

Alvellaina stared up at him. "No. I don't think I would like that party. Are the Miguls fun? Their invitation looks very dull, somehow."

"They are, indeed, the dullest race I know of. But their musical evenings are as uplifting as a Havassit blessing. Anything in that batch from the Antrians?"

"Yes. It's very confusing."

"Read it to me."

" 'Will you join the dance? Current Third and Seventh Levels approaching Creation. Patterns above 1900 are cordially invited to partake of the energy exchange. Others may observe.' That's all. No date, nothing. What does it mean?"

He was not surprised at her ignorance. Despite the vast variety of worlds within and without the Kardusian Empire, most planet-dwellers were quite provincial. And the Antrians were rather off the beaten track even for a spaceman. "It is the Antrian Creation. They believe the dance mirrors the universe. Level Three is the 'Animal Kingdom' and Seven is 'Angels and Demons.' The reason there is no date is that it is continuous. The card is just to tell one where they are in the pattern. They will probably do Four and Eight next. That's 'Plants and Emotions.' And, if you ever see a card which says they are dancing Nine, you might just say your prayers, because, theoretically, the end of all things is at hand."

"It's religion, then?" She was still puzzled.

"If religion can be said to be life, then, yes. Would you like to go? Level Seven, of course."

" 'Angels and Demons.' It doesn't sound very exciting."

"You might be surprised. I shall go, in any case. I could not pass up an opportunity . . . to be myself. Come, stand up with me in the Antrian Creation. I think you'll like it. Consult the communicator for the pattern. It's not difficult and Buschard says you are a quick learner."

"Alright, yes. It obviously fascinates you, and that makes me curious. What is the appropriate garb?"

"For you? Something white, of course, Halba Vanity." They smiled at each other.

_____ *Chapter XI*

"Hurry up, woman!" Gilhame shouted across the apartment that evening as they prepared to go to the ball at the Kalurian Embassy. "You've had time enough to dress three times over. Buschard just called to say he and Derissa are on their way up."

"Yes, master. In a minute," came her voice.

"'Master,' indeed," he muttered, smiling. They were beginning to joke with one another, which he thought a very hopeful sign. He paced back and forth, slipping the little knife in and out of its sleeve sheath. He turned at the faint rustle behind him.

He barely prevented himself from gasping as he saw her. The gown she wore was green, cut high in the waist. The bodice was a pale silvery green, almost, but not quite, transparent, and sparkling with flecks of gold. The skirt was made of many panels, alternating the material of the bodice with a darker green stuff also flecked with gold. She wore no jewelry except a spray of sparkling flowers in her unnetted hair. The thousands of burnished copper curls framed her face and emphasized her lovely eyes.

Alvellaina eyed him a trifle apprehensively. "You look very handsome tonight," she said, fiddling with the enormous green feather fan on one wrist.

Gilhame bowed slightly. "A ravishing creation, my dear. Lefair has outdone himself. I had no idea he had so much talent. He is quite wasted on uniforms.

"Do you like it?"

"Very much. A tantalizing garment. More discreet than your nightdress—but very lovely."

"I took that to Lefair and told him what you said—about riots and all."

"If you wish to cause a stir, you will certainly succeed. Where did the material come from? It is quite out of the ordinary."

"Lefair said he found it on Colocos."

"I see I must . . . That must be Buschard and your sister." He opened the door.

Derissa twirled through the door, laughing at some remark of Buschard's. Gilhame studied her, noting the high-waisted deep-blue gown with short, full sleeves. The skirt was made in many layers, each one a different shade of blue and sewn round the edge with tiny white beads. She had electro-netted her hair, braided it with long blue ribbons and coiled the braids over her ears. Buschard came in, his eyes intent on Derissa, looking very elegant in his dress golds.

"So, that's why you wanted that fan," Derissa exclaimed as she looked at Alvellaina. "You utter wretch." But she smiled as she said it.

"Yes," Alvellaina answered calmly.

Buschard stared at the two sisters for a moment, then turned to Gilhame. "They make quite a picture, don't they? Shall we go?"

"Do you have a wrap, m'alba?"

Alvellaina went back into her room and came out with a flimsy thing of silvery lace, and they left.

The Kalurian Embassy was a rather modest structure set on piles in the middle of an artificial lake. The little air taxi which had brought them from the shuttle to City Two circled over the lake and landed on a tiny platform. They could hear strains of music as they entered.

Alvellaina looked around her. Derissa and Buschard were a few steps ahead of them. "Admiral, how do I behave?" she whispered.

"We will be announced as we enter. You will stand up with me in the first pattern dance, presuming it is one you have learned. After that, you may dance with whomever you wish. When your feet are tired, we will leave. In all likelihood, a number of underbred persons will try to discomfort you. Try to deal with them without coming to blows. Do not drink too much Kalurian punch; you will regret it in the morning. Do not share drugs with strangers. If you can't find me, find Buschard or one of my officers."

"I just got . . . frightened for a moment."

"I understand. Just remember who you are, and you will survive handily: the Halba Alvellaina Curly-Krispin, nothing else."

"Will people tell me who they are?"

"Usually. Ask, if they don't. Now, if you would do me the kindness to put your hand on my arm as we descend the stairs. Very good. Now, look up at me and smile. Think of me covered with Corlian jelly and with a malus in my mouth. There, you see how easy it is."

She laughed her deep laugh. "You are a monster," she whispered.

"So you keep telling me."

"Admiral Gilhame ur Fagon! Halba Alvellaina Curly-Krispin," boomed the loudspeaker.

"How did they know me?"

"It is the herald's job to know such things. Ah, the set is almost over. You may remove your hand if it pleases you."

"I must say, I never expected such scrupulous observance of my demands, Admiral," she answered, and left her hand where it was.

"A man who would break his word a little, would break it completely. I look forward to the day when you will feel safe enough to release me from my promise. Great Yardell's Balls! It's Marpessa Devero. Smile and put up your guard."

As he said these words a handsome, black-haired woman in a red gown walked towards them. As she approached, Gilhame could tell she was in a mischief-making mood. Her lustrous black eyes darted between them, and her heavy brows rose in query.

"Well, Gil, it has been a long time, hasn't it?" she purred, ignoring Alvellaina.

"Hello, Marpessa. Has it been a long time? It seems like only yesterday. May I present Halba Krispin? Alvellaina, Captain Marpessa Devero of the Sixth Fleet. Tell me, are you still bucketing around in the old *Caldos,* or have they given you a ship worthy of you yet?"

"The *Caldos* gave up the ghost six months ago. No, I am commanding Gyre's flag these days, the *Buskin.*"

"Really? I see I am behind the times in my information. The *Buskin*? I had no idea she was still in service. You don't seem to have much luck with your equipment, do you, 'Pessa?"

The woman colored, making her make-up stand out in uneven patches. "It's alright," she said a little sulkily.

Gilhame could feel the tension in the hand Alvellaina had on his arm. She did not appreciate being snubbed. "The *Buskin*?" she said suddenly. "That must be an old ship, even older than you, Admiral, for I seem to recall that my father trained in her." She sounded like an innocent child, but Gilhame was not taken in. As he and Marpessa were of an age, the insult was carefully studied.

"It is, child, it is. It was commissioned before you were born," he answered solemnly. "No wonder you are in dry dock," he added to Marpessa.

"So, Alvellaina, if I may call you that, how do you find life now that you have the great ur Fagon?" Marpessa asked.

As restricted as her life had been, Alvellaina was sufficiently versed in matters of etiquette to know that Captain Devero was presuming that, though her father was in exile and she herself was a chattel of ur Fagon, she was still the social superior, as Gilhame had reminded her only moments before. "I do think undue familiarity is the worst of bad manners, don't you, Admiral?" Alvellaina asked, offering Marpessa the same snub she had been given.

Gilhame stifled a guffaw. "It is one of the symptoms of the decay of our civilization," he intoned as solemnly as he could. "First manners, then morals. Sad, truly sad."

"In reply to your query, *Captain* Devero, I do not 'have'

the Admiral. He is privileged to have himself. I do find his company rather amusing, however. He keeps me in hysterics with tales . . . of his experiences." She threw Gilhame a glowing look, and he swallowed to hold back his laughter.

Marpessa glared at her. "You mustn't believe everything you hear."

"It quite depends on who is speaking, doesn't it?" Alvellaina answered sweetly.

"I believe they are forming up the set for the next dance, my dear," Gilhame said before Marpessa could speak.

"It certainly looks that way, doesn't it?" Alvellaina answered, fanning herself gently. "I do hope it is less *stuffy* on the dance floor." They left the outraged Captain Devero with her mouth open.

"Stuffy! You little fiend," he hissed.

"You said not to come to *blows*, Admiral."

"You did very well, but be careful. She is a bad enemy."

"Who is she?"

"In the tale of my 'experiences,' you mean?"

"Yes."

"We were . . . lovers back when I got my first command. She was very annoyed when I didn't keep her with me."

"Why didn't you?"

"Too erratic. Oh, she's occasionally brilliant, tactically speaking, but she takes unnecessary chances. That's why she keeps getting space junk. She's had four ships shot out from under her."

The music began, and the long line of couples began an intricate pattern dance called Wanderer's Return. Alvellaina acquitted herself well enough, although she was distracted by the transparent dance floor beneath her. Colored lanterns were hung beneath the floor, and they reflected on the water of the lake, making curiously colored patterns. Gilhame and Alvellaina had danced up and down the set before the music ended.

Gilhame led his companion off the floor and smiled at her. "Buschard was right. You are very good."

"Thank you. I would never have believed it, but you make an elegant figure on the dance floor, Admiral."

"Praise, indeed. My, what a gathering of vultures we

have tonight. This handsome fellow tearing through the throng to us is none other than the unadmirable Admiral Gyre. Ah, you have your polite smile upon you already. What a very quick student you are, indeed. Now, why do I mistrust that look? Good evening, Gyre."

"Ur Fagon! Still in one piece, I see. May I have the pleasure of an introduction to your charming companion?"

"Certainly. Admiral Gyre, Halba Curly-Krispin." The omission of first names was not lost on Gyre. A slight frown crossed his undeniably handsome face.

Admiral Guthry Gyre was a broad man, yellow-haired and ruddy-skinned, with oddly black eyes. He gave a half-bow and grinned, displaying neat, even teeth beneath his large mustache. "Might I have the pleasure of the next dance, Halba-vera?" he asked, adding the honorific for "highborn" to the title "lady."

Alvellaina cast a quick, sidelong glance at Gilhame's face, but found no clue for her answer in it. She fanned herself lightly, bestowed a ravishing smile on Gyre and said, "That would be delightful."

Captain Frikard walked up and bowed. "Halba, would it be presumptuous of me to ask for your next available dance?"

With a decided gleam of mischief in her eyes, Alvellaina laughed softly. "Dearest 'Captain'—so stiff and formal, and we were *such* good friends on the ship. I would love to stand up with you, Ven, as soon as I dance with Admiral Gyre here. You did tell me that it is all equal at a dance, did you not, ur Fagon?"

"I did, indeed," he lied.

"There, you see, Ven. And we are such old friends now. Still, you have lovely manners. Oh, yes," she said, gazing at Gyre's extended hand, "the dance." She left with him, turning her head to wink broadly at the still-stunned captain and ur Fagon, who was having a time controlling his face.

"What the hell was all that, sir?" Frikard asked.

"I do believe m'alba, having practiced the fine art of insult on me for several weeks, is about to play kickball with the inside of Gyre's head. Serves him right. They are to do an *onteem*. It should be an education for both of them. Now, let me see. A partner. Don't fuss your mind, Ven. She was just using you to put Gyre in his place. I believe I see Elioz Mayhew over there. Boring female, but an admirable dancer. Excuse me."

"Certainly, sir," Frikard said to his departing back. He stared at his superior as ur Fagon cut through the crowd, and speculated on his purpose in surrendering Alvellaina for the *onteem*. It was not a dance to do with strangers. Then he shrugged and went looking for a partner, wishing Ganna Ottera were there. Ganna hated cities and was, as usual, holed up in her quarters, reading and sleeping.

The lights dimmed until the room was in twilight, though still faintly lit from the lanterns underneath the floor. The music began softly at first, then swelled in volume as the tempo increased. The couples, their arms entwined, their hands on their hips, began the spinning *onteem* "Tender Caresses." Gilhame, partnered with the lovely Elioz Mayhew, caught glimpses of Alvellaina as he spun. He saw her lips move and caught the snarled answer which Gyre made before the dance moved him out of view. Because of the propinquity created by the stance assumed by the partners, the *onteem* was a brief dance, lasting no more than seven minutes; also, because of its nature, it was not danced in all social circles.

"Tender Caresses" lasted less than four minutes. The lights came up as the music faded. Gilhame saw Alvellaina already standing on the side of the room, her face pale and without expression, fanning herself. He walked the tedious Elioz off the floor and went to Alvellaina.

She glared at him over the feathers. "That is an obscene dance!" she snapped.

"It is considered so in many circles, yes. But, you did practice it with Buschard, did you not?"

"I did, in the recreation room, with all the lights on. And Commander Buschard is a gentleman. He kept his hands on his own body and he did not make lewd suggestions. It is hard enough being that close to a man. I came very near to 'accidentally' kicking that bastard right where it counts. And he stinks. His breath is like a dead rat. Do I have to dance that again?"

"No, of course not. Many refuse it for the very reason you spoke of, the closeness. So, Guthry has started using *choon* has he? What did he say to you?"

"He asked me how much I charged, as if I were a common whore."

Gilhame quirked an eyebrow. "Well, you did sort of lead him on, making bedroom eyes at poor Frikard. How did you reply?"

She gave him a tense grin. "I told him I was a give-cruiser woman. He nearly choked."

Gilhame's boisterous laugh caused several people to stare at them. "M'alba, you are a wonder and a delight. Absolutely perfect. Now, climb down off your high horse. The insult was aimed at me. I think I have just used you, *again,* and I apologize. But, you see, I could not prevent him from asking you to dance."

"I had no idea it would be so complicated. I just thought it would be fun, like in a book."

"And so it should be. We tend to muddy even our social waters with rivalry and politics."

"I wish I had taken the veil!"

"Do you really?" He grinned as she shook her head. "Here is Frikard to claim you for the dance. If you do not wish to dance, ask for some refreshment."

"I hope that carrion-eater tries that approach with Armanda. She'll freeze his testicles."

"Your aunt or your sister?"

"Either. Hello, Captain. Do you know, I am very thirsty." She dropped the fan on its cord and extended both hands in a friendly manner.

Frikard bowed, slipped her hand onto his arm and said, "I think you will find Galagian wine very refreshing, m'alba. Besides, they are doing a *milkos* next, and that is too vigorous for my taste and your gown. By your leave, sir?"

"Shoo. I love a good *milkos*, and I know just the partner." Gilhame used his superior height to scan the crowd, then cut through several groups to reach Marpessa Devero.

"Come on, Marp. We have not done a *milkos* in years."

"Still a dancing fool, Gil?"

"I plan to dance at my own wake."

"Alright. Just a minute." She bent down and lifted the two sideseams of her gown, securing them at her hips with electro-net clips and revealing shapely legs. He took her out onto the floor as the music began.

Gilhame began the tattoo, his boots banging out the rhythm while she clapped and stood still. Then he stood while she danced around him. They began the springing leaps in perfect time, fingertips touching. When he picked her up for the spinning carry, she was panting. They repeated the whole three times, and she almost stumbled in the last set of leaps.

"You are out of condition, Marp," he commented as they left the floor.

"Shut your ugly mouth and give me your handkerchief."

Gilhame silently handed her the object and watched her mop her face and chest. Her black hair clung damply at her scalp and around her face. When she returned the cloth to him, he stuffed it into his beltpouch.

Marpessa looked at him. "What the devil has happened to you? I hardly know you anymore."

"Did you ever know me, I wonder?" He felt a stir from the other Gilhame in his mind.

"Intimately."

"But not well. *Choon* will ruin your figure, you know." He had caught the distinctive smell on her breath as they danced.

"You, lecturing me, about drugs. That's a laugh. You have changed. What happened? Did you get religion?"

"No. I just grew up."

"Then why don't you run for the Diet?" she snapped and strode away.

Gilhame danced another couple of dances, then went to get himself some wine. He watched Alvellaina in a *vane,* a slow walking dance, and spoke to the Havassit ambassador. The being was solemnly thanking him for his treatment of the priest, ben Gessar.

"I did not like to discommode His Reverence," Gilhame answered, his attention on the dancers.

"You did not, Admiral. He said, under the circumstances, that you were very kind. In fact, he was quite startled. Good quarters, attention to his dietary needs, everything. He had all expectations of incarceration."

"Why? He's a noncombatant."

"Others in this room would not view his presence on the Coalchee flagship with such charity."

"I must admit a certain curiosity as to what a priest of his status was doing on a ship of war, *any* ship of war. It puts Havassit neutrality in a very odd light, I must say."

The Havassit gave ur Fagon a look from his triangular eyes. "Admiral, are you aware of the Tides?"

Gilhame felt a kind of terrible stillness come over him. "Yes. I am familiar with that part of your faith."

"They are turning." The Havassit spoke with great sincerity.

"I see. Then, the Antrians will dance Nine soon?"

"They will."

"I see. I even believe you. How soon?" He meant it. The Dragon had seen the End of All Things before, and he never ignored its portents.

"In your lifespan, Admiral."

Gilhame gave the Havassit a hard stare. These were a people who did not lie, could not lie. They were respected as truth-sayers everywhere, and used as such. Their Tides, like the Antrian Patterns, were predictions of the future. Part religion, part philosophy, very accurate and almost incomprehensible, those Tides and Patterns. Perhaps, this time he would not survive the end. He rather hoped he would not, but thought of all the people who did not dwell on the immortal level.

"Is there any point at which the Last Tide might be turned again, Ambassador?"

There had to be a purpose to the Havassit's conversation, for the Havassit were not in the habit of making small talk about the Tides. Their discretion was almost as famous as their honesty.

"Certainly," he answered.

"Can you tell me?"

The ambassador smiled, displaying his mouth ridges. "Tradition states that when the Lion and the Dragon join hands to fight the Darkness, the Last Tides will recede, and the Pattern will begin anew."

For a moment, the room vanished from Gilhame's view. He saw a field plowed by a red-bearded man. A horse reared on a hill behind him, trumpeting and kicking. The man looked at the horse and left his plow. He mounted the horse, and the vision vanished.

Gilhame shook himself and looked at the ambassador. The Havassit was watching him intently. Gilhame cleared his throat. "Good. I have long wished to meet old Red-Beard. We do keep missing one another."

"It is very difficult for the Darkness and the Light to abide one another, ur Fagon."

"Quite." He had recovered his composure now. "But I am tired, and it is about time, don't you think?"

"What I think has nothing to do with the matter, Admiral. My Tide is almost run away as we speak."

"Then I thank you most graciously for the time you have honored me with, sir."

"I have discharged my last obligation now, speaking to you." The Havassit bowed, and Alvellaina came up beside them cautiously.

"Ambassador, may I present Halba Alvellaina Curly-Krispin. M'alba, Ambassador ben Jurrat."

She dropped a deep curtsy, gripping Gilhame's arm as she sank down. She was very white as she arose.

Ben Jurrat bowed. "A thousand sons, m'alba," he said formally.

"A thousand years," she offered the ritual reply.

"Will you excuse me? I must speak to the Rosean envoy," ben Jurrat said.

"Certainly, sir." Gilhame watched him leave, then looked at the woman. "Are you tired, little one?"

"All that dancing. My feet are like hot knives."

"Then, away. Was it as much fun as you hoped?" He offered his arm and began walking her out of the room.

"Parts of it were."

"And the rest?"

"Boring."

"Boring doesn't make you white around the mouth."

"Some of them were very cruel. That Devero female trapped me in the dressing room and regaled me with . . . explicit incidents. And others as much as said I had sold myself, like Niyarkos's wife. I didn't hit them, but I wanted to. I wanted to cut out their ugly tongues and stuff them down their throats.

"Poor little one. How intolerable that continued association with me has made you quite bloodthirsty. It would have been much kinder if I had let you go with your father."

"No! I see now that I would have exchanged one prison for another. I'll be just fine, once I grow up. Besides, this gown would be quite wasted on the Exile World, wouldn't it?"

"Yes. You were quite the most beautiful woman in the room tonight, m'alba," he said softly.

"More than Marpessa?"

"Much, much more. She uses *choon* and will soon become fat and sluttish."

"You danced with her."

"She used to do the *milkos* with some grace. That is an accomplishment. That reminds me." He opened his beltpouch and removed the soiled handkerchief. "I am about to defile the Kalurian lake," he said as they reached the taxi area. He dropped the offending object into the dark waters. "Were you jealous?"

"No. Not in the least. Remember, I know you." They got into the taxi, and he smiled into the darkness.

Chapter XII

There was a knock on his door. "Admiral?"

"Yes?"

"May I come in?"

He grinned to himself. "Certainly."

Alvellaina opened the door and entered. Gilhame was seated at his dressing table, cleaning his nails. He looked up and smiled at her.

"Are you alright?" she asked.

"I am." He got up slowly, the hem of his gray dressing gown swirling around his ankles as he rose. "That's very pretty," he said, looking at the white dress she was wearing.

"What's the matter?"

"I really don't know, m'alba. A faint sense of unease—like a storm coming over the horizon, but not yet arrived. But there is no weather on Attira. Whatever it is, it has not happened—yet."

"Yes. I feel that too. Itchy."

"Are you prepared for the Antrian Patterns?" He wanted to distract her, flattered that she would brave the intimacy of his chambers because of her unease but annoyed that nothing else would force her to enter them. Their friendship seemed to progress in fitful starts, with as many steps backward as forward. It frustrated him.

"I think so. I studied the book carefully, and it seems

straightforward enough. I am still not quite sure why I am going, except it will make a nice change. There doesn't appear to be much opportunity for . . . unkindness in the Patterns." She sounded a little wistful.

"True. Has it been very difficult, little one?"

"Yes and no. Some people have been very nice, and some have been terribly cruel for no reason I can discern. That's what is hard. Not knowing as you meet each person if they will bite or not. A few times I've wanted to cry, and other times I've been furious. Will it always be like this?"

"Until a new whipping boy appears, yes; and with a few people, always. There are those individuals in the race who feel that children should suffer for their parents' sins. And there will always be people who hate you because of your presumed relationship with me. That you were not permitted to choose exile is irrelevant. And then there are . . . I believe that the Narvan ambassador was trying to extract information from you the other evening."

She giggled. "No, he wasn't. Or, at least he didn't get that far. He was inquiring if I was available and for how much. He seems to have taken quite a fancy to me, the toad."

"I see that it did not offend you the way Gyre's similar inquiry did."

"I have become rather accustomed to it. The Narvan was the eighth."

"In three days? What do you tell them?" His amusement hid the knot of rage in his stomach.

"I told the men I wasn't interested. The two women . . . I basically acted dumb and changed the subject. If that Calvina Rost pinches my rear one more time, though, I may redesign her face."

The thought of Halba Rost, with her sad canine eyes and her drooping chins, pressing her attentions on Alvellaina first infuriated and then amused him. "Poor Calvina. She basks in reflected glory. A very silly, pathetic woman. But no questions about me, my strengths, my weaknesses, where the Fleet is off to next? My vanity is piqued." Gilhame desired nothing more than to steer the conversation away from his own jealousy without sending her away.

He wanted their talk to continue until her lingering rose-scent filled the room.

"I didn't say that. The Narvan didn't want to know about you, but a great many others did. The women want to know if you make love well, if you exercise *droit du seigneur* over my sisters, if you are available, approachable and desirable. The men want to know how you react to *var*. Well, most of the men did. A few wanted to know about sex, too."

"And what did you tell them?" He noticed the time and realized that he should be dressed. He turned his back to her and removed the dressing gown. Alvellaina watched his reflection in the mirror, blushed faintly, then stared at the even crisscross stripes on his back above the line of his shorts.

"Admiral, what are those marks on your back?"

"Whip marks. Cadet floggings."

"Didn't you have a Healer?"

"The sergeant who did all that kept me in detention until I had self-healed and therefore scarred." He took up the uniform he was going to wear and began to dress. "Now, tell me what you tell people who ask nosy questions about my personal habits." He didn't want to talk about flogging either.

"I say I have never been able to tell when you are using the drug and when you aren't. This makes them very nervous. I am not sure why."

"*Var* produces the effect of out-of-body travel and long-distance telepathy. While you are traveling, you are also subject to precognitive experiences. The notion that I might be *var*-led at an embassy ball would make my enemies uncomfortable, to say the least, particularly if they could not tell what state I was in. There is no way to guard yourself against *var*-made invasions of privacy, but many people like to think there are and that they can . . . but only if they know someone is using the drug." Gilhame closed the electro-net fastenings on his garment and turned around.

The jet-black uniform was bare of any piping or decoration save where the dragon was picked out on the chest in golden brilliants. Gilhame wore no belt to bisect his lean-ness, but had a pouch clipped at the small of his back. He turned back to the mirror, and the two of them stared at his face for a moment. Then he sat down and pulled on his boots.

His boots on, he walked back to the dressing table and picked up the little sleeve knife and put it into its sheath. He opened a drawer and took out a pair of longer knives and slipped them into his boots.

"Do you *have* to carry those?" she asked.

Gilhame stood up and looked at her reflection in the glass. The golden flecks in his green eyes seemed to coa-lesce at his pupils. "You are the only person in the cosmos who can disarm me, my heart," he replied huskily.

Alvellaina turned a rosy pink and fled. Gilhame looked after her and shrugged his shoulders. Her nearness always made him forget how much she feared and hated him. 'One step forward, two back,' he thought. 'Damn my impatience!'

Gilhame's boots rang on the stone walkway leading to the Antrian Pattern Hall. The stone was green, veined with gold, and had been imported from the Antrian home world. It felt very odd, to walk from the bustling, synthetic shore-leave city into what was clearly a park. The distant light of other buildings cast faint shadows on the silvery trees.

The Hall was a circular building made of dark stone with veins of red or perhaps gold in it. It was very still and ap-peared to be uninhabited.

"It's very dark," said Alvellaina. She had recovered her countenance, but she had also withdrawn into cautious for-mality again.

"It will be even darker inside," he replied.

"Are you still feeling . . . spooky?"

"I am." They came to the great door, six man-heights tall, and it swung open silently. The blackness of the vesti-bule yawned at them.

She shivered. "It feels like a trap."

"I don't think so, m'alba."

They crossed the vestibule slowly, accompanied only by the echoes of their footfalls, their eyes adjusting to the darkness. Beyond, they could make out the shape of the central room. It was cool inside. The great domed vault was pierced by tiny pinpricks of colored light.

There was a rustling, and someone approached. "Welcome," said a voice.

"Admiral ur Fagon and Halba Krispin come to join the dance," Gilhame answered.

"Level Seven, of course," the unseen greeter answered.

"Yes."

"This way, please. Try not to disturb the energy of the other dancers, won't you?"

They followed the dark shape down nine steps and across the floor. The floor was made of some shiny black stuff which faintly reflected the standing forms of many people. A distant tinkling might have been music.

"Here is your place, Halba," the voice murmured. Alvellaina saw a sort of glow on the dark floor and stepped over it.

The room seemed to vanish around her. She felt frozen and fought down a terrible panic. Why had she ever agreed to come? Now the darkness was total, impenetrable. She battled the claustrophobic terror. She closed her eyes . . .

. . . And *saw* the dancers.

Strange shapes wheeled through the now silver air, calling to her. They were dancers indeed, moving in some complex pattern, their wings folding and unfolding. None were recognizably human, though bilateral symmetry seemed common. Their faces were fair or hideous in turn, the colors of their bodies altering constantly.

A woman-thing with drooping breasts and claws for arms made lazy circles, moving upward, but always falling back beyond some invisible point. Alvellaina thought she had never seen such a sad face. And there was a black man-horse with leathery wings who seemed always to be falling, but somehow never reached the floor.

She "heard" the dancers call her to join them, and she

wondered what shape she would take. After a time, which was either a moment or an eternity, Alvellaina released her spirit.

The feline thing which arose from her was startling. It was green, with golden-yellow wings and eyes like drops of molten gold. It hovered at the edge of the pattern, spitting and hissing at the other dancers, dripping tears from the hot eyes, which seemed to burst into flame as they fell.

And there *he* was, always the Dragon, quartering across the pattern, his huge golden wings sending off sparks of light. Now he was beautiful, strong and wise and magnificent. How had she never seen it before? He beckoned her to join the Pattern.

There was some form to it, she knew, as the Cat and the Dragon rose, circled, almost collided and circled again. The two figures seemed to go higher and higher until they were almost lost in the stars.

She spiraled around his larger form, studying the huge cruel pinions, the great toothy jaw, the cavernous mouth, the wicked spiked tail. But the green eyes seemed always to be before her, smiling.

Then there was another, a cat-thing almost her twin, but silver and blue. It flew, tiny and fast, between them, and she felt it scream. Something called her down, and she felt herself plummet down past the other dancers. Quite suddenly she was standing to one side of her glowing circle.

Alvellaina saw the outline of the dragon on Gilhame's chest moving through the darkness quickly, but carefully avoiding the other participants. He grasped her elbow without comment and led her out into the entrance. She drew back a little from his touch, but then was caught in the intensity of his emotions.

"Did you hear her?" he snapped as they passed the doors.

"I heard . . . someone."

He broke into a trot, the tattoo of his heels on the stone shattering the silence. She grabbed a handful of skirt, pulled it up and lengthened her stride to keep up with him. In a few minutes they were out of the park and entering the edges of the apartment-building complex. "This way."

He led her away from the building they occupied,

across a busy street, crowding past revelers and shoppers without courtesy. There was an alley. He paused, and his feet seemed to falter. His face was very white. Then he went into the alley.

"What is it?" she gasped.

"Damn it! I don't have room." Then he took a deep breath and moved purposefully down the alley.

Room? Had he gone mad?

"Come on. It's just down here. He removed the sleeve knife and handed it to her. "You will need this, and you will use it!"

"Yes." She felt his focused anger and knew better than to question it. "Room for what?"

"Me, *him* and Derissa."

"Derissa?"

"Come on. I don't want her camping inside my skull forever. It's that next doorway. Stay behind me, try not to get in the way, and try not to get killed. Here we go."

Gilhame had pulled the pouch off the back of his uniform. He yanked out several small, flat disks. He gave the portal control a hard stare, then pressed several buttons. There was a hissing, and it opened.

There were six men in tan recreation uniforms crouched over something on the floor. Two rose as Gilhame entered. The little disks spun through the air, catching one man in the throat and the other in the chest. They collapsed, looking surprised.

Someone shouted. "It's too late, ur Fagon. She's beyond the Healer's art." There was a short bark of laughter.

Within his mind, Gilhame heard a whisper and "felt" a giggle. "All is illusion," said the whisper. His hands, meanwhile, had spent the rest of his killing disks and had gone to the boot knives. He glanced at the three men still standing, and took the stance of a skilled knife-fighter.

One of his opponents leapt into the air, kicking. Gilhame crouched and sprang straight up under the arc of the other's body. He felt the man's knife slash his left shoulder as he buried his own in the kidneys of his attacker, then yanked it out.

Gilhame whirled to face the two men remaining, but one

was moving rapidly toward the open portal and the other was backing away from Alvellaina. Blood spouted from his throat, and he sank to the floor. As he sent one of his knives flying into the back of the man near the door, Gilhame realized that Alvellaina must have stabbed him from behind, slashing at the man's neck with her little weapon. The man staggered to the portal and fell.

The laughter, the terrible, loud, ugly, raucous laughter which he had heard faintly throughout the brief fight, took his attention. He looked around and saw Marpessa Devero bending over Derissa's body, making tidy slashings with her knife.

He crossed to her in three long strides, caught Marpessa's hair in one hand and knocked the knife out of her hand with his foot. He snapped her head back sharply. Alvellaina stood silently staring at Derissa.

"It's too late. I've severed all her leg joints, and she'll be a vegetable," snarled Marpessa. Then she saw Alvellaina. "What?"

Alvellaina knelt down next to Derissa. "Wrong victim, Marp," Gilhame said. Derissa stirred within him. "You never could do anything right. M'alba, call a team of Healers."

Alvellaina scrambled to her feet and looked for a comm-link. Finding none, she turned toward the door, the bloody knife still in her hand. "Don't kill her before I get back," she said as she stepped over the fallen man and disappeared into the alley.

Gilhame grinned his terrible grin and said, "I won't," to the emptiness.

Marpessa looked from the still form on the floor to the door where Alvellaina had left, her face puzzled. Gilhame understood her confusion, for Derissa had worn her hair unnetted, with a spray of jewels in it. Her likeness to her sister was intensified by the hairstyle, and he supposed that the men Marpessa had chosen for the abduction had been given a description, but they could not have been chosen for brains. Gilhame had confused the two girls a few times himself.

'I can go back now,' the words whispered in his mind.

'To that?' He gazed at the ruined woman on the floor.

'It is not as bad as it looks. I must disengage the eye-scatter before the medics come. Poor Alvee. She's very angry.'

'Wait. Why the hell did you pick my head to hide in?'

'It seemed like the right thing to do at the time.'

'Where is Buschard?'

'He was called back to the ship for some reason. I came down to meet my aunt, and those goons got me.'

'Cosmos! In the lobby?' As this silent conversation continued, the gaping wounds on Derissa's body vanished one by one. Gilhame saw that she was indeed hurt, but that none of the cuts was very deep except the one on her wrist.

'No. On the street outside. If you don't mind, I'll stay "here" until the Healers get to work. I think I probably hurt like blazes.'

He chuckled out loud. Marpessa jumped at the sound. *'As you will, halba. Just don't go nosing around up there, will you?'*

'I am very good at keeping secrets, dear old Dragon.' The phrase was like a caress. *'What is going to happen to this miserable female?'*

'I have no idea yet. Perhaps your sister can offer some suggestions.'

"Let me go, Gil," Marpessa said.

"Later, perhaps, my pretty. Tell me, was this entirely your own notion, or did Gyre put you up to it? No answer. Ah, but your face tells me it was a joint effort. Do you know, I think an Admiralty court and some *truth* is an excellent prescription for what ails you. Such a simple thing, *truth*, but so exquisitely painful."

"You wouldn't!"

He continued in a silky voice. "You seem to have forgotten a thing I told you years ago. The cosmos is divided into *my* people and *other* people. I always look after my own."

"You didn't look after me, you bastard."

"No, I didn't. But your intriguing proved you to be 'other.' I simply don't have time for 'other' people. Ah, I believe I hear the medics. Yes, here they are."

Marpessa tried to twist her head away from the painful

angle at which he still held it. She clawed her hands towards Derissa's body, seeking her knife. Not finding it, she balled her left fist, slammed it into ur Fagon's testicles and jerked away from his hand to grab the knife he had kicked away. He gasped a little at the pain, doubled forward, then rolled backwards as she got the knife near his chest, kicking her full in the jaw as he somersaulted backwards. Marpessa's knife missed his chest and just tore the edge of the dragon motif. He came back to his feet only inches from where he had begun and back-handed her with his good arm as he came up. Marpessa sprawled in an ungainly mass on the floor.

The small room suddenly seemed very crowded. Alvellaina came in, leading four medics, a Chief Healer and a security team of six. She went straight to Derissa, looked down and then turned to Gilhame questioningly. The Healer pushed her aside and got to work.

"I believe the term is 'eye-scatter,' m'alba. Never seen it myself. You there, Major, put Captain Devero in custody. Wake her up, put her in restraints, and you needn't be gentle. I want all the men in this room dead-brained."

"Sir?" It was a rather pale-looking corporal.

"Yes."

"This one's still alive. It looks like he fell backward, trying to get out of the way of your *kuumi*, and knocked himself out."

"Typical of Gyre's men. Falling over their own feet. What do you want?" he snapped at a medic.

"Sir, if I may get to work on that shoulder. You've got a knick on your chest too."

Alvellaina was standing next to him, watching the Healers put Derissa to sleep. "Yes, yes. Get on with your laying-on-of-hands mumbo jumbo. Get out of the man's way, m'alba."

"Sorry." She stepped back. "I was trying to sort things out. I . . . just never knew Derissa could . . . do that."

"We'll discuss it later. She will be alright."

He smiled at her as the young and rather nervous Healer began his work. The point where Marpessa's knife had penetrated the cloth of his uniform hurt as much as the cut on his shoulder. That puzzled him. He had a faint distrust of the Healer's art, for it demanded that he submit to the control of another, a thing difficult for both the man he was and the man he had been. He could feel his "other self" squirming at the Healer's touch.

Gilhame studied Alvellaina instead of resisting the medic. Her electro-net had slipped during the short fight and one side of her hair was its curly self, while the other was long and straight. It gave her a very odd appearance. There was dirt and blood on her hands and dress, and an ugly scratch on her face. He thought she was the most beautiful woman in all creation.

She caught his look, the tenderness in his eyes, and colored.

'*So, that is how it is,*' came Derissa's thought.

'*Try to remember you are a guest and behave yourself.*' He made his retort without the awareness that he was speaking telepathically and was confused for a moment when no one in the room "heard" her delightful laughter. It made him realize how exhausted he was.

The medic was staring at the wound on Gilhame's shoulder, sending waves of healing into it, but the pain persisted. Gilhame glanced at the Healer, his brows narrowed in concentration, and wondered what the problem was.

"Are you finding the same thing I am?" the medic asked the two now tending Derissa.

"Never seen anything like it before. What do you think? Organic or not?"

"I don't know. You'd better call the Chief."

"Right." The kneeling medic took out a short-range communicator and spoke into it.

Gilhame could feel a slight dizziness now. The medic looked up into his face. He tried to smile but found that the side of his face was stiff.

"Paralyzed," he said to the other medics. "Admiral, permission to put you to sleep."

'*No!*' Derissa's thought startled him.

"Denied, medic."

"Begging the Admiral's pardon, I can do my work more effectively if you are out."

'*Is this the kind of pain I will find in my body?*'

'*Apparently.*'

'*Cosmos! Oh, well, it must be endured, I suppose. I will go back then. Thanks for the ride, Admiral.*'

'*Next time, try to find another vehicle, will you?*'

'*Where else would I find so much room?*'

'*So I have a swelled head, do I?*'

Her giggle. '*You said it. I didn't. Thank you, brother.*' Again, the caressing quality of her words flowed over him. He wondered for a moment if, somehow, he had chosen the wrong sister. Then she was gone as suddenly as she had arrived in the middle of the Antrian Pattern.

Gilhame looked around him. The security team had re-strained Marpessa Devero and were removing the corpses. Alvellaina was staring at him wide-eyed. He was curious how much of his interchange with Derissa she had picked up.

"I think, m'alba, you will have to stop wearing white when we are together. I fear your dress is beyond repair—like the other which you seem to treasure. Yes, Healer, you may put me to sleep. But only until you have the pain under control."

The short medic stood on tiptoe to reach Gilhame's wide brow. He placed his fingertips on the forehead very lightly and looked into Gilhame's eyes.

"Please, sir, you are resisting me."

"Am I? How very tiresome of me, to be sure." He heard Marpessa's insane laugh. Then he slept.

The Barren Plain. How long had he wandered here? A moment? Forever? Sometimes he almost left it, and then there were voices, voices he almost knew. But one, one interior voice, always called him back onto this empty place—a woman's voice, a siren song of death.

'You are the Darkness. You are the very spirit of war. You are Chaos masquerading as Law. Die, die, die.'

Was this the lesson he had not learned, had misunderstood? If he left now, before the war, whatever war it would be, left her, denied that still-to-be-conceived child, died now, would that be the end? No more Glass Castle? No more turns upon the wheel? No further love and betrayal? Was this, then, the Path? The Dragon passes and returns not?

"Why isn't he better?" The voice, the one which urged him to death, was near, but not *here*. The Barren Plain receded.

"Halba Krispin, I don't know. He isn't fighting the poison. He is fighting me, fighting my most skilled medics. Perhaps he is fighting himself. In any case, he is dying." Vraser. The name came across the Plain to him, but it meant nothing.

"I don't understand. Derissa was much worse, and she's mending. Why isn't he?" There was a kind of panic in the well-remembered voice.

"Child, I do not know. He does not care to heal. It is as if he doubts himself. All I hear are distant questions. He is so far across the Plain . . ."

"I see. Let me sit with him awhile. You are dead on your feet, Vraser. He will be fine with me here."

"There is nothing more I can do," the voice sounded sad and a little desperate. "Perhaps, a Circle . . ."

"No, don't. He would hate it. A Circle is such . . . an invasion. Perhaps he will come back."

"Have *you* called him, halba?" the voice was stern now.

"No."

"Why not?"

"Go away and leave us alone." Shuffling noises. The rub of cloth on cloth. Then *she* said, "Interfering old busybody!"

Hands, very cold hands, and silence. A wind moved across the Barren Plain, and he smelled something. It was a distant, tantalizing scent, strange and familiar at the same time. There was a name for it, if he could only remember. It was important to remember.

The cold hands moved over his own. The voice began, sharply.

"Don't you dare die, you black-blooded bastard! You can't have the last word. I won't permit it! You come back here, right now, and stop feeling sorry for yourself. I am not finished with you yet, damn it! You can't leave me. Wake up and fight with me. Open your eyes. I *know* you are in there. Look, the pard is here. She's waiting for you. Open your damned eyes. Don't go back to the Castle. Come back to me!"

He felt a hard slap. Where? On his face. His face. What was that? Then he remembered the name of the smell. Roses. There was another slap. What did the word mean, roses? The very smell of love. The Plain shrank.

"Halba Krispin! What are you doing? Stop that! It was an unknown voice, male and angry.

Gilhame forced his eyes open to find Alvellaina snatching her hands away from a medic. The medic leapt forward to catch her hands again and was rewarded with a sharp kick in the shins for his efforts. He watched them tussle for a moment. The pard, nestled at his right side, gave a dreadful yowl, arched its back, stood and bottled its tail.

"Roses," he murmured. Alvellaina was still struggling with the medic. "Here! Stop that!" Gilhame croaked. He tried to sit up, but his shoulder burned like fire.

Alvellaina and the medic jumped at the sound of his voice. The pard sprang off the bed and marched away, spitting and hissing.

"You're awake!" Alvellaina sat down on the edge of the bed and he winced at the pain in his shoulder.

"So it would seem." His voice sounded rusty to him. "May one inquire into the meaning of this brawl?" He decided he didn't care what his voice sounded like. As long as he talked, he wouldn't go back *there*.

"I found the halba striking you, Admiral," said the medic stiffly.

"Yes, I know. My face will be sore for a while. Stop bouncing on the bed, will you? Can't I turn my back on you for a minute without you finding some mischief to get into, woman?" He had to say anything.

She gave him part of a smile. "No. I need an experienced hand to guide me."

"Get me something to drink. My throat is dry." They both jumped to answer his demand, and water got spilled on the floor before it got to his mouth. Alvellaina held the cup to his lips and watched him intently. "I shall have to have the Combat Master give you some instruction in hand-to-hand, m'alba. You were glaringly wide, but you have potential."

The Healer, who was as tall as Alvellaina and somewhat heavier, touched his face gingerly. One side was red, and there seemed to be a good promise of a black eye in the future. "Please, sir, she is quite formidable as she is."

"True, but shockingly untrained. Why am I being starved? I could eat almost anything. How long have I been asleep?"

"Days and days," she answered.

"A week and a day, sir," replied the medic. "I'd better call Chief Vraser and tell him you are awake, so he can get to work."

"What the Bless has he been doing for eight days?" Gilhame asked, but the medic was gone.

"Lie still, please," Alvellaina said. "You see, the Healers couldn't do a thing while you were asleep, and you wouldn't wake up."

"What? Why couldn't they?"

"The knives those bastards used were covered with something—they haven't decided whether to call it a poison or an infection yet—anyhow, it is an organic radiation. Now you know as much as I do. I can't even pretend to understand it, though Derissa seems to. But it can't be treated while you are unconscious, at least not with the standard healing techniques. They . . . they almost lost Derissa before they found out, but at least she was willing to wake up. You weren't."

He remembered the Plain and the siren voice. "I must have had something on my mind. Organic radiation? Where did it come from?"

"I think you'd better rest until some food arrives, Admiral." Her voice was cool now.

She had withdrawn again. Gilhame settled back on his pillows and smiled at her. "You cannot beat me about the head and shoulders and call me dreadful names and then go back to calling me 'Admiral,' child. Let me see. There was 'black-blooded bastard.' I rather like that one—poetic and alliterative. Now, try it. Say 'Gilhame.' The word won't choke you, I promise."

She glared at him. "No, but I might choke *you*."

"What? After all the trouble you went to to get me back? Such ambivalence."

"You are needed. I only did my duty."

"I am sure the Emperor will be pleased at your devotion. Strange, how the mind plays trick on one. I could have sworn you cared about the matter *personally*. Now then," he said as she blushed, "when do I get some good food? It quite saddens me that the consumption of flesh is such a so-cial solecism in these civilized times. See if you can get me some fish, at least, will you? I feel as if I could eat a horse . . . or even a camel."

"Don't be disgusting!" Her eyes were bright with anger, for it was impolite to even discuss the eating of flesh.

"Failing that, I could leap upon you and bite you on the throat—as I was once reputed to have done. I have the very real feeling that you would rather watch me eat an equine, hooves and all, than for me to nibble away at your lovely neck. I feel quite primitive. And you won't remember at all, will you, my haughty one? Never mind. Get me a bowl of soup and some bread. And then you can tell me whatever it is you don't want to tell me."

She did remember other times and places, he could tell. The light in her eyes was as unfriendly now as it had been warm a few minutes earlier. "You carrion-eater!" She left the room stiff-backed.

He did not regret provoking her. There was a time in his memory, though he could not give it a name or a place, when they had eaten great bleeding slabs of bovine and deer together. That meal ended in a rather greasy but intimate encounter. 'At least,' he thought, 'she didn't call me a cannibal.' That was the ultimate insult across the cosmos now. At least among the upper classes. The peasants, he knew, were not nearly as nice in their notions of polite behavior, and often enjoyed a "shovel supper" of some small rodent hacked to bits and roasted in a field on the end of their tools. There were no peasants on Attira, a fact Gilhame had not previously regretted.

A few minutes later, old Farren Vraser stumped into the room and glared at him. "You're awake."

"So it would appear."

"How do you feel?"

"Ghastly. I am starved to death, my head aches like I had been on a very long and very cheap drunk, my shoulder burns and my face feels sore from m'alba's rough-and-ready therapy. And you just stand there looking like a disapproving *gautama*. Is it true you wax your dome? How do you expect me to feel?"

Vraser ignored the reference to his baldness. "We should have the problem of your shoulder fixed in a day or so. I can see that at least the tenor of your disposition as a patient has not changed, Gil."

"Changed? Should it have?" Damn, the old man was a truth-hearer!

"You are . . . different these days."

"You may blame that on the positive influence of m'alba," he answered.

"I think not. It began . . . well, no matter. Let me see if I can do something about that shoulder." He came to the bed and held his big hand over the injured shoulder for several minutes. "Nasty weapon, that," he commented as he finished. "Better?"

"Some. There are no nice weapons, Farren. Where did it come from, anyhow? Alvellaina clammed up when I asked her. I don't permit my people to keep things from me, even for my own good. *Especially* not for my own good!"

"No, you don't. The dead-brained men all *say* Pordallas." Vraser answered slowly.

"Pordallas. But that's a restricted world. Do you think they were misled, Farren?"

"Those men had no direct knowledge. They had been *told* Pordallas. I examined the tapes myself."

"And Captain Devero?"

"Is *truth*-blocked, Gil."

"The Devil you say! *Truth*-blocked, is she? That means we can't be certain if Gyre had anything to do with this, as I suspect he did, or if it was Marpessa's own initiative. She was always terribly jealous and much too impulsive. But the block is almost incriminating by itself, isn't it?"

"On one level, yes. But she was with Kurrian long enough that it could have been done during that tour and not have any connection with Admiral Gyre."

"Kurrian? That old fart? I don't think he's ever even thought of *truth*-proofing his staff. No, I see Guth's fine Denebolian hand in this, but finding evidence is going to be quite difficult. But not impossible. Do you know, I have spent almost as much of my life in the litigation of various suits as I have in battle? It is a curious reflection on our times, isn't it? Ah, nourishment."

Alvellaina entered with a tray. She set it over his lap and

stepped hastily away with a funny expression on her face. Gilhame removed the dish covers and looked at the stuff on the tray.

"I spoke too soon," he said. "It is not nourishment. It is pap. Unsweetened, pasty cereal; bitter-fruit; dry, naked bread and something hot and foul-smelling in a cup. No wonder you drop the tray and back away, m'alba. Would that I could do the same. What an infernal stink! I am almost tempted to throw the tea—it is tea, isn't it?—across the room, but I think the odor would linger on and on—like roses, but not so nice." He held his nose and gulped down the offending liquid. He finished with an outraged expression on his face. "It tastes worse than it smells."

The pard jumped up on the bed. It sniffed the tray tentatively, then drew back on three paws. It turned haughtily with its tail held aloft and marched down to the foot of the bed.

"You see. Even the pard disdains it," Gilhame said, munching a piece of bitter-fruit. "But, I see your plan. You are trying to force me to get well be feeding me things you would not feed your worst enemy. Gah! Glue would taste better." He glared at the cereal after he tasted it, then ate it as quickly as he could, gulping it down without pausing. He tried a bite of his toast, masticated solemnly, then put the rest back on the tray.

"Please, take it away, m'alba." He leaned back on the pillows and found Vraser staring at him. "Well?"

"You can begin eating normally in a day or so," the Healer said. Gilhame could tell that the old man was quite puzzled over something, and he wondered what.

"Normally? I don't want to eat normally. I want Guthry Gyre's heart spitted and roasted, or perhaps he would taste better in a Denebolian ragout. And Marpessa, dear Marpessa. No, instead of cooking her goose, I think I'll give it to the fleet." The puzzled expression on Vraser's face faded, but Alvellaina went green under her white skin. "Forgive me, m'alba. I was speaking in jest. I've no doubt at all that a single drop of Gyre's blood would be quite fatal to anyone."

Alvellaina bent her head and looked at her hands. She

found she was unmoved by the prospect of Marpessa Devero's fleetwide prostitution. Her father had occasionally used such a punishment for mutinous officers of both sexes. The concept of Gyre's heart roasting made her a little queasy, but she found, on consideration, that she was troubled by feelings which had nothing to do with meat, cooked or otherwise.

Gilhame watched the two of them through nearly closed eyes. Alvellaina looked as if she had not had much sleep in several days. There were deep shadows under her eyes, and she had lost weight. Vraser was still uneasy about something. "How is Derissa?" Gilhame asked.

"Mending, mending," Vraser answered. "There will be very little scarring, and she is in good spirits. I had a bit of trouble with Buschard, which should not surprise you. I'll go now. Try to stay put and keep out of mischief, will you, Gil?"

Gilhame was startled at the genuine affection he caught in the older man's voice. "Of course. Why should I do otherwise?"

"The last time I had you as a patient . . ."

"Yes, I know. I was quite impossible. But I didn't have m'alba then to bully me into drinking stinking messes. She isn't afraid of me, which is rather a pleasant change."

Vraser scowled. "I would be much more settled in my mind . . . if you were not acting so . . ."

"Prim and proper," Gilhame cut in. "I am a reformed character. Quite soon now, I expect I'll get religion."

Vraser raised his heavy eyebrows, snorted like a baited goat and limped out. Alvellaina continued to stand at one side of the bed, clenching her hands into fists. Gilhame wondered what was upsetting her so much.

"He thinks I am making game of him. Can you tell me, m'alba, now that Derissa will not be a helpless cripple for the rest of her life, how it happened? I am sure I saw the wounds and I have some vague memory of . . ."

"Derissa made an illusory self. It's quite hard to explain. She made a projection of herself. Her body appeared to them to be bigger than it actually was. They 'saw' themselves cutting into the sinews, but they were really only slashing her skin."

"Yes. She said . . . 'mind-scatter,' but I didn't understand."

"She '*said*'?" Alvellaina's voice was tense.

"Your sister, or a fair portion of her, housed inside my . . . what—head, mind? She didn't just call for help; she came and got it!"

"And she didn't . . . mind?"

"What? Oh, I see what you mean. No, contact with me doesn't seem to have soiled her. Your sister is a remarkable woman, m'alba. Would you not sit down and tell me what troubles you now?"

She sat down and looked at him. "The only thing which has ever troubled me. You!"

"I believe we have been over what an evil and murderous person I am sufficiently that we need not go into it again." He looked at her—very young and very vulnerable. His pulses behaved in a very un-Admiralish manner. "I see you are . . . confused, little one. Tell me, won't you, what bewilders you?"

"I am not confused about anything!"

"Little liar. I'll wait. You look very tired, m'alba. Why don't you go off to bed? I'll be quite alright."

"I . . . couldn't sleep."

"Why not?"

"Whenever I close my eyes, I have your dreams."

"How dreadful for you. Come, sit beside me on the bed. There, that's better. Is it the dreams which disturb you or the closeness it implies?"

"Closeness? Don't be disgusting."

"You don't *have* to dream my dreams or think my thoughts, little one. Well then, let me change the subject. Why did you call me back? I would have thought you would leap at the opportunity to be rid of me once and for all. And spare me any fairy tales about your duty, please. Now is not the time to break your habit of reviling me at every encounter."

She bit her lower lip. "I . . . I didn't want your blood on my hands."

"How could you?"

"I 'heard' myself, my words, in your mind all the time you were asleep. Even my voice. They were killing you!"

"You are, I believe, a contact telepath. I have, as you know, kept our physical intimacy to a minimum so that you would not be bothered by my thoughts. So, do you 'hear' my thoughts very often?"

"No. That first evening, in your cabin, when we talked, I did. I hated it and I shut it off as well as I could. But . . . when you were wandering in your sleep, like the night you had the nightmare on the ship, and this past week, I could not keep you out. I never knew what a two-edged gift I had. With Derissa and Armanda, there was never any need to . . . filter anything. And my father was not a physical man. And I do not eavesdrop. I was ever so careful at the dances that week not to peek. I was properly brought up." She sounded like a very young girl now.

"I keep forgetting that you are untrained. No doubt there is someone on Vraser's staff who could teach you never to 'hear' me again. And I know you would not spy on your dancing partners, though others are not as nice in their manners. Still, since I do not read minds, you might have mentioned the problem to me. But that's not what is eating you up. What are you afraid of, truly?"

Alvellaina looked directly at him, thoughtfully. The bones of his skull were more prominent now. She wondered how much weight he had lost. The color had faded from his skin, and it looked like parchment. His big, square teeth seemed huge in the thinner face. 'Truly, an ugly man,' she thought. 'Except his eyes. And his voice! Every time he speaks, it is a caress. I wouldn't let him touch me, and yet he touches me with every word.' "Who is the Lion?" she asked suddenly.

"Someone I have never met. Another . . . being such as I am, but different. Why?"

"I kept 'hearing' the words, 'Let the Lion deal with it.' Where is he?"

"I haven't any notion. Somewhere, on some world, plowing his fields, no doubt."

"What does he do?"

"What I do."

"More war?"

"Yes. But the Lion doesn't disturb your dreams. If you wish precise information concerning him, apply to the Havassit. They say he is coming. They say his Tide comes."

"How do you know?"

"A curious little conversation I had with the Havassit ambassador at that first ball we attended. It would appear that the End of All Things—at least things as we know them—is at hand. I can't say the prospect fills me with anything but relief. Enough. Tell me what *really* troubles you."

"You."

"It is always the same answer, isn't it? Why?"

Alvellaina interlaced her fingers and held her hands close to her chest. She whispered, "Because you love me—and I can't bear it. I don't want to be loved like that."

"Like what?"

"Like *her*. You don't care about *me*. You are in love with all the women I have ever been. You don't see me, only all the echoes of long-dead heroes and their ladyloves. If I were some filthy streetwalker, up to my armpits in gore, you would only see your 'White Lady.' You love me out of habit, not affection."

"Do I? I had not noticed. Perhaps you are correct. But I think not. At first, yes. When you tumbled through the door with a sewer pipe in your arms that time, yes. I said to myself, 'There she is.' I had been wondering, you see, just how far the play had progressed."

"The play? This isn't some cosmic drama! I will not be cast in a role for your convenience—or for anyone else's. I want to wear my own face."

"You always do. It is one of your principal characteristics."

"Damn you!"

"Halba, I cannot cease to be the Dragon. And, as long as I am that being, I will love you—now and forever. I am sorry it is such a burden to your spirit."

"Love? You don't know the meaning of the word. It isn't an automatic response. Look at me. I am not any of those women who have been before. I am Alvellaina Curly-Krispin, daughter of your enemy."

Gilhame refrained from pointing out that this too was part of the pattern. Instead, he said, "But how could I fail to adore you? You are so loving and gentle." He touched the side of his face where she had slapped him.

Alvellaina clenched her teeth. "If you weren't sick, I'd hit you again."

"Of course you would. All the way to the Day of Judgment. I cannot see, yet, what is so terrible in my love for you. Tell me."

She frowned. "What if I give in to you? Then what? I am lost. Alvellaina vanishes. I live out my life, barren and used. Because, somewhere, sometime, it will come to a choice between me and the war, and the war will win. It always has. I will fail you and betray you. I always do. And I don't want to. I want you to care for me, only me—not memories, not our fabled past. I don't want to be a romantic legend."

"I can see that. We have contributed quite enough to the literature of our races, have we not?" *Barren.* The word held him. Then she had not "seen" the dream of the sturdy little boy and the terrible white light. Or, perhaps, it was his son, but not hers. Gilhame tried to imagine seducing Derissa or Armanda, and failed. Betray Buschard? Never. "So, you would have me beat my ships into plowshares and set my hand to tilling the land? An interesting notion. And what of the anonymous millions whose lives will be lost because I have decided not to fight? What about their children and their worlds?"

"It always comes to that, doesn't it?" She almost snarled the words. "I am always second to the war, the cause, whatever. And you say you love me. How dare you!"

"A man cares for many things in his life."

"You only care for one thing: Glory. You may dress it up in any garb you choose, but you worship war and fame, the fame which comes with war. You speak of lives destroyed. What of the lives you will spend in defense? What of the love and loyalty you will use like bits of money? I don't

want any part of them. I will not lend my countenance to
your foul deeds.''

"Have I asked you to?"

"Yes."

"How?"

"If I would accept this 'love' you have for me, then I
would be approving of you—and I don't."

"Do you think you will alter the future by keeping me at
a distance?"

"Yes. It may seem very selfish to you, but I can find no
other way to stop you."

"Am I to interpret what you say to mean that part of you
enjoys my love?" She didn't answer, but turned quite red.
"But only on your own terms. Why?"

She pleated the skirt of her gown in her hands. "You
have such gentleness sometimes. It is very hard to hate
you. Even though I know that it is that very gentleness
which is part of the way you use people. Still, it is very
seductive. Here, on Attira, going with you to balls and
teas, listening to you speak of music and recite poetry, I almost forgot who you were. Then I saw those little edged
disks appear in your hands, like a conjuror's trick, and
watched them fly into the air and kill people, and I remembered. And even though you were saving Derissa, you
were still a killer. In fact, she was hurt because of you."

"True. They thought they had you. Marpessa has always
had a rather nasty temper. And, if you submit to me—for I
am sure it seems to be a submission to you—you have lost?
Well, it is gratifying to know the flame burns within you
also. Silly girl, you are almost dead with fatigue. Go to bed.
We have all the time in the cosmos to continue this
debate."

"No."

"You can hardly keep your eyes open."

Alvellaina looked into her lap. "I . . . don't . . . want to
leave you." The whispered words were dragged out of her
slowly. He could see that her legs were shaking beneath her
dress.

"I see. You really are in a state, aren't you? I won't slip

away to my death, I promise. Glass Castle is not nearly as interesting as you are. Lady Silver Wheels is a charming hostess, to be sure, but she sets a very spare table. Go to bed.''

"No."

"Then lie down here. The bed is large enough for a small army. My dreams need not trouble you. I swear I won't lay a hand on you.''

"No, you wouldn't. You have been very good, honoring my wishes. They must seem very foolish to you.'' She rose and went around to the far side of the bed. "If only you would not look at me so. I never thought that it could be so terrifying.'' She lifted the covers and slid her body under them, disturbing the pard, who was now in the middle of the bed. The animal gave her a disdainful glance, rose and re-arranged itself in a new position. Alvellaina put her head on a pillow, her back to Gilhame. "Every autumn we burn the fields on my father's estates. All the straw on the ground is burned off.''

"I have seen such things. It is a very old custom.''

"I feel like straw.''

"Go to sleep, little one. No one will touch the field.''

"I could almost smell the roses in your mind," she murmured sleepily.

"Sleep, then, and dream of roses.''

Gilhame studied the line of her back, her spine straight even in sleep. He longed to reach out and touch her with his whole being. The smell of her warm body was almost unbearable, so close and touchable. He looked away, staring up at the ceiling, and tried to remember some other scent. He closed his eyes, tired now, and thought of all the flowers on all the worlds he had known.

Apples. The word came unbidden into his mind. He saw Alvellaina's mother, golden-haired and azure-eyed, smiling at him. Her gown was blue, and she held a golden apple in one hand. A scrap of verse bubbled up from some time past.

> *I am the ancient Apple-Queen*
> *As once I was, so I am now,*

Forevermore a hope unseen
Betwixt the blossom and the bough.

Then slumber captured him and bore him away.

Gilhame awoke because he could barely breathe. Alvellaina had rolled over and pillowed her head on his good shoulder. Her eyes moved beneath her eyelids, and her arm, flung across him, twitched. The pard had curled up almost under his chin and was purring happily.

He debated whether to wake her, then took advantage of the moment to hug her a little closer. It was difficult to see her, the pard being very much in the way, in the manner of its race, but he hesitated to attempt any alteration of the arrangement, lest the sleeper awake and end the unexpected but welcome intimacy.

Alvellaina stirred and muttered in her sleep. Gilhame lifted the pard off his chest and set it on the bed beside him. Then he rolled Alvellaina off his chest, brushing her forehead with a kiss, and pulled himself a little further up in the bed. He sighed and tried to relax his injured shoulder. The pard rearranged itself in an unlikely position, and the woman seemed to settle back to sleep.

He stared and thought of roses and apples and the symbols of love on a thousand worlds. Finally, he realized that his body was in need of immediate relief. Gilhame ruthlessly disturbed the pard and got out of bed. He was surprised at how weak his legs were as he went into the privy.

He was still sitting there, wondering if he could make it back to his bed unassisted, when he heard a slight slithering noise in the room. Gilhame envisioned assassins coming to complete the job Marpessa had botched, and looked for a weapon.

"Gilhame!" Alvellaina appeared at the door of the bathroom, looking frightened and knuckling her eyes.

"Yes?" He felt glorious. She had finally used his real name!

"I woke up, and you were gone!" She sounded peeved.

"I did not mean to frighten you, m'alba, but nature called."

"Why didn't you wake me?"

"I did not realize I needed permission for my bodily functions."

She looked at him and chuckled. "Come on, brave soldier, let me help you back. You are the color of a winding-sheet."

"Well, I was wondering how I would manage it," he said, with as much dignity as the situation permitted. He tugged up his shorts.

Alvellaina drew his right arm over her shoulder and tried unsuccessfully to stop laughing. He leaned against her, glad that she was a tall woman, and enjoyed the nearness.

When she had gotten him back into bed, Gilhame asked, "What are you laughing at?"

"Is there anything sillier in the cosmos than an undressed male? I wonder what the Creatrix was thinking of?"

"Even the gods have a sense of humor," he answered calmly. "You have a real talent for making me feel foolish. But, enough of that. I am hungry, still—'yet,' 'again'? Please, no paste this time. Could you get me a bowl of rice meal, with milk, sugar and dried grapes? And some real tea. No more vile herbs. I am still burping that whatever-it-was. Ugh! And get me a medic. The shoulder is driving me crazy."

"Yes, master," she said with a suppressed smile.

"Was I peremptory?"

"No, just your normal self."

"Oh." She was gone.

The next four days consisted of eating, sleeping and

arguing, the latter with Alvellaina and old Vraser. They insisted on constraining him; he pushed himself and then was forced to admit that they had been right.

Alvellaina did not share his couch again, but returned to her rooms on the other side of the suite. Gilhame offered no comment on this nor on her single use of his given name. Alvellaina went back to "Admiral," and he continued to call her "lady."

On the fifth day, Vraser grudgingly declared him fit, if not completely recovered. "I would appreciate it if you would not damage yourself again! I would rather single-handedly nurse a platoon with blood-flukes than you!"

"Farren, you act as if I got my shoulder hurt just to aggravate you."

"And you behave as if I were forcing you to bed for my pleasure."

As there was no answer to this, Gilhame just got dressed in a black, floor-length caftan embroidered with golden dragons doing a number of unlikely and obscene things. The lack of a weapon fretted him, even in the safety of his apartments, but he could not find the little wrist-knife which Alvellaina had used, and his boot-knife was gone too.

He went to the comm and called a meeting of his senior staff. Alvellaina found him there a few minutes later. She looked at the gown in wonder, moving around him and studying the embroidery. "Where in the cosmos did you get *that*?"

"I believe it was made for me by . . . her name escapes me . . . in commemoration of an incredible affair. Where is my small knife?"

"Your knife? I don't know. I think the security people may have it. How much of that is possible?" She seemed fascinated by the caftan.

"I would like it back. It has a good balance. Possible?" He looked at the reflection of himself in the mirror. "I suppose, if one is sufficiently athletic, highly trained in the arts of sexual gymnastics and has a reptilian spine, all of it. I personally find the achievement of this sort of extraordinary couplings rather unpleasant. One is so busy concentrating on subduing one's muscles to reach some exotic climax that all the intimacy vanishes and one is left with an odd kind of emptiness. Still, if you are intrigued? No, I see you are not. But I am glad the gown amuses you."

Alvellaina gave him a cold green stare, then returned to her study of the work. "If you didn't do all those things, why did she put them on the gown?"

"She had quite an imagination, I seem to recall. Or perhaps she was rebuking me for my pedestrian tastes."

"There's the door. I'll be in my room if you need me."

Gilhame looked into her face. "I always *need* you, m'alba." Alvellaina blushed and fled. Gilhame went to answer the door.

It was Ven Frickard, his flag captain, wearing his tan recreation uniform and frowning. He looked at Gilhame's caftan, checked his timepiece and frowned more deeply. The buzzer sounded again, and Gilhame admitted E-varit and A-gurit. Gilhame quickly adjusted the lights to accommodate the Coalchee sensitivity. Buschard arrived. He gave ur Fagon a careful appraisal as he entered.

Frikard and Buschard had both visited him a few times during his recovery, supervised somewhat hostilely by Alvellaina, who tended to behave like a pard with one kitten. Each man had behaved quite characteristically. Frickard had struggled to determine precisely what data was absolutely necessary to impart and which could wait, and Buschard had tried not to fuss, and failed signally. Vraser had commented that Buschard had been more trouble than he was worth during Derissa's illness— Bushard had a fairly high Healer potential, but was untrained.

Gilhame waved the men towards the refreshment center and waited until they had each gotten their particular preferences.

"Shall we begin then? Frikard, you go first. Whatever is bothering you may be less painful if shared."

"Yes, sir. As I was coming over, a *fac* arrived. It appears . . . appears that an invasion of *curthels* is about to occur in the Faldarian sector."

Gilhame attempted to rein in his very active imagination. Faldar, the world of the Living Dream, turned into a world of nightmare, despite his efforts? The *curthels*—the plague which had, to some degree, caused the Kardusian Empire to exist! Only a name, for no one had ever seen one, but the planet-wide madness they created was a matter of history. The madness had sent dozens of worlds back into savagery. But, for over two hundred years, it had seemed that the threat no longer existed.

Gilhame ur Fagon felt a stirring of the being whose body he inhabited. "He" had grown up on Faldar. There is sister Coralys and his son Hamecor still lived. Once in its history, Faldar had been a rather ordinary world, engaged in commerce and agriculture. But after the last *curthel* invasion, the culture had retreated into aesthetic contemplation. Now all Faldar exported was dreams and drugs. Oaths on Faldar were sworn "until the *curthel* return." Unless dreams were a shield, there was no defense.

"I see. What, precisely, has occurred?"

"A ship—a trader called Himez—came into Copia three days ago. That's a little mining world at the edge of the Faldar sector, where it abuts Nabatean space. He, this Himez, was concerned when he couldn't raise anyone on the comm. Copia used to have a population of a little more than a thousand. When Himez and his people arrived, there were three. One was still engaged in violating the dead. The other two were busy hammering themselves to pulp. Typical *curthel*-insanity, historically speaking. Himez froze the survivors and ran like the devil for Narbute. It's the closest world with proper medical facilities."

"What is the status of the fleet?" Gilhame asked.

"We can be out of here in six hours."

The communicator made a rude noise. Gilhame rose to answer it. "What about your people, E-varit?" he asked as he crossed the room.

"We are ready, sir."

"Good." Gilhame picked up the pack of flimsies which the machine had coughed out. He turned over the pages swiftly. "We have twelve hours." He continued to read. "I had no idea the Admiralty had a sense of humor."

"What the devil are you talking about, Gil?" Buschard demanded.

"Our orders are to work in concert with the Eighth Fleet. That should be fascinating. No doubt dear old Guthry is as charmed by the notion as I am. Speaking of Gyre, what has been done with Marp—Captain Devero? Since she's Gyre's flag, has she been returned?"

Buschard grinned. "Gyre has registered several complaints—with us, not with the Admirally—but we seem to have 'lost' Captain Devero. He seems to want her back rather badly. So, she isn't in the fo'c'sle of the *Harbinger,* which, I believe, is the impression you had. She's in the deep freeze."

"Now, why would he want her back, other than because she's his flag captain? It needs consideration, but it will have to wait. Meanwhile . . ." He began outlining the order of the fleet. The five men spent half an hour in this discussion. Then they emptied their cups and glasses and left.

Gilhame walked to the door of Alvellaina's rooms and opened it. "Pack!" he shouted.

She came out in the green-and-silver uniform of a noncombatant attached to a fighting force. "I already have," she said coolly. "Shall I pack your things?"

"If you would be so kind. The shoulder is still touchy, But, how . . .?"

"Frikard *broadcasts.*"

Fourteen hours later the command staff of the Twelfth Fleet and their seconds sat in the darkened theater on board the *Black Dragon* and watched history tapes of the *curthel* invasion and the film taken by the trader Himez on Copia. A number of people left the room rapidly and returned white-faced and sweaty. A few didn't make it to the privy, and the room began to smell of nervous perspiration and vomit. Gilhame watched it all with a dispassionate eye as he paced back and forth at the front of the hall.

The lights came up, and he looked over his audience, noting the range of pallors from chalk to chartreuse. He waited until everyone had stopped fidgeting and coughing. "Are there any questions?"

"Has anyone ever seen one of these things?"

"No record of any sighting exists," Gilhame answered. "Lieutenant Darkcut?"

She was frowning. "This is not precisely a question. It occurred to me that . . . what happened on Copia was somehow different from the tapes. I realize that the tapes are reconstructions and that there must be inaccuracies, but . . ."

"Sir?"

"Yes, Major Hameth?" Hameth was a historio-technician.

"If the Lieutenant is asking if the tapes have been

modified, the answer is no. The tapes are reconstructed from the Faldarian Dreamers, and record the actual memory of some of the survivors. The Kardus Historical Academy feels they are accurate. I have also seen records kept by the Havassit and the Orcadians, and they are identical."

"Thank you, Major Hameth," Gilhame said. The sturdy little man looked startled. Gilhame frowned over Darkcut's question. It was the psycho-historians' job to interpret data, the historio-techs' to gather and sort it. As a result, the two arms of the discipline rarely communicated and exhibited a rather muted hostility. 'Herodotus, where are you now when I need you?' he thought.

"I think I see what disturbs Lieutenant Darkcut. If the film sent by the trader and the records are both accurate, then the *curthel* have . . . what, mutated?"

"Sir?"

"Yes, Lieutenant Darkcut."

"All the records show that *curthel* attacks have caused widespread hysteria and madness, but it appears that they were uniformly inner-directed. The incident on Copia is clearly otherwise. The bodies, particularly those of the women, show they were brutally abused, repeatedly raped, then smashed a little at a time with a blunt object. That they fought back is also clear. All of that is inconsistent with a *curthel* invasion. In a *curthel* invasion, the victims appear to have either battered themselves to death or immolated themselves in the fires of the cities."

"Quite. There is a distinct, if subtle, difference in the actions of the Copians," Gilhame answered. "Do you have any conclusions, Darkcut?"

"No conclusions, sir, but I do have some ideas I want to think about," she answered.

"Think quickly, will you?" he replied, smiling. He glanced around at the raised hands. Of the hundred or so people in the room, only about six seemed to have questions or comments. He chose one. "Major Avillar?"

Avillar—a tall, bony woman somewhere between forty and a hundred—stood up, the oyster-white of her Foreseer Corps uniform contrasting badly with her sallow skin and unkempt hair. Gilhame wondered why being a full-time precognitive always seemed to produce such desperately unhealthy-looking people. Still, he saw, she carried herself with a kind of fragile dignity.

"Admiral, it was not a *curthel* invasion. It was intended to simulate one."

One did not question a foreseer's pronouncements. Unlike his *var*-produced visions, a foreseer's were considered admissible in a court of law. They were a cautious, closemouthed bunch, and the problem was not the accuracy of their foresight, but getting them to say anything at all. It was rare that they volunteered information. Still, he felt relieved that he was not facing a *curthel* invasion. But what was it, then? "Thank you, Major."

"It was in the nature of an experiment," she continued as if he had not spoken. "A one-eyed . . . woman oversaw the preparation. She is an ally planning betrayal. The next attack will be on the Rope Dancers." She crumbled back into her seat like a collapsing air sack.

Gilhame watched the frightened glances go from face to face around the room. Foreseers spoke in riddles and metaphors much of the time, which was one of the reasons they rarely volunteered information. Much of the knowledge they received was subjective, like his *var* visions. Always, the problem was interpretation.

On this occasion, there was little doubt as to Major Avillar's meaning. The Emperor's sister, Araclyde, whose name meant "one eye," and who was the wife of the Nabatean monarch, came into everyone's mind. Araclyde had been a problem to her family almost from the moment of her birth. She had grown from a strong-willed and spoiled child into a woman of ungovernable passions and ambitions, ruthless and cunning.

The Rope Dancers? That was not clear. "Does anyone have any other questions or anything else to add?" He was suddenly very weary.

"Admiral?"

It was the chief of his chemistry staff, Lieutenant Commander Greyfus. Greyfus was a long, narrow man with a vague expression on his thin face. His eyes were so pale that from a distance they seemed to be all white. "Yes, Greyfus?"

"Were water, soil and air samples taken by this trader fellow?"

Gilhame looked at the written report in his hand. He turned the pages over rapidly. "Yes. No analysis yet. Some samples are coming to us soon. Captain Leelial?"

"Were any of the victims dead-brained?"

"No. Himez didn't have the facilities."

"I'd like my people to go over a few of the victims, then."

"Fine. Frikard, will you take over?" He handed the papers to the man and left the room. He loped through the corridors, wondering exactly what to report to the Admiralty. One did not accuse the wife of a ruling monarch lightly.

Alvellaina was curled up with the pard on her lap when he came into his rooms. He unbuttoned the front of his tunic and reached in to scratch the still-healing shoulder. Gilhame twisted his head from side to side to loosen his neck muscles, then noticed the table was set with food and drink.

"Are we expecting guests, m'alba?"

"Admiral Gyre wants to see you. They wouldn't let me tell you during that meeting. He says . . . he wants *her* back, or you'll be sorry. I thought that wine and food might make the meeting a little less ugly."

"Less ugly? With the odious Guthry? You have the instincts of a great political hostess, little one. It almost seems a shame to waste them. Damn! I wanted to get out of this uniform. It itches like madness. Ah well, duty before pleasure. What do you call that garment you are wearing?"

"I don't know. A pseudo-uniform?" She was wearing a gray, high-necked, long-sleeved single-suit with wide legs. It had the dragon symbol at the top of each sleeve but was otherwise plain. "I get bored, just sitting around. I can't read all the time. So I go down to Lefair's shop and nose around. He says I have the makings of a good tailor's mate. I don't really enjoy feeling . . . like a ship's woman. And

Lefair says he hasn't enough work to keep him busy."

"I am glad you have found an occupation to suit you, though I would never have chosen that one for you, myself. In fact, I am surprised that Vraser hasn't copped you for his work."

"Oh, no. Derissa is the Healer in the family."

"I meant your other talent."

Alvellaina gave him an angry look. "I never want to do that again, so don't even bother to ask me."

"So, Lefair complains of lack of work. I suppose that being a master tailor on a naval vessel must be . . . unchallenging," he said, changing the subject from Alvellaina's capacity for forced rapport.

"What happened at the meeting?"

"A great deal. It needs sorting out yet." He went to his communicator. "Have Commanders Buschard and Frikard and Chief Vraser report to my quarters."

"Yes, sir."

"Are you planning on staying for the party, m'alba?"

"If that is alright with you."

"Certainly. It will brighten the room considerably. You know, since that animal," he said, pointing at the pard, "seems to have decided to make his home in my quarters, do you think we should offer it a name?"

"Offer?"

"Pards all have their own names, secret names, and the labels which people give them are quite arbitrary and often wrong. So, it is more polite to offer a name than to give one."

"Yes, it might be more convenient to have something to call it, though it's so independent. What do you think Gyre wants?"

"Who knows? My vitals on a platter, no doubt. But, beyond that is anyone's guess. I would give a great deal to know the precise extent of his involvement in Marpessa's little adventure, however."

The communicator beeped. "Admiral Gyre is arriving, sir."

"Have him brought to my quarters," he answered.

"Speak of the devil."

"And he *will* appear." Alvellaina rose gracefully and smoothed the front of her garment. "At least I don't have to dance with him."

She busied herself carrying trays from the sideboard to the table. He watched her arrange the fruits and vegetables to make interesting patterns. Then she put out carafes of wine and juice. Gilhame picked up a carafe and sniffed it.

"That's Grentarian or I'm no judge. Where did it come from?"

"I . . . took the liberty of ordering some things while we were on Attira. There's *durek* and *vidar* for Buschard, Rurian for Vraser, and four kinds of elixir. Commander Frikard is very fond of Mardean elixir."

"You behave like a wife in every way but one."

"Elfdun, your commissary officer was a little . . . nonplussed, but I did not think you would mind," she answered, ignoring his remark. "Besides, though we entertained very rarely, I was my father's hostess for three years. It is a thing I *can* do. I prefer to be something more than an ornament in the crown of your achievements."

"Forgive me, m'alba." He bowed his head. "I am a selfish brute."

"Save that twaddle for someone who does not know you in and out," she answered sharply. "I trust my choices of refreshment do not displease you?"

"No, of course not." He had noticed that they both backed away from the sharp debates which had marked their early acquaintance. They had not had a proper fight since the night he recovered consciousness. Gilhame was not sure if he missed them or not. "It just seems a shame to waste good things on the likes of Guthry Gyre. Don't we have some . . . Paladomian cream?"

"What's that?"

"A perfectly dreadful drink which resembles canine urine in both taste and smell."

She giggled. "No. And I wouldn't put it on the table with Vraser here if I did. I wish to have a good reputation about my table. Do you know, all that time you were asleep, he talked of nothing but food and drink and the history of same. I believe he was trying to distract me, but it was most educational."

"Were you worried, little one?"

"I . . . cannot lie to you. I was frantic, both for Derissa and for you."

"An odd attitude for a woman who professes to hate me."

"I don't think I precisely hate you. I rather like the person I was with on Attira. I just don't like Admiral ur Fagon, the Black Dragon. You can be quite charming when you're not killing people. Close your tunic. They're coming—rather a lot of them," she said with a frown.

"What does it feel like . . . mind-seeing?"

"Right now it is like many candles in a dark hall. I am not 'seeing' thoughts—for that I need contact—but am visualizing life forces. I have to know someone fairly well to actually divine his thoughts at a distance. Here, let me. You missed a button and you are crooked." She unbuttoned several buttons and redid them. She looked into his face for a moment, then reached up and brushed back a lock of hair that had fallen on his forehead.

The door intercom sounded. "Admiral!" The voice on the other side was strained.

Gilhame released the lock. There were indeed a large number of people in the corridor. Two frightened-looking midshipmen, one of each sex, wearing the dragon emblem, escorted Admiral Gyre and his escort of eight heavy troopers and three line officers. The troopers were wearing enough battle gear to sack a small city, and Gilhame could see a platoon of his own marines coming quietly into the corridor behind them, armed and anxious-looking.

"Precisely what the devil do you think you are up to, Gyre?" he roared.

"Didn't your whore deliver my message?"

"You know I am not in the habit of taking you seriously, Guthry. Now, unless you really wish to cost the Emperor *two* Admirals, I suggest you send your braves away. I have you surrounded—again!"

"What?" Gyre turned around and saw the marines and

the portable cannon. At that moment, six of ur Fagon's troopers in heavy armor entered the corridor. "Damn you!"

"The element of surprise has never been your strong suit, Guthry. Come in, won't you, and have some wine? The smell of burnt meat would be so distasteful in these close quarters. Send your troopers away. You know I never bargain at gunpoint. Let me see." He pointed at one of Gyre's officers. "I seem to remember you. Mafrin, isn't it? Please, Guthry introduce me to your officers, and try to behave as if you were well brought-up."

Gyre, red-faced, motioned to the troopers. "Return to your ships," he said in a voice almost strangled with rage.

"I am sure my men will be happy to escort them off the *Dragon* after they have had a little refreshment. Wearing all that gear must be very tiring. Major Freedel," he said to one of the marines, "will you see that our guests get something to eat and drink before they leave?"

Gilhame was aware that Alvellaina was standing behind him and to his right, out of the doorway, and seemed to be staring at the wall. He could not tell if she was angry or near laughter. He watched the troopers and the marines vacate the corridor. Frikard came into the end of the hall, looking harassed.

Alvellaina walked to the portal. "Come in, won't you, Admiral Gyre?" she said prettily. She slipped her arm through his and drew him ruthlessly into the room.

Gilhame turned his attention to the three officers and Frikard a little uneasily. He mistrusted Alvellaina in that sugary mood. Out of the corner of his eye he saw her lean over Gyre as she sat him down at the table and whisper something into his ear. The flush on Gyre's face indicated that she had not said anything loving.

Frikard and Mafrin, Gyre's officer, made introductions. Then Vraser stumped in, looking grumpy, and introductions were repeated. Alvellaina cut the Healer out and herded him over to the table. She served him some wine, ignoring the protocol which demanded that all the guests be seated before wine was served. Buschard came in, and everyone went to sit down.

Gilhame half-smiled at Buschard. "Ah, there you are, Pers," he said to his handsome friend. "Let me do the introductions this time. Frikard is quite worn down with it. Commander Mafrin, who was leaving the Academy as I entered, Commander Villiam, and Captain Dunegan. Formalities are so exhausting, but they do keep society running smoothly, don't they?"

He knew that his languor would alert his three officers. Buschard had once told him, "I never trust you when you get polite, Gil. You're like a damned pard at a rathole, playing. You've gotten me into more brawls with that polite voice of yours!" Gilhame smiled. Certainly, it was one of the aspects of the real ur Fagon's personality which he understood.

Vraser raised his face from a rapt olfactory examination of his wine and nodded genially. Commander Mafrin, seated beside him, nodded back.

Vraser put down his glass and said, "Would you like some wine? Here, try some of this. That wine in the blue jar is pretty poor stuff. You wouldn't like it."

Mafrin laughed. He was a small man, square and solid, with stiff, crinkly brown hair and a ruddy complexion. "So, of course, from politeness, you are forced to drink the contents of the blue jug yourself. Really, Vraser, your reputation as a wine expert is almost as respected as your talent as a Healer. Let me at least taste the stuff in the blue jar before you sacrifice yourself and drink it all."

Vraser balked, then poured a generous amount into Mafrin's glass. "It's nice to know my opinions are appreciated." He glanced up and down the table benevolently and stopped in horror as he watched Admiral Gyre open his belt pouch and remove a sizable wad of *choon*. "Admiral . . . that will ruin the taste of your wine."

Gilhame, sitting at the head of the table and on Gyre's left, reached out and grasped Gyre's wrist. "Put it back. No drugs at my table, Guthry."

Gyre just stared at him for a moment, then shrugged and put the stuff back. "You didn't used to be so particular, Gilhame."

"I was younger then, and less aware of my mortality."

Gilhame looked down the table. Alvellaina had seated herself at the foot and was serving Captain Dunegan and Frikard, saying something which made them laugh. Buschard and Commander Villiam appeared to have found some common ground on the right side of the table below Gyre, while Vraser and Mafrin on the left seemed amiably engaged in wine talk.

"Have you studied the trader's films on Copia, Guthry?" Gilhame asked as he picked up a tray of fruit and offered it. "Try the vidar grapes. They are quite tasty for having been grown in a tank."

"Thank you." Gyre had apparently decided to control his temper and observe the amenities, as if he had not entered the ship with an armed force. He took some grapes and a kimis-fruit, a kind of peach. "No, I'm letting my staff handle that." He lowered his voice and looked across at Vraser. "Why is that old cripple on your staff?"

"Good Healers are hard to come by, and Vraser is one of the best. Besides, he's been with me for years."

"He gives me the creeps."

"You never cease to amaze me, Guthry. I had no idea you were an aesthete. Do you prefer Rurian or Grentarian wine?"

"Pard-lap! Oh, well, give me some of the Grentarian."

"There is *durek* down the table. We can probably pry it away from Buschard if we try."

"Don't bother."

Gilhame, watching his fellow admiral carefully, poured some wine into his cup. The man's hand trembled slightly when he raised it, draining the vessel in a few swallows. Gilhame refilled Gyre's cup, then took some for himself. He noted the absence of the elegant, long-stemmed glasses which usually graced his board and wondered at Alvellaina's choice of table setting. Still, it presented a pleasant and unified picture—no cloth, so the high shine of the wood of the table showed, carved wooden trenchers, earthenware cups, no utensils except fruit knives. All very rustic. Gilhame wondered if Gyre read any insult into the table setting and contrasted it with the almost indecent luxury of the party they had given for Niyarkos. 'She has a bit of the devil in her,' he thought irreverently, lifting his cup and toasting her silently. Alvellaina caught his gesture and gave him a tiny smile.

"Well, since you didn't come to talk about the *curthel*, is this a social call, Guthry? No, I suppose not. I was forgetting the troopers. One doesn't bring troopers, however well-behaved, on a social call."

"You know very well I want Marpessa back."

"Dear Guthry, I would give her back in a moment, but I haven't the faintest idea where she is. I cannot quite comprehend why you are so anxious to have returned to you such an unreliable officer. Sentiment has never been one of your characteristics. Oh, I admit, her tactics were occasionally brilliant. But so erratic. Now, if it were Captain Letitia Branwen, say, or Commander Kylaa Vitz'erbert, I could understand your frantic desire. They are officers anyone would be proud to have in his command. In fact, I would not be surprised if Vitz'erbert doesn't make admiral soon. She has the brains, the drive and the discipline to do it. But Marpessa? Or is there sentiment involved?"

Gyre clenched his teeth. "Don't play games with me, ur Fagon!"

"After Feebus? I wouldn't think of it. I never kick a man in the same place twice. But I swear I have not seen her since that unfortunate evening two weeks ago when I found her trying to make chopped meat out of Derissa Krispin."

Gyre slammed his hand down on the table, making the cups bounce a little. Gilhame was now quite glad for the rustic table setting. "Where have you put her?"

"I believe I recommended fleet prostitution. You might, after moderating your voice, inquire of Commander Frikard. He was managing the store at the time. Really, the whole subject bores me. Let us change it, shall we? You were, I believe, patrolling the Nabatean interface before you put in for repairs. What is their ship strength these days? I've heard some curious rumors about a new chemical weapon they're using."

Gyre was white and tense now. "Weapons? I don't know about that. But then, I didn't have any actual encounters with their fleet—except on Muria."

"Muria? That's one of the neutral worlds, isn't it?"

"Yes. We sent a few of our ships there for some rec-time. There were a couple of Nabatean ships in at the same time."

Gilhame could tell that Vraser was listening to their conversation while appearing to talk to Mafrin. Gyre, ignoring formality, refilled his own cup.

The pard, which had continued to sleep on the chair, woke, stretched and leapt onto the table. It looked around, sniffed and started towards Gilhame. The little animal scented Gyre's still extended hand, spat, bottled it's tail and gave a hideous yowl. It's paw raked Gyre's outstretched hand before he could snatch it back.

Gilhame hauled the pard off the table and into his lap, ignoring several scratches he got from the still-growling beast. He stroked it beneath the table, feeling its trembling, and said, "I'm afraid my friend doesn't like you, Guthry. There, there, my pretty. He didn't mean to frighten you." The pard made a number of untranslatable but obviously rude remarks in gutter-pard and dug its claws into Gilhame's leg. "Pards are such temperamental creatures, aren't they?"

Gyre sucked his hand meditatively. He put his hand down from his mouth. "That one is!"

"Don't worry. I am certain her claws aren't . . . septic. She's quite fastidious," Gilhame answered, enjoying the ghastly color Gyre turned at the suggestion. "Frikard, we've been so busy. What did you finally do with Captain Devero?"

"Sir? Oh, Captain Devero. Well, sir, we packed her in 'cold' and shipped her off to the Havassit Institute before we left Attira. She was *truth*-blocked, and they're the only ones who can reverse the process. She should be as good as new in a week or so."

"I protest," said Gyre. "You had no right to do that."

"My dear Guthry, we had every right in the cosmos. She was found doing damage to one of the fleet's personnel."

"That's nonsense. Ship's whores don't count."

Vraser cleared his throat. "Halba Derissa Krispin was made a member of my staff two days after she came on board, Admiral. We gave the standard tests and found she had a very good 'healer' index. The paperwork is still in the works, but I doubt if the Admiralty would pass over any Healer, even if he or she were blind or lame. The need is too great, you know. I also take offense at your language. I think you should apologize quickly.''

"The devil I will!"

Buschard, with Villiam between himself and Gyre, leaned forward and looked at him. He frowned and seemed to consider the matter with his usual gravity. Then he took up his wine and said, "The Admiral is entitled to his opinion, Vraser. 'Names break no sinews,' you know." He paused while everyone at the table absorbed the implication of his use of one of the Healers' Proverbs.

Gilhame pursed his lips to keep from smiling. 'Good old Pers, always makes his words count,' he thought. "Still, one must consider that any man who countenances an attack on a woman, whatever her station, is a coward."

Gyre half-rose from his chair. "You . . ." Gilhame grasped Gyre's arm and forced him back into his seat.

"I think the insults are even now, gentlemen. Guthry, I suggest you drop the entire matter. Surely you have someone to replace Captain Devero on your flagship."

"That's not the point!"

"Yes, I know. The point is that you have gotten into the habit of thinking of yourself as beyond the law. That's a very dangerous position to take, my dear. But, you always were headstrong and heedless. I recommend you eat a little less *choon* and moderate your actions."

Gilhame tucked the pard into the curve of his arm and stood up. He smiled lazily. "Well, Guthry, I think we are done."

Gyre's officers arose from the table with unseemly haste. Admiral Gyre took his dismissal a little more slowly, but finally stood up. Frikard and Buschard came to their feet. Only Alvellaina and Vraser remained seated.

"You haven't heard the last of this, ur Fagon," snapped Gyre.

"I didn't think I had. Oh yes. I commend the Copian

tapes to your attention. There are some features you might find fascinating.''

But Gyre was already opening the portal, Frikard escorting him. Gilhame watched, amused, while Gyre's officers quivered between polite farewells and a need to accompany their commanding officer. They finally mumbled thanks and left in undignified haste to pursue the Admiral. Buschard left with them, closing the portal behind him.

Gilhame put down the pard and began unbuttoning his tunic. "Damned itching. Can't you do anything about it, Farren?" he asked the Healer.

"It's normal," said the old man, filling his cup again.

Alvellaina got up and came down the length of the table. She picked up Gyre's trencher and cup and took them to the disposer. She shoved them into the slot and gave the two men a radiant smile.

Gilhame enjoyed her smile. "Now, what is all this about Derissa being a medic? No, don't say a word. I can't stand this uniform a minute longer. It's a straitjacket." He went into his bedroom and changed his clothes.

When he came back into the room, Buschard and Frikard were entering. Alvellaina had reset the table for five, grouped at one end.

"Will you satisfy my curiosity, m'alba?" he asked as she sat down on his right. "What did you say to Guthry when you sat him at the table?"

She blushed lightly. "I was hoping you weren't watching."

"I always watch you, little one," he said ignoring the suppressed smiles of his officers.

"I told him that if I ever heard him call me a whore again, I would cut his liver out, cook it on the end of a shovel and feed it to the pigs."

"Brava! I see I underestimated your worth. A fleet at least, with perhaps a duchy or two thrown in for good measure. But, why would you cook it?"

"I rather like pigs, and I wouldn't want to make them ill." The room was filled with masculine laughter.

"And now, you old eavesdropper," Gilhame said to

Vraser, "what did you get out of Gyre's conversation?"

"There were . . . indications. Captain Devero is privy to whatever mischief Gyre is up to, and he is very worried about that. He lied directly about the matter of the Nabatean weapons. He knows what those weapons are and probably has a good idea how and when they will be used. I would say that contact was made while he was on Muria."

"Any conclusions?"

"I believe . . . he has come to some agreement with the Nabateans. He will do something for them in return for some consideration on their part—if he doesn't come to pieces altogether first. The *choon* delusions are affecting his judgment. He wanted to know what you knew. He's afraid of you, Gil, and he hates you."

"Anything else?"

"His staff is very . . . spooked. Commander Mafrin almost certainly does not know what is going on, but he is worried. Also, I believe that Captain Devero acted without Gyre's knowledge or permission. The premature use of that organic-radiation poison . . . uh, tipped his hand."

"Alright. Good. What do we know, or think we know? Gyre has made a deal with the Nabateans; he has knowledge of at least one weapon which is not part of the Kardusian arsenal. He probably knows that the incident on Copia was not a *curthel* invasion.

"I think we can safely assume that the *curthel* thing is chemical and that, combined with the radiation matter, it points a rather bony finger at Araclyde. Her talents in that area are well-known.

"I can just see my report now. 'To His Imperial Majesty, Clyven the Fourth, greetings. Evidence indicates that Your Majesty's sister, the Nabatean Empress Araclyde, is planning chemical warfare against the Kardus Temporal Empire. To this end, she may have purchased the services of Your Majesty's own Admiral Guthry Gyre. Obediently yours, Admiral Gilhame ur Fagon.' By the imperishable blood of the Savior, the Ten Nations Compact would fly into a million pieces if I sent that out. The war that would follow would make a *curthel* invasion look like a school dance. And really, we have no evidence, just a lot of unhealthy suspicions. Did you really send Marpessa to the Havassit Institute, Ven?"

"We told you she was on ice, Gil," Buschard answered instead.

"Yes, I believe you did. Cosmos protect me from my well-meaning subordinates. My enemies I can take care of. I am still somewhat puzzled. Of what possible use is this radiation stuff outside of armed combat? We don't do enough of that to justify a weapon for just hand-to-hand."

Vraser cleared his throat. "That's not quite how I see it being used. I believe it could be distributed as an airborne mist, tasteless and odorless. It would have no effect while one was awake. But, when one was asleep, it would invade the sinews, destroy them and you would never even know you had been poisoned. The stuff acts like a disease we only know from medical history, a wasting disease where the lifeblood actually destroys the body."

"You mean the stuff could be put in the air or water supply of a city—or a ship."

"Precisely."

"Can it be detected?"

"It seems that a few individuals can 'see' it. One of my staff, Gurian, can. That was how we actually determined how to treat you and Derissa."

"I want everyone who can 'see' that damned substance checking out every ship in the fleet. I wouldn't put sabotage past dear old Guthry. He's always been a cheater. That is, if you haven't anticipated me already."

"I have and I haven't. The *Dragon* was checked out before we left."

"Check it again. I want everyone on full alert until every ship in the fleet has a clean bill of health. Nobody sleeps."

"Yes, sir." Vraser gave him a wide grin.

"Now, tell me about Derissa being on your staff."

"All the girls are officially noncombatant personnel of the fleet, Gil," Buschard put in.

"Oh?"

"It seemed the wisest thing. After all, the irregularity of their positions could only be unpleasant. So, Armanda is listed as a musician, Derissa is studying healing, and

Alvellaina is officially part of Lefair's work staff."

"I am still unsure as to why you felt this was necessary."

"Suppose you dropped dead right now."

"A gruesome thought, but go on."

"Alvellaina would have been an unprotected ship's woman."

"I am occasionally quite dense. I am glad I have subordinates who aren't afraid to keep me out of trouble. Tell me, what do you think Gyre will do, Pers?"

Buschard thought for a moment. "I think he'll go renegade."

_____ *Chapter XVI*

Renegade. The word seemed to echo inside his head long after Buschard had spoken it. The guests were gone, his staff departed, the table cleared, the room silent except for the pard's purring. Turncoats were not unique or even novel, of course, but ur Fagon found the concept offended him. Somehow, betrayal was worse than death.

He put the pard down from his lap and got up. He paced back and forth in the room, mentally sorting and resorting all the information. Finally he went to a little niche in the wall and opened the cover.

Var. Gilhame stared at the bottle. The hideous, wormlike red parasites swam around in the bottom of the vessel. Over them floated the thick, gray fluid which was the by-product of their existence, the *var* which provoked some visions of the future, if one was foolhardy enough to desire them.

The parasites and their excretion disgusted him. He understood why the original ur Fagon had become dependent on such a device, but it still repelled him. Gilhame remembered a tall man with a shaven head wearing a necklace made of red leeches implanted around his throat. The man's eyes were glazed but not empty, distant eyes which saw a constant world of tomorrows. The bloated red leeches lived on the man's blood and, in return, he saw the future, or perhaps his most cherished dreams. That was the danger of *var*. Sometimes one saw what one wished to see.

Gilhame knew that that other ur Fagon who still whispered in his mind had been fortunate in his use of the drug. Of fantasies and outré desires, he had been moderately free. All he had cared for was winning and serving the Emperor, in that order. *Var* had been a tool to shorten the odds a little, to give an edge, as it had at the Battle of the Vardar Straits. Now he needed that edge, and he hesitated to use it.

Gilhame wished he were free of his need to anticipate the future or that he could leave the matter in the hands of those more competent to deal with it, like Major Avillar. He could not. So, he poured a minute amount of *var* off the top of the bottle, watching the red worms react to the disturbance, recapped the bottle, closed the niche and carried the glass back to the table.

He swallowed the stuff, barely a mouthful, in a single gulp. Time stopped.

Fast-rushing darkness. The splendid power of the Black Dragon's body, leathery wings beating across the Void. Voices? No, thoughts. 'How much does the bastard know? Damn Marp and her temper. Must move up the attack. Release the ingarit *now. They'll never know what hit them. Gilhame ur Fagon will wake up dead. I am going to murder an entire fleet!' Pleasure. 'I only wish I could see it happen.' Faint regret.*

Eyes. The Black Dragon saw through eyes not his own. The corridor of a ship all twisted and distorted, full of colors and shapes he could not name. A tiny room full of dials. The faces of the instruments seemed to crawl around, the lights bounced up and down. There was a timepiece on the wall. The numbers on it seemed to have left their places and to be engaging in a pattern dance. With great difficulty, the Dragon disengaged himself from the mind he was riding. The colors vanished. The dials were dials, the numbers on the chronometer just numbers. 1407 hours, Nelis 9, 4702. The blackness swirled past him, the leathery wings flapped home, then faded into nothing.

Gilhame opened his eyes. Alvellaina sat across from him, looking disapproving. He looked straight into her green eyes. "It was needful, m'alba."

"I know."

"But you still don't like it."

"I still don't like it."

"Neither do I. Especially the mixture of *var* and *choon* I just experienced. Gah! My mouth tastes like a locker." He picked up the little cup and took it into the bathroom. He washed it out, then rinsed his mouth several times.

Gilhame returned the cup to its niche and got a bottle of wine and two glasses from the refreshment cabinet. "How much did you get?"

"All of it, I think. I felt you 'go' and came across immediately. I just could not sit still. At least I understand a little better now why you use it.

"Do you? I don't."

"The Dragon. It was rather like the Angels and Demons Pattern. I wish we had finished that. It was a wonderful feeling of freedom, don't you think?"

"I suppose. Well, with any luck, I won't need the blasted stuff again. Nelis 9. That's tomorrow. I wonder why he is waiting?"

"I don't think he's supposed to do anything yet. I think he's supposed to wait. And I think the drug is affecting his judgment."

"Has anyone ever told you you are as smart as you are beautiful, m'alba?"

"I don't believe so." She smiled at him, then sipped the wine he had poured. *Damn you, don't look at me that way.* Alvellaina felt her thoughts go into their usual confusion when Gilhame turned the full force of his affection upon her. *I don't want to love you and be used by you. No, that's not true. I want you, but on my terms. Has it always been like this, this battle for supremacy? Probably. But he's so damned brave and so disciplined. He makes me feel useless. All I'll ever be is an object of affection. I can't compete with the war for his love. Why can't I just settle for the crumbs, why must I have the whole cake? Or, do I want to reform him? And would I feel like this about him if he were all tame and nice? Why couldn't I have gone with Father? Exile couldn't possibly be worse than this.*

"Have you ever used drugs, little one?" His deep voice broke into her reverie.

"I've been smoky on field-weed a few times. The wind was in the wrong quarter and brought the fumes up to the house when they were burning off the land. Nothing else."

"Did you enjoy the sensation?"

"Yes and no. I like the slight out-of-body feeling it gave me. But it also . . . excited me. I understood why the landfolk have orgies." She was blushing.

"That's a very common reaction. But you didn't like it."

"I didn't say that. It was frustrating and confusing. It made me feel undignified."

He grinned at her. "I regret to say that there is never anything dignified about sex. Grace, occasionally, can be achieved by the knowledgeable, but never dignity. Still, I cannot deny I would like to see you in such a state."

"Don't be crude."

"I can't help it. You arouse all my healthy animal nature."

"I know that."

"Have you been snooping in my skull again, woman?"

"I would hardly call it snooping when any telepath within a mile can 'hear' you shouting."

"Do I shout? Mentally, I mean? And I thought I was being very discreet."

"Discreet! About as subtle as a boil. My sisters are starting to give me evil looks. Derissa has become quite *fond* of you, since . . . And Armanda, well, she has always had a romantic disposition. But, total strangers are glaring at me and I 'hear' them whisper, 'Who does she think she is?' in their minds. As if I should be honored. No, Admiral, you are not discreet!"

"I do not think I have ever made so many black marks with a woman when I have been on my best behavior. Forgive me, m'alba."

"For what? Your feelings are your own. I've been being a little . . . spoiled, but I am used to having things my own way. I should just have capitulated instantly, when you laid your heart before me. I think anyone else would have."

"And why didn't you?"

"Because you never asked me."

"Asked you what, m'alba?"

"If it was alright with me to be loved by you. You just assumed that since you loved me, everything was as it should be. Just because you love someone, doesn't mean they want it."

"Presumptuous of me, to be sure."

"Yes, it was. But I have made up my mind." Alvellaina smiled at him in her heartrending way.

"I can see that, m'alba. What a botch we have made of our beginning. Hello, little friend," he said as the pard came walking up the table. "I think she earned a title today, don't you, m'alba?" He scratched the animal between its ears.

"For clawing Gyre? I do. I just wish she had gotten his face!"

"For a lady who professes to loathe violence, you have a nasty, bloodthirsty streak in you."

"It must be the company I've been keeping. What shall we offer the pard for a name?"

"I've no idea. I wish you could have seen Guthry's face when I told him her claws weren't septic."

"What do you think of 'Capsia'? That means 'traitor's bane' in Gretarian."

"Short and poetic. I like it. Do you think you could bear to be called Capsia, my small ally?" he asked the pard. The beast yawned at him, curling a pink tongue. "I suppose that is an affirmative."

Alvellaina looked at him. "Why did you leave Faldar?" she asked abruptly.

"Because I could not see the Dream."

"I don't understand."

"My home world, 'his' home world . . . this body's world of origin is, what shall I say? A massive racial delusion? After the last *curthel* devastation, the Faldarians created a new religion or philosophy. It is an odd combination of fatalism and despondency. They decided not to rebuild. After all, who knew when there would be another wave of planet-wide hysteria?

"They have not rebuilt a single building. The only new

construction on the planet is at Fanar, the out-worlder's city. That is where the spaceport is, and the embassies and government offices. The rest of the world is precisely as it was at the end of the last *curthel* invasion, except for a couple centuries of erosion and plant growth. I was breached between the roots of a great tree which has been the ur Fagon 'keep' for six generations.

"But the Faldarians do not see crumbling cities and vine-encrusted buildings. They have the Dream. They have a world of perfect beauty. Each fire-gutted building is a fairy castle—light, airy, complete. Every family-tree-keep is a palace. I could never see the Dream. By the standards of my race, I was crippled or mad or both."

Alvellaina heard the sorrow in his voice. She could imagine a younger Gilhame longing for some kind of acceptance from his people and receiving none. "Do you hate them?"

"I don't believe so. I used to be vastly impatient when my mother would send me up to her 'bedroom' to fetch her fan, and I would climb up to her sleeping platform and get a large fern branch. I would catch glimpses of what she 'saw'—the beautiful drapes blowing lightly in a breeze, the soft bed covered with furs, the gleam of candlelight off polished floors. I would see the hard, bare, plaited platform and the sleeping covers woven out of grasses at the same time. The elders did everything they could to 'cure' me, but by the time I was fourteen, they gave it up. I fathered my sister-son, as required, went to Fanar and entered the Academy a year later. The rest of my life is a matter of public record. You may consult the ship's library if you are curious."

She heard the shift in his voice, the quick harshness to hide an old hurt. Alvellaina felt the motes of the Dragon's lifetimes, the pain he must have suffered before, all drawn together in the story of Gilhame ur Fagon's failure to be a man of his people. '*I thought he was immune to pain. How many other ways have I misjudged you, old friend*?'

"You did hate them for seeing beauty when there was none."

He shrugged, then winced at the ache in his shoulder.

"As you will, m'alba. I am going to bed. Please, let yourself out." Gilhame drank down the last of his wine and bowed as he rose from the table, then left.

Gilhame sensed a faint stirring in the suppressed personality whose body he inhabited. The original man flooded him with the pain of rejection by his own family. Seated on the edge of the bed, he pitied the misery of his host-man.

Gilhame heard the whisper of the portal as Alvellaina left. He realized that he missed her, but was too caught up in the emotions of the suppressed ur Fagon to feel more than a vague regret. He removed his garments, hanging them neatly as he had been taught at the Academy, remembering how he had prized his first uniform, his first real clothing.

Alvellaina stood at the portal. She had walked to it, opened it, then closed it again. She leaned against the wall, feeling excited and frightened at the same time. Her nipples were hard under her uniform. 'My body has its own mind,' she thought. 'Well, maybe I won't go up in smoke.'

She turned, pulling the net off her hair and fluffing the curls with her fingers. Then she released the closing on her uniforms and folded it neatly, putting it on a chair. She walked towards the bedroom door.

There was a tiny noise behind him. Gilhame spun around, half-crouched, hands raised to strike. Alvellaina came into the room rather slowly. He straightened up, feeling somewhat foolish, as she walked up to him. She stood directly in front of him, wearing a faint smile and nothing more. He could feel her breath on his chest and smelled her sweet scent. "I told you I had made up my mind," she said.

"You should never come up behind a trained fighter without giving him some warning, my dear. I might have hurt you." He said the words huskily as he looked at her small, high breasts.

"Scold me later. Right now I think I would like to be kissed. Or don't you want me to kiss you?"

Gilhame slipped an arm around her gently and waited for a moment. There was no feeling of resistance. He kissed her brow very tentatively, then her cheek and finally her mouth. She responded by putting both arms around him and pressing her body against him.

"When you decide something, you really do it, don't you?" He asked. "Now, just what are you up to?" Gilhame had the distinct feeling that he had lost control of the situation.

"Don't ask stupid questions. Just kiss me again."

He did, and she kissed him back, as she had not done the first time. It was an eager kiss, unskilled, but responsive. He drew back and looked down at her, suspicious at her sudden capitulation. The matter, he decided, was definitely out of his hands. He was not sure he liked that.

After several more kisses, she drew him towards the bed. She slid in beside him and pressed her body against his insistently. Alvellaina caressed his chest and kissed his throat.

He ran his hand along the long, smooth stretch of her leg, filled with the suppressed desires of the previous weeks. His own needs nearly blinded him. But he forced himself to proceed slowly, waking her body into excitement.

That first coupling, between the skilled man and the completely untutored girl, was as painful and as awkward as such things usually are, but neither partner was left unsatisfied. Gilhame was as gentle as he could be, and found her eager but unsubmissive. His patience was rewarded finally by a sharp cry of pleasure.

Afterwards, she pillowed her head on his chest, stroking it and humming softly to herself. All he could see was her mass of curly hair and her elegant hand on his chest. Her face was entirely out of his view.

"I . . . feel I should warn you, m'alba, that if you continue to do that, I shall be moved to repeat my performance."

"Promise?"

"Greedy wench. Trying to make up for lost time?"

"Not exactly."

"Will you tell me now just what prompted you . . . great cosmos, I've been seduced! Not that I was unwilling, you understand."

"Good. Think how mortifying it would be to have the great Admiral ur Fagon crying rape."

"True. I doubt my reputation would stand the strain. Now, stop distracting me and tell me what this sudden change of heart is all about."

"It's not sudden."

"Oh?" He smiled at her as she turned her face up to him and gave her a kiss.

"It's all very confusing. I wanted to hate you. And I did for a while. But, after you saved Derissa's life . . . I . . ."

"This is a wonderful way to show your gratitude, but I don't require charity."

"It's not gratitude. If it was that, then Derissa should be here, not me."

"I don't think Pers would like that, do you?"

"Him? He'd give you anything you wanted, including Derissa. And I don't believe she'd mind. She's more flexible than I am—and more realistic. She saw past the monster long before I did."

"Eros and Psyche."

"What?"

"A very old legend, older even than we. Eros was the god of love, son of the goddess Aphrodite, who was the goddess of love. And Psyche was the most beautiful woman in the world. Aphrodite didn't much care for that, since people began comparing her beauty to Psyche's. Anyhow, Eros saw Psyche and fell madly in love with her, which annoyed his mother no end, and he married her. Only, for reasons which elude me now, poor Psyche was not allowed to see him. She thought he was a terrible monster. But her curiosity got the better of her, and one night she stole into his bedroom with a candle. Imagine her surprise when her monster turned out to be a very comely young man."

"Did they live happily ever after?" She sounded like a little girl with that question.

"Not immediately. Aphrodite, being the petty, jealous female that she was, made Psyche perform some nearly impossible tasks. But, eventually, yes, Eros and Psyche were reunited—happily, one assumes, if living with those particular gods and goddesses can be called happy. They were a fractious bunch, always cheating on one another and tossing thunderbolts about. It always sounded rather noisy and uncomfortable to me.''

"Well, you are not the handsomest man in the cosmos.''

"Thank you.''

"But you are not quite ugly, either.''

"I am relieved to hear it.''

"Don't be smug.''

"Sorry. I am still stunned by your about-face. Of course, I don't know why I should be. I have never understood women. I don't know any man who does. I still suspect you of some ulterior motive.''

"I just . . . decided to try being grown up.'' She kissed his throat. "I am tired of being called a spoiled brat. What happens if I do this?'' Alvellaina asked as she slid her hands down between his legs.

"For a virgin, you are very knowledgeable.''

"I read a great deal.''

He grasped her and kissed her with all the pent-up frustration of many weeks. She answered in a way that made argument or even talking impossible for some time.

He knew there was some reason he should not sleep, but his eyes refused to stay open. Alvellaina was awake, saying soft words he could not focus on.

Roses and apples. He drifted into a light dream. And saw her again, the beautiful golden-haired woman with the branch of apples in her hand. Her blue gown was bright with stars, and she lifted her branch in benediction.

> *I am the ancient Apple-Queen.*
> *As once I was, so I am now,*
> *Forevermore a hope unseen*
> *Betwixt the blossom and the bough.*

> *Ah, where the river's hidden Gold!*
> *And where the windy grave of Troy?*

Yet come I as I came of old,
From out the heart of Summer's joy.

The words comforted him, and Gilhame passed into dreamless sleep.

Gilhame snapped awake. He was alone in his bed and wondered if he had dreamt the whole encounter. What if it had been a *var* hallucination? No. There was a faint smell of roses on him, and a bright red hair coiled into the black ones on his chest.

Then Alvellaina came into the room, carrying a tray with two mugs on it. She had put on the dressing gown embroidered with obscene dragons. It was too big in the shoulders and almost too long for her, but he thought she looked wonderful.

"I must have fallen asleep," he said as she set the tray down on the bed. "I wasn't supposed to."

"I know. You were disobeying your own orders. But Gurian had already found Gyre's little presents, so I didn't wake you. You snore, you know."

"Do I? One night of passion, and already she's complaining. Presents? Plural?"

"Plural. His troopers 'left' three oxy tanks, only they weren't."

"Is my staff reporting to you now, Admiral?"

She giggled. "I am not trying to wear your hat, *Admiral*. No, a yeoman brought a written report from Vraser and I peeked. Drink your tea."

"When I am old and useless, I shall write my memoirs. All old fighters do. I shall call them, *Under the Pard's Paw:*

My Life and Loves.'' He sipped his drink as ordered. ''The rest of the fleet?''

''Every ship has now been checked—and they all had the same kind of oxygen cylinders in with the battle gear. But Vraser doesn't know how to dispose of the stuff. So, drink up and think.''

''Where is the . . . what did Gyre call it . . . *ingarit*, now?''

''In an unmanned shuttlecraft out in space. Vraser says that was the best he could think of.''

''How long have I been asleep?''

''Oh, only a couple of hours.''

''Do you know, I am very tempted.''

''Tempted to do what? Stop looking at me like a hungry beast and pay attention. Well, don't. I haven't kissed you in hours!'' Alvellaina surrendered with poor grace to the demands of his hands. But she kissed him until they were both breathless. She pulled back. ''You are more easily distracted than I would have believed. Tempted by what?''

''Besides you? Oh, just the notion of sending that shuttlecraft over to Gyre's flag about 1400 today. Then he could do himself in—and my hands would be fairly clean in the matter. But, I can't wait. There are lots of good men who would die with him.'' He gulped the rest of his drink and got out of bed.

Two minutes later he emerged from the bathroom still drying his lean body. Alvellaina had curled herself up on the bed and was finishing her tea. Gilhame pulled on his duty uniform.

He found the report next to the communicator and flipped through it. He sent for Frikard and punched up some data on the computer while he waited.

Alvellaina watched him. ''I take it you have a solution?''

''Yes, I think so. Next time, wake me. I love you to distraction, but you aren't trained to make command decisions.''

''Are you angry with me?''

''No, not really,'' he smiled at her. ''But we'd better have one thing clear before we go any further. The fleet is my prime responsibility. Nothing comes before that. If an alarm comes in the middle of making love, I go. Do you understand that?"

"Yes." It was a sad whisper.

"I know. It is very hard to play second fiddle to a bunch of ships and men you don't even know. I wish that it were otherwise. But these people serving under me deserve my best."

She looked at him very sternly. "It's alright, Gilhame. If you didn't put them first, you really would be a monster. That was my father's mistake. He was willing to kill your men to get at you. I just forgot for a moment who you are—and thought you were like other men."

"Perhaps, someday, I can be. Here's Frikard."

"Oh!" Alvellaina got off the bed, fled into the dining room and returned clutching her uniform. He raised an eyebrow at her. "I like my privacy."

"Good. I do too." Then he left her and went to let Frikard in. "Good morning, Ven. Have you gotten Vraser's report?"

"Yes, sir."

"No need to look so grim. Have two destroyers escort the shuttlecraft. Tell them to drop out at these coordinates. There's a nice red dwarf very close to the exit space. That should cook the little buggers, but if it doesn't, no matter. There's no decent planets around that star, anyhow."

"Very good, sir. However, I just got word from Gretry VI. The whole planet has gone berserk. Someone started tossing nukes. It looks like the same thing which happened at Copia. Except someone kept his head long enough to get word out."

"I see. Any report on the movements of the Nabatean fleet?"

"No, sir. It seems to have vanished."

"The devil you say! Where was it last seen?"

"The Nabatean Fleet left the Telfar system two days ago."

"Telfar?" Gilhame went to the computer and got some coordinates. "Why wasn't I told?"

"We only just found out ourselves."

"Who took over Gyre's patrol on the Nabatean sector while he was at Attira?"

"No one, Gil. He left behind eight of his heavies under Captain Millaise."

"That old bastard? And where are those ships right now?"

"They've vanished too."

A slow smile played over Gilhame's face. "Where were they?"

"They left Gretry twelve hours ago."

"I rarely indulge in vain regrets, but I suspect I should have killed Guthry Gyre years ago. My old martialist at the Academy, Nikodar—remember him?—always said that clemency to your enemies was a fatal form of stupidity."

"That was one of his favorite maxims."

"It was. Well, let's see what this marvel of a machine has made of all this data." The screen of his computer was printing a list of several planets and suns, each followed by a number indicating probabilities in response to Gilhame's query. "Suesoo. Well, that makes sense of a sort. It's just inside the Faldarian sector. It's fairly isolated. Hasn't it been in contention between the Emperor and the Nabateans for quite some time?"

"Yes, Gil. It's more like a Nabatean colony than a Kardusian world."

Gilhame punched another query. "And it will take us fourteen hours to get there from our current position. Let me see. Where would they go?" He jabbed some more buttons. "Of course. I've been away from home so long I've forgotten the sector configurations. Gemna! The crystal supplier for half the Empire. The loss of that would cripple Kardus for years. They won't use that fake *curthel* stuff there. Too destructive. The *curthel* threat is a diversion. I see the pattern now. We have been ordered to Gretry?"

"We have."

"It was so so sweet of Marpessa to tip Guthry's hand. Set course for Gemna, signal the Admiralty that we expect an attack there and get rid of that shuttle."

"What about Admiral Gyre?" Frikard was still worried.

"What about him? He can tag along or not, as he wishes. I'd blast him to bits right now, but I don't have time. We may be able to beat the Nabatean forces to the Gemna system, but not if we stop to slap Gyre's hands."

"Yes, sir."

"Have I ever led you wrong, Ven?"

"Well, not *wrong* precisely."

"But, you are worried."

"If Gyre renegades, we are badly outnumbered, even with the Coalchee."

"That's very true. Well, I shall just have to see if I can't remove his stinger. Set the new course. I'll deal with Gyre."

Alvellaina came out after Frikard left. "I heard what you said. Just what are you going to do?"

"I am not sure. Bluff. Lie. Confuse. Where is the weak point in old Guthry?"

"Would he come here again?"

"It is possible."

"Couldn't you just . . . do what you did to my father? Keep him here?"

"I could, if I knew for certain what his subordinates would do. Your father was a single individual, acting alone in one sense. In fact, I'll never understand why he came on board the *Dragon* at all. Oh, I am sure he intended to be long-gone before the battle began. But I must know if Mafrin and Dunegan are in on this . . . conspiracy. Mafrin's very able, Dunegan is an unknown. I must also assume that sur-Melasar is admiral of the Nabatean fleet. He is more than able; he's brilliant. Is there any more of that tea?"

"Yes. I'll get it. What about . . . using some *var*?"

"Too many variables. I'd only see what I wanted to see. Of course, that might be actual, too, but I'd rather not take the chance. Still, it gives me an idea. Thank you," he said as she handed him a steaming mug. "I must say, you have a certain glow about you this morning."

She smiled at him, then looked a little grave. "It was almost as nice as I had been led to expect."

"Only almost?"

"I was very . . . tense."

"Were you? I did not notice. I shall try to be more aware the next time. Will there be a next time, m'alba?"

"Yes. And stop my-ladying me. You've said 'Alvellaina' in your sleep often enough."

"Dearest Alvellaina! The light of my life! I hope I never give you reason to regret not keeping me at arm's length."

"You will, but I will learn to live with it." She smiled an odd, secret smile which disquieted him. "You don't snore very loudly."

"That's good. I would not want to disturb your beauty-sleep." The communicator beeped. "Answer that, will you? I have a premonition it is dear Guthry." Gilhame strode across the room, opened the niche, tipped some *var* into the crystal cup, poured it back and closed the receptacle. He tousled his hair and rubbed his eyes until they watered.

"Admiral ur Fagon's quarters," Alvellaina said to the little screen.

"Let me speak to him!" It was Gyre, angry by the sound of his voice.

"One moment please. I'll see if he can come." She stepped out of view of the machine and looked at ur Fagon. "What are you up to?" she hissed.

"Do I look smoky enough?"

She suppressed a giggle. "You look as if you've been on a three-day binge."

Gilhame stepped into the communicator's view. "Guthry! Your very good health." He lifted the little cup so that it could be seen. "What can I do you out of?"

"You've changed course. What's going on?"

"Did you get the report? Marpessa talked. The Nabateans are going to attack the Gemna system. We're going to meet them. What the devil is the matter with your communications?"

"What report? All I got was word of an attack on Gretry. Then my communications went crazy. There's a lot of interference. I can barely see you. Are you smoky?"

"Only a little. You're right. There seems to be a lot of interference. You'd better come over here to discuss strate-

gy. Can't work through this fog. I'll show you the report on
Marpessa. I've only scanned it lightly."

Gyre hesitated. He peered at Gilhame, trying to decide
what he should do. "Yes. I guess I'd better. I'll be there
directly."

"'Won't you come into my parlor? said the spider to the
fly!'" Gilhame chuckled. "Commander Frikard!" He said
into the communicator.

There was a brief pause, then Frikard said, "Sir?"

"What have you done to Gyre's communications?"

"Not just his, sir. The entire fleet. It struck me we didn't
want him talking to either the Admiralty or the enemy."

"Clever man. You'll be an admiral yourself, at this rate.
But he'll almost certainly try to get a ship into normal space
at our next pass-point. See if you can prevent that. He's
coming over. I'll see him, but you'd better greet him with
some marines. I don't think he'll come alone. You may use
whatever force seems appropriate."

"With pleasure, sir!"

"Don't enjoy yourself too much," Gilhame said. He
heard Frikard's rare laugh as he turned away from the communicator. "Now we know. Marpessa knew the attack
would be at Gemna."

"What if Gyre didn't take the bait?"

"'The wicked flee where no man pursueth,' my darling. I
took a gamble, though I prefer to think of it as a calculated
risk, based on my knowledge of Gyre's personality. And I
think I won. I suspect he will attempt to declare me inca-
pacitated. Either that or he'll try to board me."

Alvellaina frowned. "But why doesn't he just go along
with you? I mean, there's no hard evidence against him so
far, and he could really make the situation at Gemna rotten
if he just sat still."

"You have a good grasp of the reality of the thing,
dearest. Because he is who he is, and he can't sit still. There
are other reasons. First, he is afraid of me. Second, he
doesn't know how much I know. Third, he is boxed into a
no-win situation. You see, I don't think my participation in
this plan was anticipated. I think Gyre expected to be sent
back to his sector alone. Who could have guessed that the

Admiralty would send two fleets? Unless, of course, they had some inkling of all this. That is possible. They do have good intelligence and good foreseers. And, if one of the latter said, 'Send ur Fagon to the Faldarian sector,' they would."

"How is it a no-win place for him?"

"If he fights with me, the Empress will be very annoyed. And if he fights against me, I'll blow him to spacedust before I go. That's why he put the *ingarit* aboard. As insurance. A poor choice of weapons, actually, after Marpessa exposed it, but Gyre reasons differently than I do. Now, unless you are anxious for another audience with our *choon*-eating friend, I suggest you retire."

"Retire? And miss my chance at his liver?"

"Beautiful, but bloodthirsty."

"Only in certain cases. Why does he hate you?"

"Because I beat him during a war game years ago and cost him a promotion. He's older than I am, and I showed him up."

"But if he's such a poor commander, how did he get where he is?"

"He made a good marriage—she's dead now, poor thing—and then his commanding officer died under curious circumstances. As a matter of record, five of Guthry's superiors have died suddenly. And he is not incompetent. Far from it. When he's thinking, he is very good. But the achievements of others diminish him, somehow; he has always been eaten alive with envy. And, sometimes, he doesn't understand the consequences of his actions. He and Marpessa are well-matched in that."

"What are you going to do with him?"

"That depends on what he chooses to do." Gilhame went to the bathroom and combed his hair back into place. When he came out, Alvellaina offered him more tea. They talked and cuddled for a few minutes.

Finally, the portal buzzer sounded. Gilhame opened the comm and said, "Yes?"

"Gil, here's your package." It was Buschard's voice.

Gilhame opened the portal. Buschard and a pair of bulky security men stood outside with Gyre. The Commander had a long scratch on his face, and it had dripped blood onto his uniform. One sleeve was ripped from its armhole, and the knuckles of Pers's right hand were beginning to swell. The two security men were similarly disheveled.

Gyre's face was badly bruised. His left arm hung at an unnatural angle, and he was white with pain. "You'll pay for this," he said with difficulty.

"He tried to board with a bunch of troopers. I'm afraid hatch four is out of commission for a while. They had cannon. We dumped the survivors. Sixteen of ours dead, fourteen wounded. The only reason Gyre isn't dead is that he was leading from behind." The contempt in Buschard's voice was unmistakable.

"Who broke his arm?"

"One of his own men fell on him in full kit."

"It must have been quite a brawl. I'm sorry I missed it."

"I haven't been in that good a fight in years," Buschard answered grimly.

"Bring him in. Alvellaina, would you call for a Witness, please? And a Healer. You always were a fool, Guthry."

The security men pushed Gyre into a chair and stood behind him. Buschard yanked the torn sleeve off his uniform and wiped at the blood on his face and chest. Alvellaina spoke into the communicator, and Gilhame drank some of his now tepid tea. The only sounds in the room were the woman's voice and Gyre's heavy breathing.

A few minutes later a medic came in through the still open portal, followed rapidly by an Adjudicator's Witness carrying the impedimenta of its office—a recorder and truth-baton. The Witness wore silver robes of no particular cut, and its head was covered with a dark hood whose purpose was to mask identity. Only the shape of the hands gave Gilhame any clue as to the sex of the Witness. They were small for a man.

"Witness, you may be seated," Gilhame said formally. She sat.

The little dumpling of a medic was cleaning the blood from Buschard's face. "Sir?" Her question was almost a whisper.

"What is it?"

"Do you want me to treat . . . to treat the Admiral?" The medic's eyes were round as saucers.

"Yes. I do hope, Guthry, that the trooper's fall didn't damage the sinew. Otherwise, you'll be crippled for the balance of your brief existence. Do you know, only a few minutes ago I was regretting your wife's demise. She is fortunate, actually, to be beyond punishment. Now, why don't you just tell the Witness the names · of your coconspirators in your agreement with the Empress. I would rather not destroy your fleet entirely. It would mean wasting blameless lives."

"You wouldn't!"

"Of course I would," he answered icily. "Besides, this is only to confirm the accuracy of Marpessa's confession. It's a little garbled," he said, picking up Vraser's report on the *ingarit* cylinders and pretending to study it. "I'm afraid that considerable damage was done getting the truth out of her. Why don't you begin with your meeting on Muria?"

"I don't know what you mean," Gyre snarled.

The Witness's baton turned an ugly red. "He's trying to think of something to say, sir," came a quiet voice from behind the hood.

"Of course he is. Be reasonable, Guthry. Those troopers are already waiting for you. Do you really want to meet your whole fleet in the overworld?"

"No." Gyre's eyes were very wide with white. He was not ordinarily a superstitious man, but the pain of defeat was undermining his reason.

"Then, tell the Witness what transpired, and you can go off to a nice bed in the brig."

"Damn you! Damn Marpessa and all women! I was to get the Faldarian sector when Araclyde gained control."

"Control of what, Guthry?"

"The Empire, of course. You know that."

"Of course I do, but the Witness needs it for her records."

"What the devil are the records for? The Emperor and his whole family are dead on Dardanus by now."

Gilhame shook his head and smiled. "I hate to disappoint you, but the Emperor did not go to Dardanus." The baton went red again, and the Witness glanced at him, but Gyre did not notice the change. Gilhame exchanged a glance with Buschard, who left the room quietly.

Gilhame reflected that this was one eventuality he had not even considered, that Araclyde might be the only member of the imperial family still alive. The war that would cause could not bear thinking about. "Now, who knows of your conspiracy?" His voice did not betray either his interest or his impatience.

"The Emperor's alive?"

"Very much so." Gilhame had a sudden burst of that rare foresight which occasionally came to him without *var*. He saw himself bow before the rather ugly but august person of Clyven IV and receive from him the coveted white star given to heroes of the Empire. His tall, red-headed wife, the Empress Urlanda, smiled at Gilhame. Then it was gone.

"Damn! Dunegan knows. Chillworthy, Gorun, Hrunt, Doevidsun, Vingar, ur Selmes, Nispar and Marpessa. That's everyone."

"Not Mafrin?"

"That prig. He couldn't lie to save his skin."

"Villiam?"

"No." The baton turned red again, then back to white.

"Now, Guthry. Is Villiam also in this?"

"I don't know." The baton stayed white.

"Something about his person disturbs you?"

"Yes. I can't quite put a finger on it. I *feel* as if he knows something. I tried to get him transferred when we were at Attira, but . . . my request was ignored."

"Really? Then I would not be surprised if he was in Intelligence. I see by your face that that thought had not crossed what was left of your mind. I think you can put him to sleep now, medic."

"No!" The word was shouted.

Gilhame looked at him, looked at the timepiece on the wall and smiled. It was 1350. "Don't worry. The *ingarit* has been removed long since. Sleep, dear Guthry, and dream of . . . what? I don't think you'll be exiled."

"How did you find out?"

"You really must learn to give the devil his due, Guthry. My spies are everywhere."

The little medic placed her hand on Gyre's forehead, and he closed his eyes. She withdrew her hand and wiped it distastefully on her uniform. "Can I call for a litter, sir?"

"After you wash your hands, certainly. There's a basin in there." He pointed towards his sleeping quarters.

"Yes, sir." She scurried out of the room.

"Do you need me any further, Admiral?" asked the Witness.

"No. You may leave."

"Sir. What he said about the Emperor . . ."

". . . need not worry you."

After a few minutes the room was empty of all but Alvellaina and ur Fagon. Buschard came in, smiling.

"Well, Pers?" Gilhame asked.

"Very, thank you. As is the royal family."

"Of course they are. How could you have doubted it?" Gilhame answered with a grin.

Chapter XVIII

Alvellaina looked at the two men as they sat down across from each other at the table. Buschard was tense, nervous and ready for a fight. Gilhame was relaxed and at ease. It puzzled her somewhat that Gilhame seemed almost disinterested. Then she decided it must be a consistent facet of his personality, remembering that the more sharp-tongued she was, the more urbane were his responses.

"Now, having ascertained that the Emperor and his family are quite well, we had better decide what to do with Gyre's fleet, quickly. Much as I would like to, I cannot call Mafrin on the comm and say, 'I say, old boy, I have your Admiral in the brig for treason.' He'd want to know the details, which I am perfectly willing to share with him, but _not_ with any renegade officers. And, while I believe that Gyre told me all he knew, conspiracies have a terrible tendency to grow. It is a shame that the comm is not a more discreet device."

"But, Gilhame, he tried to board your ship and take over. Isn't that enough?" Alvellaina asked.

"If there were not seven officers who were his co-conspirators—certainly. They are what's bothering me. Ah, that must be the information I wanted." He got up and took the sheets the computer was producing.

"Now, let's see what we are up against. Damn. I said Gyre wasn't incompetent—and I was right. Technically speaking, these seven men could manipulate that fleet without Gyre's presence. Even without Marpessa to back him up, Gyre still has an effective weapon. Except for Nispar, I don't know any of these men personally, but if Nispar is typical, they'll fight alone.

"Ummm. They will have to be disarmed before we get to Gemna. They are surely becoming a little uneasy right now. We altered course three quarters of an hour ago. Right on cue. Anyone want to make a wager this is Mafrin calling to speak to Gyre?" he finished, as the comm sounded.

Alvellaina rose to answer it. "Admiral ur Fagon's quarters."

"Greetings, Halba Krispin. Could I speak to Admiral Gyre? There seems to be some disagreement . . . I mean, there's some confusion . . . well, er, could you break in on . . . I mean, is he in conference with Admiral ur Fagon?" It was Mafrin, although Alvellaina wondered if there wasn't someone out of her view prompting the man.

"I'd love to, Commander, but he's sound asleep," she answered in a low, husky voice.

"Asleep?"

Gilhame was standing beside her, but out of view, one eyebrow arched. He nodded to her and hissed, "Go on. You're doing fine. Just see if you can get him over here."

Alvellaina took a deep breath and said to Mafrin, "He came in to speak to the Admiral, chewing a wad of that dreadful stuff he likes. You know, that *choon*?" She made a face. "And bang, three minutes later he was sound asleep. The medic wondered if he could have gotten hold of something that wasn't quite pure, you see, and says Gyre should sleep it off.

"It's all so upsetting. And embarrassing. He may sleep through everything. Do you think you could send someone . . . no, that's not a good idea, is it? Look, do you think you and Commander Villiam could come over, sort of quietly, and take him back? No one would question your presence here under the circumstances, and you could save Admiral Gyre a lot of embarrassment." She smiled at Mafrin, annoyed with herself for leading the rather nice man astray, angry with herself for letting Gilhame use her to further his own ends but delighted with her first major lie. "Then Admiral ur Fagon can bring you up-to-date on the situation—which is what he was doing when Gyre fell asleep."

"I see. Yes, you're right. I'll be there shortly."

"The fewer people know about this, the better."

"True, true. Thank you, Halba Krispin." The comm went dark.

Gilhame smiled down at her and shook his head. "Beautiful, my darling. Just beautiful. Why have you never used that voice on me?"

Alvellaina drew herself up with dignity, aware of Buschard's interested gaze. "I didn't wish to arouse your beast, sir."

"But you don't mind arousing Mafrin's? My thousand-planet woman! Always keeps me in my place. Now, if Mafrin doesn't say anything to Dunegan, we may just have a chance to squeak out of this with a minimum of casualties. I think we want the Witness back. Could you next time, give me just a little warning of what you are going to do, m'alba?"

"Why should I? You never reveal your plans to me."

"I can always depend on you to depress my pretensions. Tell me, Pers, does Derissa fight you every step of the way?"

Buschard, who had been watching them in his quiet, thoughtful way, shook his head. "We have never even exchanged a harsh word."

"Strange. I assumed that all redheads were contentious. Sounds dull," Gilhame continued. He looked at Buschard's reddening face. "No, you probably like it all smooth, don't you, Pers? Excuse me." He went over to the comm and talked briefly into it. "Now, if our guests will refrain from bringing in any more troopers," he said as he came back, "we can get onto the real problem. These encounters with Gyre's folk are becoming quite tedious. Relax, Pers. I have the situation as well in hand as it can be."

By the time Commanders Mafrin and Villiam arrived several minutes later, the Witness was back. She had her little recorder in front of her and was playing back the tape.

Mafrin and Villiam arrived alone, the former fidgeting with nervousness, the latter cool.

"Where is Admiral Gyre?" Mafrin asked, looking around.

"Sit down, won't you, gentlemen? There's something I think you should hear. Witness."

"Yes, sir." The voice was muffled by the hood.

"Would you be so kind as to play the tape?"

He got a nod in reply. She fiddled with her machine, adjusting the sound levels.

"What is all this?" Mafrin asked.

"Shh." said Villiam. He folded his hands in front of him on the table and listened to the tape without expression. Then he looked at the Witness. "Can you testify that this is a true and accurate record, Witness?"

"Yes, sir." The Witness stirred uneasily. "Except for the portions where Admiral ur Fagon lied. But, since he was the questioner, not the respondent . . ." she trailed off nervously, torn between her duty to her commanding officer and her duty to the Adjudicator's Tribunal.

Gilhame gave her a smile. "It is not easy to serve two masters, Witness. You are quite correct to tell Commander Villiam that I was—what? No matter. I won't make any bones about it. I made Admiral Gyre think I knew more than I did. Have you made a transcript yet?"

"No, sir."

"Be sure you mark the portions where the baton showed I was lying. The Adjudicator's office likes accurate records. If I go on at my present rate, however, my legal cases will fill a warehouse by the time I die. Now, Commander Villiam, you are either with Admiralty Intelligence or working directly for the Empress as a watchdog for Gyre."

"Yes."

"I don't think we have time for games, Villiam."

"True. And my devotion to the Emperor is as great as your own."

"I presume, then, that you knew about this conspiracy."

"Oh, yes."

"And did nothing about it?"

"My ways are not your ways, ur Fagon. It had to be allowed to run its course."

"Why?"

"Araclyde, Admiral, must be stopped in a way that is final and effective. She was becoming a greater and greater threat to the Empire. There have been seven attempts on Clyven's life in the past year, four of which we can lay at her door."

"Then why, if I may ask, didn't you just remove her? I understand your people are very good at that."

"There are reasons. In any case, it was decided that discredit was a better political expedient than death."

Gilhame looked at Villiam with distate. "I see. What, then, would you have me do—let the Nabatean fleet take Gemna?"

"Of course not, ur Fagon. You weren't sent on this mission for your looks. You are to take command of both fleets when we come out into normal space."

"And what about the renegades who are in charge of key ships in Gyre's fleet?"

"I'll take care of them," Villiam answered.

Gilhame made a faint moue with his thin lips, then shrugged. "As you wish. Is there anything else? I have some work to do before we get to Gemna."

When they left a few minutes later, Mafrin was still upset and Villiam had no expression at all. Gilhame paced the length of the room, striking his right fist into his left hand. Alvellaina watched him tensely, but Buschard was unmoved. The Witness seemed to be frozen in her seat.

Finally, Gilhame picked up a half-empty tea mug and smashed it against the far wall. It broke, pouring the green liquid onto the wall and floor.

"Damn butcher! Filthy assassin! Pers, how many run-ins have we had with these cloak-and-dagger politicians?"

"Six, maybe seven. Yes, this is the seventh," Buschard answered thoughtfully.

"And what would you estimate was the number of lives lost through their machinations?"

"Pretty high. If you throw in the population on Gretry— about eighty million."

"Eighty million people die for political expediency. What a waste! What a desolation!" He took a deep breath. "I'll see you on the bridge later." Gilhame opened the portal and vanished.

"Buschard, what was all that?" Alvellaina asked. "Witness, I think you can go now."

"Yes, halba."

"Well, Buschard?" She studied him while she waited for an answer. Even tired and disheveled, he was a good-looking man. His light-blond hair fell onto his brow, and his generous mouth was drawn down at the corners.

"Oh, it's all of a piece with what happened between him and your father. Even at the Academy, the only thing that made him really angry, hot angry, was the useless spending of life. He's a fighter, not some pacifist, but if you read his stats, you'll find he has a fine record for keeping his men alive and his equipment intact. It's one of the reasons men are eager to serve under him.

"You see, he is aware that if he hadn't figured out what Gyre was about, that bastard Villiam would have let him go renegade at Gemna or Gretry or who-knows-where, just to get enough evidence on Araclyde to nail her hide to the wall. Gil doesn't like that—thinks it's a dishonest way to fight." He smiled and stood up. "He'll go down to the 'farm,' weed a tank or two, to the great distress of the Hydroponics staff, and come back his old sardonic self. Don't worry." He patted her on the shoulder as he got up, gave her a light kiss on the cheek and left.

Alvellaina stared at the portal after he had gone, frowning. Then she got herself another cup of tea and waited for the next development.

_____ *Chapter XIX*

Gilhame sat upon his high seat on the bridge, running data on his screen at top speed. He had a headset on, and he murmured continuously into the mouthpiece. People scurried past him or stood at their stations. A tiny portion of his mind noted the curious similarity between the silent but continuous movement around him and some fantastic undersea panorama. Then he returned his full attention to the probable tactics of the Nabatean fleet.

Finally he stopped, removed the headset and looked around. A pretty yeoman darted forward with a tray. She handed him a cup of hot liquid. "Thank you," he said absently.

Commander Frikard came up as he was sipping what appeared to be soup. "Well," Gilhame asked, "are we going to get there first, or will they?"

"We will, sir, but not by much. And, it looks like there are six dreadnought-class ships in addition to the *Star of Nabat,* their flagship."

"Six, hmm? Don't look so glum. A dreadnought is a terrific ship if you're blasting away space rabble, but if maneuvers like a beached whale. Besides, if our records of their staff are accurate, they don't have a single officer capable of managing one of those tubs effectively. Ven, I sometimes get the impression that you derive some obscure pleasure from the threat of disaster. It makes me glad it is such a frequent thing in our lives together. So, seven dreadnoughts, and Araclyde will probably be on the *Star*."

"Do you think she is actually present?"

"The computer does. Eighty-seven percent probability. I suppose I should speak to Commander Villiam, though if the truth be told, I'd rather talk to a *var*-leech." He activated the comm, and a few seconds later they were linking him to the intelligence man.

Gilhame looked at Villiam's thin face and took a deep breath. "Commander," he began without ceremony, "it is highly probable that the Empress is aboard the *Star of Nabat*. Do you have a preference as to her disposition—dead or alive?"

"Of course I don't want her killed. She must be taken! My lord, man, don't you comprehend the situation?"

"Commander, I am a simple fighting man. I have no wish to understand the situations you politicians create for whatever reasons. You want the Empress alive, and I'll do my best."

"You don't like me, do you, ur Fagon?"

"Like you? Commander, my feelings are not relevant. But I expect you have quite a welcoming committee in the overworld, Commander, from Copia and Gretry. I have my own, of course, but every man who has died serving with me knew why he died. I've never sacrificed the population of an entire world to capture one woman—whatever her political importance."

"There are factors in the matter which . . ."

". . . have been deliberately withheld from me throughout the entire venture. I am fully cognizant of *that*, Villiam. As I said, I'm a simple man. I go where I am told and destroy the Emperor's enemies. You, on the other hand, have no compunctions about removing anyone and anything to achieve whatever ends you feel necessary. The terms 'friend' and 'foe' have no meaning for you, do they? Ah, well, I don't suppose it will matter in a century or two, not one bit. Just do me a favor, will you? After this is all over, if we ever meet socially, pretend you don't know me. I am getting rather fussy about the company I keep." He cut the link and watched Commander Villiam's startled face vanish.

The screen lit up almost immediately with technical information about the Nabatean fleet. He wondered if the population on Gemna had already been infected with the *ingarit*. He also wondered where those eight ships which Gyre had left on patrol had gone off to. He put his headset back on and started running the data as fast as he could. Finally, he felt he had as clear a picture of what he would find at Gemna as could be constructed by the computer.

He and Frikard conferred, as they had done many times before, on the positioning of the fleet. Gilhame was still nagged by the eight unaccounted-for cruisers. There was no indication of them on any of the inner-space tracks leading to Gemna. Were they already there?

Gilhame suddenly asked, "How accurately can we calculate where the Nabatean fleet will emerge from inner space?"

Frikard shrugged. "Within point-oh-one percent."

"And how well can we spot the *Star of Nabat*?"

"In inner space?"

"Yes."

"I suppose we can differentiate it from the other dreadnought-class ships by its position in the line. The Nabateans are pretty conservative in their formations."

"What do you think? Can we use the trick we used on E-varit against the *Star*—just as they emerge?"

"I don't know. Cruisers aren't going to be much use against a dreadnought."

"How about before they come out?"

"In inner-space?"

"Yes."

"Impossible. It's never been done."

"Now, Ven. Impossible? The only thing which functions in I-S besides the drive units is tractor beams, right?"

"Uh huh."

"Well?"

"That's insane!"

"Probably. But if we can take out the *Star*, we may be able to save a great deal of trouble."

"Yes, sir." Frikard sounded resigned.

"Otherwise, it's all hacking and hewing, with no science in it."

Frikard gave a slow grin. "Quite so, sir." The previous year, ur Fagon had been asked to do some lecturing for the Academy on the subject of space warfare. He had done so, but he had not given the Academy either what it had expected or wanted. For ur Fagon had studied the aesthetics of ten famous space battles, had indicated to the students how an intuitive grasp of the dynamics of a situation could save lives and win battles and had played general mischief with the orthodox approaches to the subject. Frikard knew, after his years with ur Fagon, that the man saw patterns in battle formations which were not immediately apparent to others, and did not believe that they were invisible to anyone but himself. So, Frikard knew that ur Fagon's desire to capture the dreadnought *Star of Nabat* indicated neither fear nor laziness on his admiral's part, but was rather an admission that he had not yet visualized a pattern. Seizing the *Star* was the most direct way to shorten the battle and save lives. He also knew that mere 'hacking and hewing' offended his superior's sensibilities.

"The Gemna system in ten minutes, sir," said one of the helmsmen.

Gilhame punched some buttons and stared at the screen beside him. Frikard, looking over his shoulder, could see it was a schematic of the inner-space avenues leading to the Gemna system. After a moment, Gilhame said, "Tell me, Frikard, how much does it cost to reconstruct the fabric of space once it is disrupted?"

"About six million talers, sir."

"That much? That's more than some planet's gross product in a century."

"It is."

"Still, it's cheap compared with the loss of men and materials. What did Valdar Straits cost, exclusive of recompense?"

"About two million."

"And that was only because we got E-varit's flagship and stopped the battle." He scratched his head thoughtfully. "I still feel as if a critical piece of information is unknown to me. I wish I knew precisely what that bastard Villiam was up to. There are too many variables here to suit me." He whistled tunelessly for a minute.

Then he said. "Alright, Frikard. Get a warp-bomb squadron ready. I want the point of emergence that the *Nabat* will use mined as soon as we are out in normal space. And pray we have time. And pray Villiam knows what he is doing and doesn't have his cranium inserted rectally, as I suspect he does. This one is not going to be shooting fish in a barrel."

"Sir, what about using 'screamers'?"

"The noise weapons we used on the gamester machine! We don't have time to make any."

"We have plenty. Morshull got fascinated by the notion and has been playing with them ever since."

"Has he? It might just do the trick. How clever of you to think of it, Ven. What a way to even our odds! If Morshull . . ."

"He has modified the original device so that he can change the tone to disrupt the molecular structure of almost anything."

"Including flesh, no doubt. And to think, it all came out of the Elves' Parade. What a misuse of music. Still, beggars can't be choosers, can they? Alright, get some ready. We'll mine the exit point too. I'd rather trap a good portion of the Nabatean fleet where they can't get to us than try to take the whole by force."

He activated his headset and began giving orders. He was concentrating on this when the comm flashed. He finished the section of deployment he was working on and then opened the link.

The less-than-lovely features of Captain Chillworthy of the battle cruiser *Meldebone* of Gyre's fleet greeted him. Gilhame knew him from the profiles he had gotten on the conspirators hours earlier, but he decided to feign ignorance. Section captains were not supposed to interrupt Admirals.

"What the devil is the meaning of this insubordination?" he roared at the screen, reflecting that there was some advantage to having the reputation of a son-of-a-demon. "Who are you?"

"Chillworthy of the *Meldebone*, Admiral. What have you done with Admiral Gyre?"

"Done? I haven't done anything with the bugger. He's asleep—or he was the last time I looked. Get off this line. I'm busy. I don't have time to discuss Gyre's drug habits. Cosmos! What passes for discipline in your fleet would make a bird puke." Villiam was supposed to be taking care of the renegades. Why hasn't he?"

"I don't believe you."

"I don't give a damn what you believe." Gilhame reached forward to press the cutoff switch, and then he saw it. A tiny golden dart flew up behind Chillworthy's head, paused for a moment, then touched the man's skull. The screen was filled with brains and blood as Chillworthy's head exploded.

Gilhame hoped that Villiam survived this battle so that he could tell the man what a contemptible creature he was. There was something repellent to Gilhame about a weapon that could be activated anytime, anywhere, to find and kill an individual so that there were not enough pieces left to identify the body. The miniature antipersonnel mines were rarely used, but Gilhame regarded it as typical of a man of Villiam's stamp. He wondered where in the ship Villiam had planted one with *his* life-pattern on it, and whether he still radiated the same rhythm as the original Gilhame had. He did not doubt that Villiam had planned his death, just to cover the eventuality that he and Gyre might reach some partnership. The Commander was that kind of double-think, double-deal fellow.

They emerged into normal space with the usual problems of ships barely moving out of the way in time for the ships behind them. Ur Fagon's fleet was well-drilled and made the transition moderately well, but there were still close calls. Gyre's fleet was not only not as well-disciplined, it was suffering from the indecision of numerous officers who had not only lost their admiral, but had seen their commanding officers exploded in front of them.

Once in normal space, ur Fagon's ships went as quickly as possible to their positions, as did some of Gyre's forces. But many of Gyre's ships veered away from the main fleet, while others turned to offer battle to the still emerging ships behind them. There was no time when a ship was more vulnerable than when she was emerging into normal space.

"Some of Gyre's ships appear to be revolting, sir," Frikard reported.

"*All* of Guthry's ships are revolting, Ven; some are currently mutinying. And Villiam was so certain he had the matter well-in-hand. He really doesn't understand us, you know."

"Yes, sir."

"Get the portal at I-S 476 GN mined and our ships into position, and don't worry about anything else. Let Villiam handle what he can. He made the mess, let him clean it up. But, anything gets in *our* way, destroy it. I don't have time for finicking niceties on this one. And where the devil are those eight cruisers from Gretry? I don't like it that we haven't found a trace of them yet."

Gilhame began reassessing the deployment of his fleet. He had presumed that some of Gyre's people would turn on him, so he had not given them a major role in his plans. He did not believe that the conspiracy had stopped at the top level or that Gyre had any notion of what his underlings had done on their own. But Gilhame did not want to find himself fighting both the *Nabat and* Gyre's people.

After several minutes, he was satisfied that he had as good a grasp of what was happening to the two portions of the Kardusian forces as he could with a rapidly changing situation. He opened the comm, tuned it to the fleet-wide frequency and began to speak. "This is a general order to the Eighth and Twelfth Fleets from Admiral Gilhame ur Fagon. Any ship not proceeding to its assigned position will be assumed to be in mutiny and will be destroyed." He watched his words print themselves out on his screen as well as echo over the sound system. Then he waited.

It was not quite an empty threat. It was true he did not have the time to indulge in a fight with his own forces. It was also true that if he attempted to meet the *Nabat* with hostile ships behind him, he might as well surrender now.

Except that ur Fagon never surrendered. He knew that his very reputation would be a deciding factor on some of the revolting ships. He sensed that fear of him would influence the actions of many, and he almost pitied the officer who had to make the choice between Gyre's conspiracy and ur Fagon's ire. He lacked the time to fully savor the dilemma, so he went back to gathering information and giving orders.

His own ships were scooting across the edge of the Gemna system at their best speed. Some of the smaller vessels had already reached their positions, and the contingent which was to mine the 'exit' through which the *Nabat* would arrive was already at work. If only the enemy did not arrive early, it might just work!

Several of the mutinying ships fell into line almost immediately. A little destroyer winked out of existence, meaning that someone had activated the inner-space drive in normal space. But there was still enormous confusion in Gyre's fleet when Gilhame got another priority-one call on his comm.

Gilhame sighed, completed the orders he was giving and opened the comm-link. Commander Villiam's cheerless countenance greeted him as the screen focused. Gilhame could see that there was blood on his face and that the man held himself in an awkward manner.

"You've got to stop this!" the man croaked. Gilhame could hear the faint sizzling of a port-a-cannon and various shouts behind Villiam.

"Stop what, Commander?"

"Dunegan's men are taking over this ship."

"I'm sorry, Commander, but that's your problem. I have to catch an empress, remember? More conspirators than you knew about?"

"Yes. The missile . . . I didn't get Dunegan!"

"I know all about your nasty little arrows, Villiam. I watched Chillworthy come to pieces in the middle of a sentence. I hope you didn't plant one with my pattern on it, because if you did, I'll stuff it up your rectum. Where's Mafrin?"

"Here."

"Let me speak to him."

"Why?"

"Indulge my whim, Commander. Mafrin knows that ship better than you do."

Mafrin's face appeared. He appeared undamaged and unruffled. Gilhame said, "Have you ever noticed how much more trouble we get into *with* Admiralty intelligence than without it? What happened?"

"I am not entirely certain, sir. But Captain Dunegan and some of our troopers are trying to regain control of the ship."

"What is your status?"

"We are on the bridge with about forty troopers. Commander Villiam is hurt—he caught a blast in the lower back. I think the spine is damaged. But the rest of us . . ."

"I see. It seems I will have to forego the flogging I had in mind for Villiam after this is over. Did Gyre install those new sleep units the Admiralty ordered about six months ago?" He was referring to hypnotic generators which could cause deep sleep.

"He did."

"Use them."

"On the whole ship?"

"Yes. I'll send a boarding party over in a bit. 'Good night, sweet prince. And clouds of angels . . .'"

"What?"

"Nighty-night, Commander."

Mafrin frowned, sighed, shrugged his shoulders. "Yes, sir."

Gilhame watched the screen fade. "Damn self-righteous asshole," he said, thinking of Villiam. Then he used his headset again. "Get a boarding party over to the *Buskin* in about thirty minutes. Make sure they are equipped with anti-sleep plugs and helms," he told the duty officer. Sleep. "To sleep, perchance to dream." To Dream? "We are such stuff as dreams are made of." Bloody nightmare is more like it. 'What a weapon, what a gentle, kind and tender weapon,' he thought, remembering the Barren Plain.

He listened to reports on his headset and watched the display screen. Most of his own fleet was in their proper places. About half of Gyre's people were as well. The balance of the Eighth Fleet was either hanging in space or was moving away. Another ship flashed out, a light cruiser this time, and he tried not to mourn for the innocents caught in the plots of the conspirators.

The Battle of Gemna took much less time to fight than to prepare for. The Nabatean ships began emerging from the 'exit' almost as soon as ur Fagon's ships were in place, but since their orders were to hold off for the time being, they essentially ignored the enemy.

Two squadrons of Nabatean fighters came through first and dashed towards Gilhame's ships. They were followed by several destroyers. Ur Fagon's ships retreated in formation, keeping just out of effective combat range. The first dreadnought with its escort of cruisers emerged.

The battle began then, but only sporadically. Ur Fagon continued his apparent withdrawal until three of the huge Nabatean ships were out. Finally the *Star of Nabat* emerged. He gave his orders and something very like a small nova disrupted the fiber of space at the terminus of the inner-space highway.

As he had expected, the shockwaves from the explosion damaged a good part of the *Star's* escort. The flagship itself seemed to stagger, then falter. A dozen or so fighters swept in, making what appeared to be a futile sortie, but actually dropping a scatter of Morshull's "screamers." Buschard led eight cruisers to encircle the floundering vessel. They approached cautiously, for the *Star* still had a bit of fight, but she started to break up before they got close enough to use their tractor beams. There was some damage to Gilhame's ships, but less than might have been expected. About forty minutes after she had entered the Gemna system, the *Star of Nabat*—or rather, her component pieces—surrendered.

Gilhame opened his comm screen and found Buschard smiling at him. "The *Star of Nabat* is taken, sir," he said formally.

"Very good. Is Her Majesty aboard?"

"Yes, sir! We have the Empress very much in hand."

"How is she?"

"Mad as a wet pard."

"Be careful. She could have a few tricks left in her yet."

"I am always careful, Gil." They both laughed.

The news of the capture of the Nabatean flagship was broadcast. The rest of that fleet surrendered with the exception of one dreadnought and its accompanying ships. That one fought on stubbornly until it was almost blasted to pieces.

Gilhame listened to the damage-and-loss reports on his headset. "This is going to cost the Empress a pretty penny," he said to himself.

_____ *Chapter XX*

Four weeks later Gilhame ur Fagon led his fleet to the planet of the Emperor's summer home, Kardisia, to await his monarch's pleasure. They took up their positions and sat. A week went by, and they still sat.

Gilhame paced around the living room of his quarters, sensing that the day held more for him than just the reward he had foreseen before the Battle of Gemna. There had been other times in the life of the "other" Gilhame ur Fagon when he had known he was at a crisis point, and he felt his body recalling those days.

Alvellaina came through the portal, her arms filled with black garments. She looked different to him today, softer, if that was possible. "What should I wear to court?" she asked, putting the clothes on the table and holding one garment against her body.

"How the devil should I know?" he snapped.

"It has to be black. I know that. Do you like this?"

"I'm sure it's very pretty, but I suspect that you would be a little . . . over-exposed. What have you done to yourself?"

"Done?" She gazed at him wide-eyed.

"I can't put my finger on it. There's something . . ."

"I told him you'd notice," she answered inconsequentially as she brushed her red hair back from her shoulders.

She took up another dress. "This one?"

"You told *who* I'd notice *what*?" he replied, ignoring her question.

"Vraser."

"And what interesting medical phenomenon have I noticed?"

"You're in such a foul mood, I don't want to tell you."

"Am I? I suppose I am. Sorry, my dearest. Put that rag down and let me hold you. You are the best cure I know."

"Rag? I spent hours designing it." She dropped the gown and put her arms around him.

Gilhame kissed her on the mouth and stroked her hair. "You don't even feel the same," he said slowly as he drew his mouth away. "Are you ill, my darling?"

"I have never been more well in my life."

"Then, what is it?"

"If you *must* know, well . . . I . . . that is . . . I . . . promise you won't be angry?"

"I won't promise anything, but, unless you've put horns on me, I won't be angry."

"Horns?"

"Buschard."

"Pers?"

"Yes, Pers. Do you like him?"

"Oh, he's nice enough, I suppose, but he's too bland for my taste. Vraser is more to my liking, if I were shopping for a new love, which I am not."

"Vraser?"

"I prefer men who speak their own minds. No, I have not cuckolded you. Do you fear it so much?"

"I must. You are so very dear to me, Alvellaina."

"You must have a very low opinion of my feelings if you think I would ever even look at another man." Her cheeks were flushed with anger and her eyes glittered with unshed tears.

"No, just a low opinion of my own worth as a lover."

"You are an ass."

"Am I?"

"Yes. If it did not make me furious, I should be vastly

elated to have reduced the Emperor's most valuable admiral to the status of a suppliant. I love you, Gilhame ur Fagon. I have committed my life to you, my loyalties to you. I will follow you into exile or to the end of the cosmos. You are all that I will ever love. I swear it. But don't you ever dare doubt me, or I'll cut your heart out. Do you understand?" She brought her fist down on his sternum as she spoke.

"No, I don't understand at all. But I believe you—and that is all that matters. So, finally, we are allies. I am not sure I will ever get used to that. My darling, if I could squeeze the universe into a handful, I would and give it to you to wear in your hair."

"You are very silly, and terribly romantic. Now, what should I wear? Let me go."

"Not until you tell me what you are not telling me."

She blushed and lowered her eyes. "Alright. In about eight-and-a-half months, there will be a little ur Fagon."

Gilhame ignored the cold hand that seemed to grip his heart, and kissed her. The wonderful, sturdy boy and the horrible white light from his nightmare haunted him, but he forced himself to think fiercely of something else. He did not want Alvellaina picking up the memory of that dream. "My dearest," he whispered.

"Are you angry?"

"Of course not. It will just take me a little while to become accustomed to the idea, that's all. Well, it certainly agrees with you. I never thought you could be more beautiful, but you are." He kissed her again.

The comm beeped and interrupted them. Gilhame released her reluctantly and went to answer it. He left the visual off.

"Ur Fagon here."

"Admiral, the Emperor's King-at-Arms is just arriving."

"Good grief. I hardly expected that. Have him brought . . . or do I come to him? Damn! I don't know the protocol."

He heard the comm speaker, a female by the voice, give a sharp titter. He grinned. The Great Gilhame ur Fagon, caught with his pants down. Then he said, "Would you like to accompany me into the Presence, young woman?"

"No, sir!" An audience with the Emperor was not a pleasure, and were it not for the honor of the thing, anyone in his right mind avoided it.

"Then get me . . . Lieutenant Vaverly. That's the name which springs to mind when I think of Imperial protocol. On the double, and delay the herald."

"Right away, sir."

He waited, glaring at the screen. "A fine mess. The Dardanus King-at-Arms is coming on board and I feel like an eight-year-old," he muttered to Alvellaina. She had come up beside him and slipped her arm through his.

"Are you upset about . . . the baby?"

"No, not really. I just never realized how frightening close contact with his Imperial Majesty could be." He was also grateful for the distraction. Alvellaina was too ethical to "peek" and would read his agitation as "court jitters," he hoped.

"You? Frightened?"

"Nervous, at the very least."

She giggled.

"Vaverly here, sir." It was a woman's voice.

Gilhame opened the viewscreen and looked at a gray-haired woman in her early forties. He knew her, as he knew all his people by now, from her records, but they had rarely met. "The Imperial Herald is coming on board—is already on board, most likely. Do I go to him or does he come to me?"

"He will come to you."

"Fine. Get into your dress kit and get yourself to my quarters on the double."

"Yes, sir."

"Do you know, dearest," he said as he turned off the screen, "I don't think I like the exalted circles I am about to move in."

"You should have thought of that before you became a hero."

"That is not very comforting."

"I still don't know what to wear."

"The simplest thing you have, Lady Vanity."

"That's easy for you to say. You can wear your uniform."

He walked to the table, examined the gowns and handed one to her. "Here, wear this one."

"Yes, sir!" She giggled and went to her quarters.

Gilhame stood in the living room for a moment. Then he went to dress. As he changed his uniform and combed his hair, he considered the meaning of the presence of the Imperial Herald. It might mean nothing, but it sent little prickles up the back of his neck that were his early warnings of crisis. He knew enough about protocol to realize that generals and admirals were not ordinarily honored in this way.

He was still puzzling over the matter when the portal buzzer sounded. As he went to answer it, the words "too strong" spoken in a thready voice came into his mind. He stopped in midstride. He stood for several seconds, considering the words, before he opened the portal.

It was Lieutenant Vaverly. She was a raw-boned woman, almost as tall as he was, with steel-gray hair coiled in a knot on top of her head. Her gray eyes on either side of a prominent nose stared directly into his. That surprised him. Very few people looked him in the eye.

"Thank you for coming so quickly," he said. He looked at her. Her white dress uniform with its black piping had little decoration on it and was entirely devoid of the dragon embellishments that adorned the uniforms of the rest of his people.

"Certainly, Admiral." She had a deep voice which was very pleasant.

"Now, is there any reason—protocolwise—for the King-at-Arms to call on me?"

"No, there is no precedent, to my knowledge. I would assume the matter is diplomatic. Il-sabayoo, the Dardanus Herald, is a very old man. Ordinarily, he does not interface with *anyone* outside the Imperial household."

"How old?"

"He served the first Clyven."

"Then, he must be over two hundred."

"Quite so, sir."

The silence which followed her reply seemed to stretch on and on. Finally, Gilhame asked, "Do I offer him refreshment?"

"You may, sir. He is said to have a fondness for Cabellian wine. Does the Admiral know that he will not sit in the presence of the King-at-Arms unless invited to do so?"

"The Admiral does not. But that, of course, is quite consistent with my dealings with other offices of the Imperium. I find I am quite unprepared to move in these rarefied atmospheres. Sometimes I wish I were still sleeping on a platform in a tree on Faldar. Life was much less complicated then." As he spoke he went to the refreshment cabinet and opened it. "No Cabellian, I'm afraid. Rurian?"

"Always a good choice, Admiral."

He took a small white cloth, a single glass and an unopened jar of wine to the table and put them at his place, at the head, in front of the dragon-carved chair. Gilhame smoothed the cloth, then stepped back and looked at his handiwork. "It looks a little bare," he said casually. "I wish there had been some warning. We've been sitting here a week without a word, and all of a sudden this visit."

"There never is."

"I wonder what he wants? Any educated guesses, Vaverly?"

"The Emperor prefers his . . . subjects to have families, Admiral."

Gilhame stared at her. He remembered the Imperial Adjudicator's lecture on family at the trial of Alvellaina's father. Of course, his sister-son, Hamecor, was family, if one could find him. The Faldar were notoriously difficult on the actuality of any individual. Their usual response to the question of locality was, "Somewhere" or "Around."

Of course, too, as a bachelor, he was less governable than a family man. That, at least, was the theory.

Alvellaina came in, neatly dressed in her green-and-silver uniform. She had a clear glass vase with a single blue flower in it. This she set on the table. She looked Gilhame and Vaverly and asked, "Now what's the matter?"

Gilhame crossed to her and took her hand. He looked down at her for a long moment, then said quietly, "Lieutenant Vaverly has just reminded me of my . . . un-domesticated status. Tell me, m'alba, do you think, under the circumstances, you could bring yourself to marry me?"

Alvellaina looked at him, then glared. "That is the most offhand proposal I have ever . . . well, not heard! I've never heard a proposal before. But I've never even read anything so clumsy. I don't know. I'll think about it."

"I am not sure you have time to do so, my darling."

"Why? Because of the baby?"

"No. Because of his Imperial Majesty's policies. Come, say you will marry me. A short contract, if you like. A year and a day?"

"Policies? I really don't understand all this. What does the Emperor have to do with us?"

"Everything. Just say yes, and let Lieutenant Vaverly be our witness. I'll explain everything later. Otherwise, I'll appropriate one of your sisters for the thing."

"Alright. Yes. You would, wouldn't you? Armanda or Derissa?"

"When I can have you? Certainly not." He raised his voice. "Lieutenant Vaverly, we wish you to bear witness to a commitment as a legal binding of two persons."

The protocol officer looked startled. "Is this your wish, halba?"

"Yes," Alvellaina said in a dull voice.

"Then I witness this binding." She pulled out her recorder and spoke into it.

"I wanted . . . a real ceremony," Alvellaina said in a stifled voice.

"Don't cry, my darling. You shall have anything you want. Poor Alvellaina. Don't look quite so downcast, please. It is not the end of the world. You shall have the biggest wedding the cosmos has ever seen. *After* the herald has come and gone."

"I wish I knew what was going on."

"There may have been no need for this hasty business, Alvellaina, but you know that I would not want to lose you. I would not want anything to come between us. Trust me. Have I ever led you wrong?"

"Come between us? Led me wrong? That's what you always say to your officers just before you make the fleet do something crazy."

"You know me too well, dearest."

"Sometimes. And sometimes I don't know you at all. Tell me, did I just marry the admiral or the man?"

"For you, I am only a man."

The portal sounded. Alvellaina slipped out of Gilhame's embrace and answered it. The door hissed open, and Frikard ushered a party of five into the room.

A young woman in the livery of a heraldic page entered first. Behind her came fan Talba, the Imperial Adjudicator, looking just as nondescript as he had two months earlier. He was followed by a woman Gilhame recognized as the Imperial Court Justice, fan Talba's superior, and the principal judicial officer of the state.

Then the Dardanus King-at-Arms, Horabe Il-sabayoo, leaning on the arm of a pursuivant, entered. He was indeed a very old man, his face seamed with lines, his hair sparse and white, his back bent with years. But his blue eyes were lively with intelligence as he swept the room with a glance.

Gilhame, Alvellaina and Vaverly put their right hands across their hearts and bowed from the waist. The room was silent as the old man shuffled to the chair at the head of the table.

He sighed as he settled down, plucking at the folds of his robe. Then he stared at his audience. "So, you are Admiral ur Fagon," he said in a thready voice.

Gilhame recognized the voice as the one which had said "too strong" in his mind. He bowed again. "I am he."

"And you are undoubtedly wondering why I dragged my old bones up here to see you."

"Your worship is correct."

"Sit down. I hate craning my neck to talk to people. I am too old to enjoy the protocol I myself invented. There is something to be said for not out-living one's usefulness. All of you, sit down. What is this?" He pointed at the jar before him.

"Rurian wine, Excellency." Gilhame answered as the company sorted itself down the table in order of precedence. Kinterra Kinagin, the Chief Justice, sat on the right of the King-at-Arms, and fan Talba sat beside her. Gilhame took the chair to the left of Il-sabayoo, and Vaverly sat next to him. Alvellaina, taking her cue from the page and the pursuivant, did not sit down but stood behind Vaverly and Gilhame. Frikard stood next to the portal and put his hands behind him.

"I find these matters go more smoothly if conducted in a relaxed atmosphere. I presume more wine exists."

"Certainly, Excellency." Gilhame answered.

"Bring it!"

Alvellaina turned and almost collided with the page who was walking to the refreshment cabinet. The page gave her a quick wink and shook her head, so Alvellaina returned to her place behind Gilhame.

"I am weary, so I will get right on with my business, Admiral," Il-sabayoo said as the pursuivant poured some wine into his glass. "The Emperor sends you greeting. He is most pleased with your efforts on his behalf."

"It is my pleasure to serve His Majesty."

"Good. Because he is not pleased with your lack of family."

Gilhame gave a sidelong glance to Vaverly. "I find it difficult to believe that as busy a man as the Emperor should concern himself with the domestic arrangements of one of his subjects."

"Don't be insolent!"

"I beg your pardon. I intended no offense. But I do not believe that the Emperor knows or cares for my family. I do believe that certain of his policy-makers would prefer that I had some hostages to fortune. This is only fitting. But

I do not feel that hiding behind the Emperor's back is fitting."

"You are mistaken. This is a matter in which Clyven has concerned himself directly."

"I stand corrected. And, quite honestly, I am amazed." He gave Il-sabayoo his death's-head smile. "What service may I perform for His Majesty?"

The old man looked uncomfortable. He sipped his wine and looked at fan Talba, who gave him a tiny shrug. Gilhame, who now had a glass in front of him, drank too, and waited.

The Chief Justice cleared his throat. "Quite frankly, ur Fagon, your growing military success disturbs His Majesty," Kinagin said. The old man glared at her.

"Why? Is my loyalty in doubt?"

"Any man's loyalty has a price," she replied.

"Be quiet!" snapped Il-sabayoo. "Sometimes I wonder what the Creator was thinking about, inventing women!"

"The cosmos does seem to have a sense of humor, doesn't it? But I wonder who the joke is on, us or them?" Gilhame said this to the herald. Kinagin arched an eyebrow at ur Fagon and gave him a hint of a grin.

"The Emperor does not like his servants to grow too strong, Admiral," Il-sabayoo commented. "Therefore, it has been decided that you will marry one of His Majesty's unwed daughters. There are two, Clyfera and Donaclyde and . . ."

"I cannot."

"What?"

"I am already married."

"Set it aside!"

"I do not choose to do so. I am quite happy with the wife I have. I am sure the princesses are delightful and charming ladies. I doubt they would find me either. I am a simple fighting man. I do not wish to become an ornament of the Imperial Court."

"Hardly simple, Admiral," Kinagin said.

"Your wishes are of no matter. You will marry one of the princesses. Come, be reasonable. You may keep your wife as concubine," the herald growled.

"I have no wish to insult the mother of my children by such an irregular arrangement."

The herald looked at Kinagin and fan Talba. "You don't seem to understand that you have no choice in the matter," he said finally.

"Nonsense. If I didn't have any say, you wouldn't be here. Fan Talba can attest to my record in litigation. Short of killing me, you cannot prevent me from appealing to the Imperial Court of Justice against such a forced marriage. I have done no wrong. I have not sinned against the State. Therefore, I have the right to sue for recompense—even against His Majesty. I would rather not, you know, for the embarrassment to the crown would be greater than to me. Am I not correct, Justice Kinagin?"

"Your grasp of the matter is excellent."

"That is praise indeed." They smiled at each other.

"Would you consider leaving the Navy for a legal career, Admiral?" she asked.

He shook his head. "The wheels of justice are a little slow for my taste."

"What a shame," she replied.

"Who is this wife?" fan Talba cut in with his quiet voice.

"Alvellaina Curly-Krispin."

The Adjudicator looked up at Alvellaina standing behind Gilhame. "I see. It seems my decision was less unjust than it appeared at the time. You share, do you not, a common ancestor with Her Majesty, the Empress, halba?"

"Yes. My father's mother was the half-sister of the Empress's mother." Alvellaina spoke nervously, and there were two bright spots of color on her cheeks. The Herald was glaring at her.

"A traitor's daughter is not a persuasive assurance of loyalty," Il-sabayoo said.

"Isn't it? Strange. I had never heard that disloyalty was a hereditary trait, Your Excellency," Gilhame answered. "We seem to have reached an impasse. Shall we try another tack?"

"Ill-mannered pup!"

"I beg Your Excellency's pardon for my insolence. I regret my inability to place political needs," he said cooly, "before my own. I have spent my life serving the Empire. I have no wish but to continue to do so."

"Fine words," said the Herald, "are easily forgotten."

"I told you not to try to bully him," said Kinagin. "His psycho-tapes indicate a high resistance to such tactics."

"They also show ungovernable disobedience—as he has just displayed by his refusal to marry one of the princesses!"

"I told you that wouldn't work either. A man who has stayed single as long as ur Fagon would never wed for expediency's sake. You can't always get your way, Horabe. What are you so worried about? He isn't power-hungry."

"That is precisely what worries me. A man without ambition is always suspect."

"Would you like me to leave so you can carry on this argument without mincing words?" Gilhame cut in. "I feel as if everyone in the cosmos has seen my psycho-tapes but me. I wonder you don't just reproduce them and sell them as a new form of entertainment. A game, perhaps?"

The Herald slapped his own palm onto the table. "Enough! I have decided. You will leave your wife in the care of the Imperial family."

"That I will not. Because, when she was poisoned, as I am certain she would be, I should be forced to rend you limb from limb, old man, and my respect for your years makes me reluctant to do so. I *never* parlay with a gun in my guts."

"You will do as you are bid—or face the consequences!" shouted the herald.

"Let us examine these consequences. I can go on leading my fleet against His Majesty's enemies everywhere. That is one. I can accept exile. There is another. Do you think your father would be pleased to see us, Alvellaina? Or, I can resign my fleet and take a paper-shuffling job in the Admiralty. Would I be safe teaching tactics at the Academy? Would that draw my teeth sufficiently to satisfy your fears, Il-sabayoo? With no fleet behind me, I am no threat to anyone except perhaps my staff. What danger would I be behind a desk?"

"You would do that?" The Herald was amazed.

"Why not? I've been living in a ship for over twenty years. Perhaps it is time for a change. In fact, you might put me in charge of what is hilariously called Intelligence. I might do better at avoiding the kind of screw-up that almost happened at Gemna. Unless that is too dangerous a position for a man of my ungovernable disposition."

"You would retire?"

"Why not?"

"I don't believe this. You would voluntarily surrender the power you have amassed?"

"Power? Is that what I have? Strange, I have never thought of it as such. I suppose, to a man like yourself, who has grown old in the manipulation of such things, that a fleet defines itself as power. You see ships and weapons, don't you? I don't. I see people, like the Lieutenant here, laboring in a common cause, which *is* the Empire. My people serve under me, but they do not serve me. They serve His Majesty. This is an idealistic hangover from my own early service under Admiral Legardi, no doubt, but I have never found any reason to question his philosophy.

"I must say, however, that I resent the implication that *I* might renegade or, worse, attempt to hold some kind of gun to His Majesty's revered head. That's really offensive. Now, after Gyre's defection, I am not surprised that you are jumping at shadows. I quote you a maxim of Clyven II. 'One way to create enemies is to alienate friends.'"

"Very prettily said, ur Fagon. Alright, you will be relieved from command after you receive your rewards from the Emperor. Your audience is tomorrow at *treece*. You will receive a list of who is to accompany you. You are an unruly rapscallion, young man, and I hope you do not live to regret your decision."

Gilhame grinned. "With undue immodesty, I will say that I am currently the most able fleet officer in the Emperor's command, Il-sabayoo. You had better pray *you* don't live to regret the decision which your manipulations have forced upon me. You might, you know."

The pursuivant helped the old man out of his chair. "It doesn't matter. The pattern is nearly complete anyhow," he wheezed. The rest of the company stood as he moved towards the portal. "Arrogant bastard!" Gilhame heard him mutter as he left.

Gilhame smiled and saluted. "Call me if you need me," he said quietly.

Justice Kinagin caught his words. "You need not worry, Admiral. We will," she said. Then she followed the rest of the party out of the room, and Frikard closed the portal behind him.

Ur Fagon looked at the two women who remained. Alvellaina was white with strain. He could see her hands were fists, the nails cutting into her palms. Lieutenant Vaverly looked very thoughtful.

"Thank you both for your silent support, halbas. You really should receive combat pay for that encounter."

"What a nasty old man!" Alvellaina exclaimed.

"You misjudge him, my darling. By his lights, he did the correct thing. I am the vortex of Chaos, remember? My climb to success has been too rapid for his peace of mind, and he has spent centuries in the service of the Empire."

"Sir, what did he mean about the pattern almost being complete?" Vaverly asked.

"Metaphysics, Lieutenant, only metaphysics. Come and see me tomorrow at *brimas* and tell me how I should behave in the Presence, will you? Will they give me a patent, do you think?"

"Almost certainly, sir. Anything less would be an insult."

"Good. That old man will choke on my choice of mottoes. You are dismissed."

"Very good, sir." She did not move.

"What is it, Vaverly?"

"Your presence will be missed, sir."

"Why, thank you, Lieutenant."

"And I would like to wish you both all the happiness in the cosmos."

"You are too kind. We'll send you an invitation to the wedding."

"Thank you, sir." The protocol officer left.

Alvellaina sat down in the chair Gilhame had occupied and drained his glass. She refilled it and half-emptied it before she spoke. "Now, at least, I understand your unseemly haste to marry me. How did you know?"

"I didn't. But, I remembered that in the reign of Clyven III a similar situation arose. One Admiral Kinagin, the father of the chief justice, I believe, was . . . pressured, shall we say, into marrying Clyven's daughter Kanclyva. Since it was Il-sabayoo who masterminded that alliance—misalliance is a better word—I thought the same solution might appeal to him again. He is the power behind the throne. I hope you can bring yourself to forgive me for rushing you, and for using you as I did."

"Did you use me? I suppose you did. Still, I think you paid a pretty stiff price for me—your whole fleet for a five-cruiser woman."

"You are never going to let me forget that, are you?"

"Should I?" She was a little giddy from having drunk so much wine so quickly.

"Probably not. If you go on knocking back wine at that rate, you'll feel awful tomorrow."

"Tell me, should I be puffed up with conceit at your choosing me over my cousins, the princesses? The Emperor has so many daughters I get mixed up."

"Let me see. The one called Doraclyde has a face like a swine and writes epic plays. A charming and intelligent woman, probably, but quite ugly. The other, Clyfera, is beautiful, quite beautiful. I have heard, in the manner of her mother. She is also a devoted intrigant and would probably cost me my head if I didn't murder her first. She's been widowed twice before. No, my refusal should not enhance your consequence. Be satisfied with a fleet for your bride-price."

"You do regret it." The tears stood in her eyes.

He came over and knelt beside her, searching her face. His resignation hurt her more than it did him. He brushed his hands over her hair. "Alvellaina, I would count the cosmos well lost to have you beside me."

_____ *Epilogue*

The audience hall on Kardisia rang with the blowing of trumpets. Gilhame, his bride on his arm, began the long walk toward the throne. All along the sides of the room, nearly a quarter mile long, the twenty thousand families of the nobility sat in their hereditary boxes, eating, drinking, talking and watching. Some, who were impoverished, were reputed to live in their boxes.

As they progressed, with Frikard, Buschard, Vraser and a number of ur Fagon's other officers, toward the dias the murmur of the viewers became less. Finally, they arrived.

Clyven IV, dumpy and whey-faced, handed out such awards as were appropriate to the occasion. Gilhame waited his turn, for his officers were acknowledged before him.

"Gilhame ur Fagon, Admiral of his Imperial Majesty Clyven IV's Twelfth Fleet, approach the throne," bawled some heraldic functionary.

He received his medal. Then the herald continued. "Being mindful of your valor in Our service, We are disposed to offer you a patent of arms, Gilhame ur Fagon. Therefore, our heralds have devised the following arms: Upon a field of red, the head of a dragon in black, edged in gold, the throat of the dragon cut smooth. Henceforth you will be known as Durimus Gemma and Vardar. What, if any, motto do you wish attached to your arms?"

243

Gilhame was amused. A viscount! But the arms amused him more: Gules, a dragon's-head sable couped and fibriated or. He had borne that banner before his troops on a hundred worlds.

He bowed before the throne again. "If it please your Majesty, I would choose as my motto, 'In the Service of the Empire.'"

A tiny gasp went around the royal family and the heraldic officers. Gilhame could hear the whisper of his choice being hissed from box to box overhead. Il-sabayoo turned red and choked.

Clyven nodded at the presiding herald, apparently unaware of any irony. But the Empress gave ur Fagon a sharp look and just the hint of a smile.

"The motto of Gilhame ur Fagon, Durimus Gemna and Vardar, will be 'In the Service of the Empire.'"

Gilhame ur Fagon retreated from the Imperial Presence well aware that he had gotten the final word in his argument with the old King-at-Arms. It amused him, but all he could really concentrate on was his new wife and the child that would someday be theirs.

He heard a tinkly laugh in his mind. For a second he could see nothing but blackness. Then he made out the wheeled silver ornaments in *her* black hair. '*You see. You can progress.*' She said that and vanished. And Gilhame ur Fagon breathed a sigh of relief and forgot about Glass Castle.

BEST-SELLING
Science Fiction
and
Fantasy

MORE *SCIENCE FICTION! ADVENTURE*

Stories
⊱ of ⊰
Swords and Sorcery

Available wherever paperbacks are sold or use this coupon.